PENGUIN ⏺ CLASSICS

DE PROFUNDIS AND OTHER WRITINGS

OSCAR FINGAL O'FLAHERTIE WILLS WILDE was born in Dublin in 1854, the son of an eminent surgeon. He went to Trinity College, Dublin, and then to Magdalen College, Oxford, where, in the last years of the seventies, he started the cult of 'Aestheticism' – of making an art of life. His first book, *Poems*, was published in 1881, and in 1882 he went to lecture in America. After his marriage to Constance Lloyd in 1884 he published several books of stories for children, then followed *The Picture of Dorian Gray* (1891).

Wilde's first success on the stage was when George Alexander produced *Lady Windermere's Fan* in 1892. This was followed by Tree's production of *A Woman of No Importance* in the next year, and in 1895 by *An Ideal Husband* and *The Importance of Being Earnest* running at one time. *Salomé* was refused a licence in England but was published in France in 1893.

In 1895 Wilde brought a libel action against the Marquis of Queensbury; he lost the case and was himself sentenced to two years' imprisonment with hard labour. As a result of his experience he wrote *The Ballad of Reading Gaol*. He was released from prison, bankrupt, in 1897 and went to Paris, where he lived until his death in 1900.

HESKETH PEARSON was born in Worcestershire and spent 1911 and the years between 1918 and 1931 on the stage. His publications included a number of outstanding biographies, amongst which are *A Life of Shakespeare* and *The Life of Oscar Wilde*. He died in 1964.

OSCAR WILDE

De Profundis and Other Writings

WITH AN INTRODUCTION BY
HESKETH PEARSON

PENGUIN BOOKS

Penguin Books Ltd, Harmondsworth, Middlesex, England
Viking Penguin Inc., 40 West 23rd Street, New York, New York 10010, U.S.A.
Penguin Books Australia Ltd, Ringwood, Victoria, Australia
Penguin Books Canada Limited, 2801 John Street, Markham, Ontario, Canada L3R 1B4
Penguin Books (N.Z.) Ltd, 182–190 Wairau Road, Auckland 10, New Zealand

—

This selection first published by Penguin Books
(under the title *Selected Essays and Poems*) 1954
Reissued in the Penguin English Library 1973
Reprinted 1976, 1977, 1979, 1980, 1982, 1984
Reprinted in Penguin Classics 1986

—

Introduction copyright 1954 by Hesketh Pearson
All rights reserved

—

Made and printed in Great Britain
by Richard Clay (The Chaucer Press) Ltd,
Bungay, Suffolk
Set in Monotype Bembo

Bibliographical Note

'The Soul of Man Under Socialism' first appeared in *The Fortnightly Review* (February 1891), No. CCXC, New Series: No. CCCXXVII, Old Series; and 'The Decay of Lying' in *The Nineteenth Century* (January 1889). The first unabridged edition of *De Profundis* was published in London, October 1949. 'Magdalen Walks' first appeared in the *Irish Monthly*, April 1878, 'Ave Maria Gratia Plena' as 'Ave Maria Plena Gratia' in the *Irish Monthly*, July 1878, and 'Portia' in *The World*, January 1880, these together with 'Sonnet to Liberty', 'Requiescat', 'Sonnet on hearing the Dies Irae sung in the Sistine Chapel', 'Fabien dei Franchi', 'The Grave of Shelley' and '*Γλυκυπικρος Ερως*' appeared in *Poems* (London, 1881). The poem 'To My Wife' was presented by Wilde to his wife with *Poems*. *The Sphinx* was first published in London, 1894; and *The Ballad of Reading Gaol* in London, 1898.

Contents

Introduction

BY HESKETH PEARSON

ALTHOUGH Oscar Wilde started and ended his literary career with a volume of verse, his best poetry was in prose: that is, his imagination flowed naturally in the form of prose. Yet his reputation as a poet remained greater than his reputation as an essayist until both were eclipsed by his fame as a dramatist. This effect was produced by Gilbert and Sullivan's *Patience*, wherein he was supposed to be the poet 'Bunthorne', and by George Du Maurier's caricatures of him as the poet 'Postlethwaite' in *Punch*. There is no doubt that theatrical burlesques and journalistic parodies did more for Wilde's fame during his lifetime than all his works put together, and of course they drew attention to what was worst in his writings.

The popularity of *Poems*, with which he commenced his life as an author in 1881, was really due to his personality, not his poetry. Having been widely advertised as by an aesthete who, in W. S. Gilbert's phrase, had walked down Piccadilly with a poppy or a lily in his medieval hand, no one in the movement could afford to be without the authentic 'book of the words', five editions of which sold fairly quickly. Many of the literary critics had read the poems of Rossetti, Swinburne, and Morris, and their comments echoed the speech at the Oxford Union by Oliver Elton, who moved that Wilde's volume, presented by the author, should not be added to the library: 'It is not that these poems are thin – and they *are* thin; it is not that they are immoral – and they *are* immoral; it is not that they are this or that – and they *are* all this and all that: it is that they are for the most part not by their putative father at all, but by a number of better-known and more deservedly reputed authors. They are in fact

9

by William Shakespeare, by Philip Sidney, by John Donne, by
Lord Byron, by William Morris, by Algernon Swinburne, and
by sixty more, whose works have furnished the list of passages
which I hold in my hand at this moment.' The truth is that Wilde's
phenomenal memory was more in evidence than individual inspiration, and the continued demand for his verses partly results
from a general liking for anthologies. It might almost be said
that he helped to popularize a number of other poets.

Occasionally however he struck a personal note, or rather a
personal thought, in which his own destiny was foreshadowed,
as in *Humanitad*:

> Being ourselves the sowers and the seeds,
>> The night that covers and the lights that fade,
> The spear that pierces and the side that bleeds,
>> The lips betraying and the life betrayed.

Some of his lines appear to have pleased those to whom they
were addressed. On seeing Ellen Terry as Queen Henrietta Maria
in *Charles I*, he depicted her as standing

> Like some wan lily overdrenched with rain,

and she thanked him for the phrase 'wan lily', which represented
perfectly what she had tried to convey both as Ophelia and
Henrietta. No doubt too his description of Henry Irving as

> Thou trumpet set for Shakespeare's lips to blow

appealed to the actor, though the author might have considered
as more appropriate 'Thou scissors set for Shakespeare's lines to
cut'. But the point is that Wilde could on occasion produce an
effective passage in verse, and a list of his good lines would be
nearly as long as a list of his echoes from other poets.

About two years after his first publication Wilde was in Paris
writing a blank-verse tragedy called *The Duchess of Padua*, which
is as dull and flat as most blank-verse tragedies since the time of
Shakespeare, and composing a poem called *The Sphinx*, one
verse of which shows that it might now be popular among cross-
word-puzzle addicts:

> But you can read the Hieroglyphs on the great sandstone obelisks,
> And you have talked with Basilisks, and you have looked on
>   Hippogriffs.

Wilde seems to have felt that its appeal to his own age would be restricted, saying, 'My first idea was to print only three copies: one for myself, one for the British Museum, and one for Heaven. I had some doubt about the British Museum.' But the theme and treatment were queer enough to attract those poets of the rising generation who were searching for novelty, and it influenced the work of several, notably that of James Elroy Flecker.

Apart from a few occasional verses, of which the best were those addressed to his wife, Wilde abandoned poetry until after his imprisonment, when *The Ballad of Reading Gaol* by C.3.3. appeared early in 1898. Though it owes a little to Coleridge's *The Ancient Mariner* and Housman's *A Shropshire Lad*, its best verses reveal a true poet whose feeling and utterance transcend his indebtedness to others for form. Sometimes the lines are more poignant than any that have appeared in this medium since the Border Ballads:

> And all the woe that moved him so
>   That he gave that bitter cry,
> And the wild regrets, and the bloody sweats,
>   None knew so well as I:
> For he who lives more lives than one
>   More deaths than one must die.

But for the present age Wilde's wit and personality overshadow his poetry, as they did in his own day, as they will in the years to come; and there is more of the man himself to be found in his best essays than anywhere else in his work, excepting only *The Importance of Being Earnest*. The essayist came before the dramatist, his finest work in that kind being written within two years, beginning with 'The Decay of Lying' which appeared in *The Nineteenth Century* for January 1889, and finishing with 'The Soul of Man Under Socialism', which surprised readers of *The Fortnightly Review* in February 1891.

All the essays which appeared in the book he called *Intentions* are good, but the most arresting and original are in the form of duologue, which satisfied his desire to dramatize himself. 'Not that I agree with everything that I have said in this essay. There is much with which I entirely disagree. The essay simply represents an artistic standpoint, and in aesthetic criticism attitude is everything.' With those words he concluded an article on theatrical costume; but in duologue form he was able to adopt as many attitudes as he wished. The result is extremely stimulating, and as singular as the character of the author. Walter Savage Landor's *Imaginary Conversations* are lifeless in comparison, and the only writer whose dialogue at all resembles Wilde's is Thomas Love Peacock, whose characters discourse with as much animation but less wit.

The most entertaining and therefore the most characteristic of the three conversation-pieces is 'The Decay of Lying', the other two, entitled 'The Critic as Artist', being of a more philosophical nature and written in a more elaborate style. Unable to bear a man who carried his genius so lightly, the pundits of the age declared that Wilde's work was superficial and derivative, and one with whom he had been on very friendly terms, the famous painter James McNeill Whistler, erupted violently. Wilde had absorbed the painter's views on art, and set them forth with much humour in 'The Decay of Lying'. He even had the effrontery to steal Whistler's remark that 'Oscar . . . has the courage of the opinions of others' and pass it off as his own. Whistler wrote to a weekly paper about it, and informed Wilde that he had better confess and then hang himself. Instead of replying in a similar vein, Wilde stood on his dignity, in which posture he was never at his best, and Whistler won the bout.

But like other geniuses Wilde took many of his good things where he found them, either in the writings or the conversation of other men, transmuting or adapting them to his purpose, so that they became an expression of his own nature, which doubtless contained the seeds of the same thoughts before they flowered into speech. No two writers could be less alike than Wilde and Dickens; yet a student of both would perceive the mannerism of one Dickensian character and a famous saying by another reappearing in two of Wilde's plays, each so perfectly suited to the situation that the author may have been unaware of the coincidence and only a pedant would complain of it, since Dickens probably took them from life and Wilde came across them in literature. 'The true artist', wrote Wilde, 'is known by the use he makes of what he annexes, and he annexes everything.' At any rate this artist improved whatever he took and gave far more than he received. We may open his essays almost anywhere and come across sayings like these:

'When man acts he is a puppet. When he describes he is a poet.'

'Man can believe the impossible, but man can never believe the improbable.'

'For he to whom the present is the only thing that is present, knows nothing of the age in which he lives.'

'It is enough that our fathers have believed. They have exhausted the faith-faculty of the species. Their legacy to us is the scepticism of which they were afraid.'

'The only thing that ever consoles man for the stupid things he does is the praise he always gives himself for doing them.'

'One is tempted to define man as a rational animal who always loses his temper when he is called upon to act in accordance with the dictates of reason.'

'It is only an auctioneer who can equally and impartially admire all schools of art.'

Some thirty years before the publication of Freud's book on psycho-analysis, Wilde said:

'Every impulse that we strive to strangle broods in the mind and poisons us. . . . The only way to get rid of a temptation is to yield to it.'

Two truths that are not yet generally recognized as such were uttered by him:

'The sentimentalist is always a cynic at heart. Indeed sentimentality is merely the Bank-holiday of cynicism.'

'Each time one loves is the only time that one has ever loved. Difference of object does not alter singleness of passion. It merely intensifies it.'

If Wilde had written nothing but his essays, he would still be remembered as one of the wittiest and most profound aphorists, as surprising as Sydney Smith, as penetrating as La Rochefoucauld.

Two more remarkable essays, in addition to those already mentioned, were written during the two years of Wilde's main productivity in that field. 'Pen, Pencil and Poison' is a brief biography of the murderer and forger, Thomas Griffiths Wainwright, who had initiated a new fashion in journalism. 'To have a style so gorgeous that it conceals the subject is one of the highest achievements of an important and much admired school of Fleet Street leader-writers', remarked Wilde, and this style Wainwright had invented. His biographer did not seem to think that the forger's sentence to transportation for life was for the right crime: 'This heavy punishment was inflicted on him for what, if we remember his fatal influence on the prose of modern journalism, was certainly not the worst of all his sins.' Wilde's was the first biographical essay to be written in the modern semi-ironical manner, anticipating the work of Lytton Strachey by a generation.

The other essay dealt with Shakespeare's *Sonnets*, and Wilde named it 'The Portrait of Mr W. H.'[1] It illustrated one of his favourite theories: that when you convert someone to an idea, you lose your own faith in it. 'Whenever people agree with me, I always feel I must be wrong,' he said. Whether or not he believed that 'Mr W. H.' in Shakespeare's *Sonnets* was a young actor named Willie Hughes, who had inspired the poet to create his finest female characters and was the 'onlie Begetter' of the poems, does not matter, for on this point he had something illuminating to say: 'If one puts forward an idea to a true Englishman – always a rash thing to do – he never dreams of considering whether the idea is right or wrong. The only thing he considers of any importance is whether one believes it oneself. Now, the value of an idea has nothing whatsoever to do with the sincerity of the man who expresses it. Indeed the probabilities are that the more insincere the man is, the more purely intellectual will the idea be, as in that case it will not be coloured by either his wants, his desires, or his prejudices.' In telling the story on

1. 'The Portrait of Mr W. H.' is included in *Lord Arthur Savile's Crime and Other Stories* (Penguin Modern Classics).

one occasion his listeners were so deeply impressed that he said 'You *must* believe in Willie Hughes', adding after a pause, 'I almost do myself.' Fortunately complete disbelief does not lessen our enjoyment of the work.

Wilde's last essay, 'The Soul of Man Under Socialism', is not only his best but one of the greatest in the language. Certainly no other writing of the kind compares with it for versatility of theme and felicity of phrase. It has probably provoked more thought among the young of two generations than anything else written in that period. It has the outstanding quality of making people think for themselves, of jolting them out of their ruts, instead of influencing them to accept the thoughts of the writer, to sink into another rut. Until the true meaning of socialism in action became apparent, it was a sort of bible among the youthful rebellious spirits of nations whose governments frowned upon free thought; especially in Tsarist Russia, where copies were mysteriously printed, furtively circulated, and carefully concealed from authority. Its suppression would be more necessary than ever in Soviet Russia, since its real thesis is individualism, or 'The Soul of Man Above Socialism'.

The origin of this unique work is curious. The author attended a meeting in Westminster where the chief speaker was Bernard Shaw, whose address on socialism moved Wilde to write his essay. The different conceptions of socialism by the two men were as striking as was the difference in character between them. Each admired the other but neither liked the other; their temperaments clashed; and their viewpoints were radically dissimilar. Wilde regarded socialism merely as a means to an end; Shaw considered it, as an economic creed, an end in itself. Asked what he thought of Wilde's essay, Shaw replied that it was very witty and entertaining, but had nothing whatever to do with socialism. He particularly enjoyed such passages as: 'Agitators are a set of interfering, meddling people, who come down to some perfectly contented class of the community and sow the seeds of discontent amongst them. That is the reason why agitators are so absolutely necessary.' But both Fabian and Marxian socialists, declared Shaw, laughed at statements like the following:

'If the Socialism is Authoritarian; if there are Governments armed with economic power as they are now with political power; if, in a word, we are to have Industrial Tyrannies, then the last state of man will be worse than the first.'

'It is to be regretted that a portion of our community should be practically in slavery, but to propose to solve the problem by enslaving the entire community is childish.'

'All authority is quite degrading. It degrades those who exercise it, and it degrades those over whom it is exercised.'

'The form of government that is most suitable to the artist is no government at all.'

No doubt the early socialists thought such remarks funny; and now that Authoritarian Socialism is the fashion, Wilde's warnings must strike bureaucrats as very old-fashioned; but the joke is not yet over, and it may be as well to remember that he only conceived socialism as one of many possible utopias, writing: 'A map of the world that does not include Utopia is not worth even glancing at, for it leaves out the one country at which Humanity is always landing. And when Humanity lands there, it looks out, and, seeing a better country, sets sail. Progress is the realization of Utopias.'

During the last six months of his imprisonment Wilde was allowed to write, producing his final prose composition, *De Profundis*, in the form of a letter to his friend Alfred Douglas. No man is at his best when excusing or explaining his conduct; he is almost certain to blame others for his folly, to dramatize his experiences, and to romanticize himself. *De Profundis* is interesting as a disclosure of its writer's character under affliction, proving among other things that he did not over-indulge in self-pity; but lacking his humour it is the least characteristic of his major works.

Wilde had a higher opinion of his best essays than of the rest of his writings, and at the present time they are probably read more widely than his plays, poems, and stories; the reason being that his nature is revealed in them more fully than in his other works, and his fame as a personality steadily increases as the years go by.

1954

The Soul of Man under Socialism

The Soul of Man under Socialism

THE chief advantage that would result from the establishment of Socialism is, undoubtedly, the fact that Socialism would relieve us from that sordid necessity of living for others which, in the present condition of things, presses so hardly upon almost everybody. In fact, scarcely anyone at all escapes.

Now and then, in the course of the century, a great man of science, like Darwin; a great poet like Keats; a fine critical spirit like M. Renan; a supreme artist like Flaubert, has been able to isolate himself, to keep himself out of reach of the clamorous claims of others, to stand 'under the shelter of the wall', as Plato puts it, and so to realize the perfection of what was in him, to his own incomparable gain, and to the incomparable and lasting gain of the whole world. These, however, are exceptions. The majority of people spoil their lives by an unhealthy and exaggerated altruism – are forced, indeed, so to spoil them. They find themselves surrounded by hideous poverty, by hideous ugliness, by hideous starvation. It is inevitable that they should be strongly moved by all this. The emotions of man are stirred more quickly than man's intelligence; and, as I pointed out some time ago in an article on the function of criticism, it is much more easy to have sympathy with suffering than it is to have sympathy with thought. Accordingly, with admirable, though misdirected intentions, they very seriously and very sentimentally set themselves to the task of remedying the evils that they see. But their remedies do not cure the disease: they merely prolong it. Indeed, their remedies are part of the disease.

They try to solve the problem of poverty, for instance, by keeping the poor alive; or, in the case of a very advanced school, by amusing the poor.

But this is not a solution: it is an aggravation of the difficulty. The proper aim is to try and reconstruct society on such a basis that poverty will be impossible. And the altruistic virtues have really prevented the carrying out of this aim. Just as the worst slave-owners were those who were kind to their slaves, and so prevented the horror of the system being realized by those who suffered from it, and understood by those who contemplated it, so, in the present state of things in England, the people who do most harm are the people who try to do most good; and at last we have had the spectacle of men who have really studied the problem and know the life – educated men who live in the East End – coming forward and imploring the community to restrain its altruistic impulses of charity, benevolence, and the like. They do so on the ground that such charity degrades and demoralizes. They are perfectly right. Charity creates a multitude of sins.

There is also this to be said. It is immoral to use private property in order to alleviate the horrible evils that result from the institution of private property. It is both immoral and unfair.

Under Socialism all this will, of course, be altered. There will be no people living in fetid dens and fetid rags, and bringing up unhealthy, hunger-pinched children in the midst of impossible and absolutely repulsive surroundings. The security of society will not depend, as it does now, on the state of the weather. If a frost comes we shall not have a hundred thousand men out of work, tramping about the streets in a state of disgusting misery, or whining to their neighbours for alms, or crowding round the doors of loathsome shelters to try and secure a hunch of bread and a night's unclean lodging. Each member of the society will share in the general prosperity and happiness of the society, and if a frost comes no one will practically be anything the worse.

Upon the other hand, Socialism itself will be of value simply because it will lead to Individualism.

Socialism, Communism, or whatever one chooses to call it, by converting private property into public wealth, and substituting co-operation for competition, will restore society to its proper condition of a thoroughly healthy organism, and ensure the material well-being of each member of the community. It will, in fact, give Life its proper basis and its proper environment. But, for the full development of Life to its highest mode of perfection, something more is needed. What is needed is Individualism. If the Socialism is Authoritarian; if there are Governments armed with economic power as they are now with political power; if, in a word, we are to have Industrial Tyrannies, then the last state of man will be worse than the first. At present, in consequence of the existence of private property, a great many people are enabled to develop a certain very limited amount of Individualism. They are either under no necessity to work for their living, or are enabled to choose the sphere of activity that is really congenial to them, and gives them pleasure. These are the poets, the philosophers, the men of science, the men of culture – in a word, the real men, the men who have realized themselves, and in whom all Humanity gains a partial realization. Upon the other hand, there are a great many people who, having no private property of their own, and being always on the brink of sheer starvation, are compelled to do the work of beasts of burden, to do work that is quite uncongenial to them, and to which they are forced by the peremptory, unreasonable, degrading Tyranny of want. These are the poor; and amongst them there is no grace of manner, or charm of speech, or civilization, or culture, or refinement in pleasures, or joy of life. From their collective force Humanity gains much in material prosperity. But it is only the material result that it gains, and the man who is poor is in himself absolutely of no importance. He is merely the infinitesimal atom of a force that, so far from regarding him, crushes him: indeed, prefers him crushed, as in that case he is far more obedient.

Of course, it might be said that the Individualism generated under conditions of private property is not always, or even as a rule, of a fine or wonderful type, and that the poor, if they have not culture and charm, have still many virtues. Both these statements would be quite true. The possession of private property is very often extremely demoralizing, and that is, of course, one of the reasons why Socialism wants to get rid of the institution. In fact, property is really a nuisance. Some years ago people went about the country saying that property has duties. They said it so often and so tediously that, at last, the Church has begun to say it.

One hears it now from every pulpit. It is perfectly true. Property not merely has duties, but has so many duties that its possession to any large extent is a bore. It involves endless claims upon one, endless attention to business, endless bother. If property had simply pleasures, we could stand it; but its duties make it unbearable. In the interest of the rich we must get rid of it. The virtues of the poor may be readily admitted, and are much to be regretted. We are often told that the poor are grateful for charity. Some of them are, no doubt, but the best amongst the poor are never grateful. They are ungrateful, discontented, disobedient, and rebellious. They are quite right to be so. Charity they feel to be a ridiculously inadequate mode of partial restitution, or a sentimental dole, usually accompanied by some impertinent attempt on the part of the sentimentalist to tyrannize over their private lives. Why should they be grateful for the crumbs that fall from the rich man's table? They should be seated at the board, and are beginning to know it. As for being discontented, a man who would not be discontented with such surroundings and such a low mode of life would be a perfect brute. Disobedience, in the eyes of anyone who has read history, is man's original virtue. It is through disobedience that progress has been made, through disobedience and through rebellion. Sometimes the poor are praised for being thrifty. But to recommend thrift to the poor is both grotesque and insulting. It is like advising a man who is starving to eat less. For a town or country labourer to practise thrift would be absolutely immoral. Man should not be ready to show that he can live like a badly fed animal. He should decline to live like that, and should either steal or go on the rates, which is considered by many to be a form of stealing. As for begging, it is safer to beg than to take, but it is finer to take than to beg. No: a poor man who is ungrateful, unthrifty, discontented, and rebellious, is probably a real personality, and has much in him. He is at any rate a healthy protest. As for the virtuous poor, one can pity them, of course, but one cannot possibly admire them. They have made private terms with the enemy, and sold their birthright for very bad pottage. They must also be extraordinarily stupid. I can quite understand a man accepting laws that protect private property, and admit of its accumulation, as long as he himself is able under those conditions to realize some form of beautiful and intellectual life. But it is almost incredible to me how a man whose life is marred and made hideous by such laws can possibly acquiesce in their continuance.

However, the explanation is not really difficult to find. It is simply this. Misery and poverty are so absolutely degrading, and exercise such a paralysing effect over the nature of men, that no class is ever really conscious of its own suffering. They have to be told of it by other people, and they often entirely disbelieve them. What is said by great employers of labour against agitators is unquestionably true. Agitators are a set of interfering, meddling people, who come down to some perfectly contented class of the community, and sow the seeds of discontent amongst them. That is the reason why agitators are so absolutely necessary. Without them, in our incomplete state, there would be no advance towards civilization. Slavery was put down in America, not in consequence of any action on the part of the slaves, or even any express desire on their part that they should be free. It was put down entirely through the grossly illegal conduct of certain agitators in Boston and elsewhere, who were not slaves themselves, nor owners of slaves, nor had anything to do with the question really. It was, undoubtedly, the Abolitionists who set the torch alight, who began the whole thing. And it is curious to note that from the slaves themselves they received, not merely very little assistance, but hardly any sympathy even; and when at the close of the war the slaves found themselves free, found themselves indeed so absolutely free that they were free to starve, many of them bitterly regretted the new state of things. To the thinker, the most tragic fact in the whole of the French Revolution is not that Marie Antoinette was killed for being a queen, but that the starved peasant of the Vendée voluntarily went out to die for the hideous cause of feudalism.

It is clear, then, that no Authoritarian Socialism will do. For while under the present system a very large number of people can lead lives of a certain amount of freedom and expression and happiness, under an industrial-barrack system, or a system of economic tyranny, nobody would be able to have any such freedom at all. It is to be regretted that a portion of our community should be practically in slavery, but to propose to solve the problem by enslaving the entire community is childish. Every man must be left quite free to choose his own work. No form of compulsion must be exercised over him. If there is, his work will not be good for him, will not be good in itself, and will not be good for others. And by work I simply mean activity of any kind.

I hardly think that any Socialist, nowadays, would seriously propose that an inspector should call every morning at each house to see that each citizen rose up and did manual labour for eight hours. Humanity has got beyond that stage, and reserves such a form of life for the people whom, in a very arbitrary manner, it chooses to call criminals. But I confess that many of the socialistic views that I have come across seem to me to be tainted with ideas of authority, if not of actual compulsion. Of course, authority and compulsion are out of the question. All association must be quite voluntary. It is only in voluntary associations that man is fine.

But it may be asked how Individualism, which is now more or less dependent on the existence of private property for its development, will benefit by the abolition of such private property. The answer is very simple. It is true that, under existing conditions, a few men who have had private means of their own, such as Byron, Shelley, Browning, Victor Hugo, Baudelaire, and others, have been able to realize their personality, more or less completely. Not one of these men ever did a single day's work for hire. They were relieved from poverty. They had an immense advantage. The question is whether it would be for the good of Individualism that such an advantage should be taken away. Let us suppose that it is taken away. What happens then to Individualism? How will it benefit ?

It will benefit in this way. Under the new conditions Individualism will be far freer, far finer, and far more intensified than it is now. I am not talking of the great imaginatively realized Individualism of such poets as I have mentioned, but of the great actual Individualism latent and potential in mankind generally. For the recognition of private property has really harmed Individualism, and obscured it, by confusing a man with what he possesses. It has led Individualism entirely astray. It has made gain, not growth, its aim. So that man thought that the important thing was to have, and did not know that the important thing is to be. The true perfection of man lies, not in what man has, but in what man is. Private property has crushed true Individualism, and set up an Individualism that is false. It has debarred one part of the community from being individual by starving them. It has debarred the other part of the community from being individual by putting them on the wrong road, and encumbering them. Indeed, so completely has man's personality been absorbed by his possessions that the English law has always treated offences against a man's property with far more severity than offences against his person, and property is still the test of complete citizenship. The industry necessary for the making of money is also very demoralizing. In a community like ours, where property confers immense distinction, social position, honour, respect, titles, and other pleasant things of the kind, man, being naturally ambitious, makes it his aim to accumulate this property, and goes on wearily and tediously accumulating it long after he has got far more than he wants, or can use, or enjoy, or perhaps even know of. Man will kill himself by overwork in order to secure property, and really, considering the enormous advantages that property brings, one is hardly surprised. One's regret is that society should be constructed on such a basis that man has been forced into a groove in which he cannot freely develop what is wonderful, and fascinating, and delightful in him – in which, in fact, he misses the true pleasure and joy of living. He is also, under existing conditions, very insecure. An enormously wealthy merchant may be – often is – at every moment of his life at the mercy of things that are not under his control. If the wind blows an extra point or so, or the weather suddenly changes, or some trivial thing happens, his ship may go down, his speculations may go wrong, and he finds himself a poor man, with his social position quite gone. Now, nothing should be able to harm a man except himself. Nothing should be able to rob a man at all. What a man really has, is what is in him. What is outside of him should be a matter of no importance.

With the abolition of private property, then, we shall have true, beautiful, healthy Individualism. Nobody will waste his life in accumulating things, and the symbols for things. One will live. To live is the rarest thing in the world. Most people exist, that is all.

It is a question whether we have ever seen the full expression of a personality, except on the imaginative plane of art. In action, we never have. Caesar, says Mommsen, was the complete and perfect man. But how tragically insecure was Caesar! Wherever there is a man who exercises authority, there is a man who resists authority. Caesar was very perfect, but his perfection travelled by too dangerous a road. Marcus Aurelius was the perfect man, says Renan. Yes, the great emperor was a perfect man. But how intolerable were the endless claims upon him! He staggered under the burden of the empire. He was conscious how inadequate one man was to bear the weight of that Titan and too vast orb. What I mean by a perfect man is one who develops under perfect conditions; one who is not wounded, or worried, or maimed, or in danger. Most personalities have been obliged to be rebels. Half their strength has been wasted in friction. Byron's personality, for instance, was terribly wasted in its battle with the stupidity and hypocrisy and Philistinism of the English. Such battles do not always intensify strength; they often exaggerate weakness. Byron was never able to give us what he might have given us. Shelley escaped better. Like Byron, he got out of England as soon as possible. But he was not so well known. If the English had realized what a great poet he really was, they would have fallen on him with tooth and nail, and made his life as unbearable to him as they possibly could. But he was not a remarkable figure in society, and consequently he escaped, to a certain degree. Still, even in Shelley the note of rebellion is sometimes too strong. The note of the perfect personality is not rebellion, but peace.

It will be a marvellous thing – the true personality of man – when we see it. It will grow naturally and simply, flowerlike, or as a tree grows. It will not be at discord. It will never argue or dispute. It will not prove things. It will know everything. And yet it will not busy itself about knowledge. It will have wisdom. Its value will not be measured by material things. It will have nothing. And yet it will have everything, and whatever one takes from it, it will still have, so rich will it be. It will not be always meddling with others, or asking them to be like itself. It will love them because they will be different. And yet while it will not meddle with others, it will help all, as a beautiful thing helps us, by being what it is. The personality of man will be very wonderful. It will be as wonderful as the personality of a child.

In its development it will be assisted by Christianity, if men desire that; but if men do not desire that, it will develop none the less surely. For it will not worry itself about the past, nor care whether things happened or did not happen. Nor will it admit any laws but its own laws; nor any authority but its own authority. Yet it will love those who sought to intensify it, and speak often of them. And of these Christ was one.

'Know thyself!' was written over the portal of the antique world. Over the portal of the new world 'Be thyself' shall be written. And the message of Christ to man was simply 'Be thyself.' That is the secret of Christ.

When Jesus talks about the poor he simply means personalities, just as when he talks about the rich he simply means people who have not developed their personalities. Jesus moved in a community that allowed the accumulation of private property just as ours does, and the gospel that he preached was, not that in such a community it is an advantage for a man to live on scanty, unwholesome food, to wear ragged, unwholesome clothes, to sleep in horrid, unwholesome dwellings, and a disadvantage for a man to live under healthy, pleasant, and decent conditions. Such a view would have been wrong there and then, and would, of course, be still more wrong now and in England; for as man moves northward the material necessities of life become of more vital importance, and our society is infinitely more complex, and displays far greater extremes of luxury and pauperism than any society of the antique world. What Jesus meant was this. He said to man, 'You have a wonderful personality. Develop it. Be yourself. Don't imagine that your perfection lies in accumulating or possessing external things. Your affection is inside of you. If only you could realize that, you would not want to be rich. Ordinary riches can be stolen from a man. Real riches cannot. In the treasury-home of your soul, there are infinitely precious things, that may not be taken from you. And so, try to so shape your life that external things will not harm you. And try also to get rid of personal property. It involves sordid preoccupation, endless industry, continual wrong. Personal property hinders Individualism at every step.' It is to be noted that Jesus never says that impoverished people are necessarily good, or wealthy people necessarily bad. That would not have been true. Wealthy people are, as a class, better than impoverished people, more moral, more intellectual, more well-behaved. There is only one class in the community that thinks more about money than the rich, and that is the poor. The poor can think of nothing else. That is the misery of being poor. What Jesus does say, is that man reaches his perfection, not through what he has, not even through what he does, but entirely through what he is. And so the wealthy young man who comes to Jesus is represented as a thoroughly good citizen, who has broken none of the laws of his state, none of the commandments of his religion. He is quite respectable, in the ordinary sense of that extraordinary word. Jesus says to him, 'You should give up private property. It hinders you from realizing your perfection. It is a drag upon you. It is a burden. Your personality does not need it. It is within you, and not outside of you, that you will find what you really are, and what you really want.' To his own friends he says the same thing. He tells them to be themselves, and not to be always worrying about other things. What do other things matter? Man is complete in himself. When they go into the world, the world will disagree with them. That is inevitable. The world hates Individualism. But that is not to trouble them. They are to be calm and self-centred. If a man takes their cloak, they are to give him their coat, just to show that material things are of no importance. If people abuse them, they are not to answer back. What does it signify? The things people say of a man do not alter a man. He is what he is. Public opinion is of no value whatsoever. Even if people employ actual violence, they are not to be violent in turn. That would be to fall to the same low level. After all, even in prison, a man can be quite free. His soul can be free. His personality can be untroubled. He can be at peace. And, above all things, they are not to interfere with other people or judge them in any way. Personality is a very mysterious thing. A man cannot always be estimated by what he does. He may keep the law, and yet be worthless. He may break the law, and yet be fine. He may be bad, without ever doing anything bad. He may commit a sin against society, and yet realize through that sin his true perfection.

There was a woman who was taken in adultery. We are not told the history of her love, but that love must have been very great; for Jesus said that her sins were forgiven her, not because she repented, but because her love was so intense and wonderful. Later on, a short time before his death, as he sat at a feast, the woman came in and poured costly perfumes on his hair. His friends tried to interfere with her, and said that it was extravagance, and that the money that the perfume cost should have been expended on charitable relief of people in want, or something of that kind. Jesus did not accept that view. He pointed out that the material needs of Man were great and very permanent, but that the spiritual needs of Man were greater still, and that in one divine moment, and by selecting its own mode of expression, a personality might make itself perfect. The world worships the woman, even now, as a saint.

Yes, there are suggestive things in Individualism. Socialism annihilates family life, for instance. With the abolition of private property, marriage in its present form must disappear. This is part of the programme. Individualism accepts this and makes it fine. It converts the abolition of legal restraint into a form of freedom that will help the full development of personality, and make the love of man and woman more wonderful, more beautiful, and more ennobling. Jesus knew this. He rejected the claims of family life, although they existed in his day and community in a very marked form. 'Who is my mother? Who are my brothers?'

he said, when he was told that they wished to speak to him. When one of his followers asked leave to go and bury his father, 'Let the dead bury the dead,' was his terrible answer. He would allow no claim whatsoever to be made on personality.

And so he who would lead a Christlike life is he who is perfectly and absolutely himself. He may be a great poet, or a great man of science, or a young student at a University, or one who watches sheep upon a moor; or a maker of dramas, like Shakespeare, or a thinker about God, like Spinoza; or a child who plays in a garden, or a fisherman who throws his net into the sea. It does not matter what he is, as long as he realizes the perfection of the soul that is within him. All imitation in morals and in life is wrong. Through the streets of Jerusalem at the present day crawls one who is mad and carries a wooden cross on his shoulders. He is a symbol of the lives that are marred by imitation. Father Damien was Christlike when he went out to live with the lepers, because in such service he realized fully what was best in him. But he was not more Christlike than Wagner when he realized his soul in music; or than Shelley, when he realized his soul in song. There is no one type for man. There are as many perfections as there are imperfect men. And while to the claims of charity a man may yield and yet be free, to the claims of conformity no man may yield and remain free at all.

Individualism, then, is what through Socialism we are to attain. As a natural result, the State must give up all idea of government. It must give it up because, as a wise man once said many centuries before Christ, there is such a thing as leaving mankind alone; there is no such thing as governing mankind. All modes of government are failures. Despotism is unjust to everybody, including the despot, who was probably made for better things. Oligarchies are unjust to the many, and ochlocracies are unjust to the few. High hopes were once formed of democracy; but democracy means simply the bludgeoning of the people by the people for the people. It has been found out. I must say that it was high time, for all authority is quite degrading. It degrades those who exercise it, and degrades those over whom it is exercised. When it is violently, grossly, and cruelly used, it produces a good effect, by creating, or at any rate bringing out, the spirit of revolt and Individualism that is to kill it. When it is used with a certain amount of kindness, and accompanied by prizes and rewards, it is dreadfully demoralizing. People, in that case, are less conscious of the horrible pressure that is being put on them, and so go through their lives in a sort of coarse comfort, like petted animals, without ever realizing that they are probably thinking other people's thoughts, living by other people's standards, wearing practically what one may call other people's second-hand clothes, and never being themselves for a single moment. 'He who would be free', says a fine thinker, 'must not conform.' And authority, by bribing people to conform, produces a very gross kind of overfed barbarism amongst us.

With authority, punishment will pass away. This will be a great gain – a gain, in fact, of incalculable value. As one reads history, not in the expurgated editions written for schoolboys and passmen, but in the original authorities of each time, one is absolutely sickened, not by the crimes that the wicked have committed, but by the punishments that the good have inflicted; and a community is infinitely more brutalized by the habitual employment of punishment than it is by the occasional occurrence of crime. It obviously follows that the more punishment is inflicted the more crime is produced, and most modern legislation has clearly recognized this, and has made it its task to diminish punishment as far as it thinks it can. Wherever it has really diminished it, the results have always been extremely good. The less punishment, the less crime. When there is no punishment at all, crime will either cease to exist, or, if it occurs, will be treated by physicians as a very distressing form of dementia, to be cured by care and kindness. For what are called criminals nowadays are not criminals at all. Starvation, and not sin, is the parent of modern crime. That indeed is the reason why our criminals are, as a class, so absolutely uninteresting from any psychological point of view. They are not marvellous Macbeths and terrible Vautrins. They are merely what ordinary respectable, commonplace people would be if they had not got enough to eat. When private property is abolished there will be no necessity for crime, no demand for it; it will cease to exist. Of course, all crimes are not crimes against property, though such are the crimes that the English law, valuing what a man has more than what a man is, punishes with the harshest and most horrible severity (if we except the crime of murder, and regard death as worse than penal servitude, a point on which our criminals, I believe, disagree). But though a crime may not be against property, it may spring from the misery and rage and depression produced by our wrong system of property-holding, and so, when that system is abolished, will disappear. When each member of the community has sufficient for his wants, and is not interfered with by his neighbour, it will not be an object of any interest to him to interfere with anyone else. Jealousy, which is an extraordinary source of crime in modern life, is an emotion closely bound up with our conceptions of property, and under Socialism and Individualism will die out. It is remarkable that in communistic tribes jealousy is entirely unknown.

Now as the State is not to govern, it may be asked what the State is to do. The State is to be a voluntary association that will organize labour, and be the manufacturer and distributor of necessary commodities. The State is to make what is useful. The individual is to make what is beautiful. And as I have mentioned the word labour, I cannot help saying that a great deal of nonsense is being written and talked nowadays about the dignity of manual labour. There is nothing necessarily dignified about manual labour at all, and most of it is absolutely degrading. It is mentally and morally injurious to man to do anything in which he does not find pleasure, and many forms of labour are quite pleasureless activities, and should be regarded as such. To sweep a slushy crossing for eight hours on a day when the east wind is blowing is a disgusting occupation. To sweep it with mental, moral, or physical dignity seems to me to be impossible. To sweep it with joy would be appalling. Man is made for something better than disturbing dirt. All work of that kind should be done by a machine.

And I have no doubt that it will be so. Up to the present, man has been, to a certain extent, the slave of machinery, and there is something tragic in the fact that as soon as man had invented a machine to do his work he began to starve. This, however, is, of course, the result of our property system and our system of competition. One man owns a machine which does the work of five hundred men. Five hundred men are, in consequence, thrown out of employment, and, having no work to do, become hungry and take to thieving. The one man secures the produce of the machine and keeps it, and has five hundred times as much as he should have, and probably, which is of much more importance, a great deal more than he really wants. Were that machine the property of all, everybody would benefit by it. It would be an immense advantage to the community. All unintellectual labour, all monotonous, dull labour, all labour that deals with dreadful things, and involves unpleasant conditions, must be done by machinery. Machinery must work for us in coal mines, and do all sanitary services, and be the stoker of steamers, and clean the streets, and run messages on wet days, and do anything that is tedious or distressing. At present machinery competes against man. Under proper conditions machinery will serve man. There is no doubt at all that this is the future of machinery; and just as trees grow while the country gentleman is asleep, so while Humanity will be amusing itself, or enjoying cultivated leisure – which, and not labour, is the aim of man – or making beautiful things, or reading beautiful things, or simply contemplating the world with admiration and delight, machinery will be doing all the necessary and unpleasant work. The fact is, that civilization requires slaves. The Greeks were quite right there. Unless there are slaves to do the ugly, horrible, uninteresting work, culture and contemplation become almost impossible. Human slavery is wrong, insecure, and demoralizing. On mechanical slavery, on the slavery of the machine, the future of the world depends. And when scientific men are no longer called upon to go down to a depressing East End and distribute bad cocoa and worse blankets to starving people, they will have delightful leisure in which to devise wonderful and marvellous things for their own joy and the joy of everyone else. There will be great storages of force for every city, and for every house if required, and this force man will convert into heat, light, or motion, according to his needs. Is this Utopian? A map of the world that does not include Utopia is not worth even glancing at, for it leaves out the one country at which Humanity is always landing. And when Humanity lands there, it looks out, and, seeing a better country, sets sail. Progress is the realization of Utopias.

Now, I have said that the community by means of organization of machinery will supply the useful things, and that the beautiful things will be made by the individual. This is not merely necessary, but it is the only possible way by which we can get either the one or the other. An individual who has to make things for the use of others, and with reference to their wants and their wishes, does not work with interest, and consequently cannot put into his work what is best in him. Upon the other hand, whenever a community or a powerful section of a community, or a government of any kind, attempts to dictate to the artist what he is to do, Art either entirely vanishes, or becomes stereotyped, or degenerates into a low and ignoble form of craft. A work of art is the unique result of a unique temperament. Its beauty comes from the fact that the author is what he is. It has nothing to do with the fact that other people want what they want. Indeed, the moment that an artist takes notice of what other people want, and tries to supply the demand, he ceases to be an artist, and becomes a dull or an amusing craftsman, an honest or a dishonest tradesman. He has no further claim to be considered as an artist. Art is the most intense mode of Individualism that the world has known. I am inclined to say that it is the only real mode of Individualism that the world has known. Crime, which, under certain conditions, may seem to have created Individualism, must take cognizance of other people and interfere with them. It belongs to the sphere of action. But alone, without any reference to his neighbours, without any interference the artist can fashion a beautiful thing; and if he does not do it solely for his own pleasure, he is not an artist at all.

And it is to be noted that it is the fact that Art is this intense form of Individualism that makes the public try to exercise over it an authority that is as immoral as it is ridiculous, and as corrupting as it is contemptible. It is not quite their fault. The public has always, and in every age, been badly brought up. They are continually asking Art to be popular, to please their want of taste, to flatter their absurd vanity, to tell them what they have been told before, to show them what they ought to be tired of seeing, to amuse them when they feel heavy after eating too much, and to distract their thoughts when they are wearied of their own stupidity. Now Art should never try to be popular. The public should try to make itself artistic. There is a very wide difference. If a man of science were told that the results of his experiments, and the conclusions that he arrived at, should be of such a character that they would not upset the received popular notions on the subject, or disturb popular prejudice, or hurt the sensibilities of people who knew nothing about science; if a philosopher were told that he had a perfect right to speculate in the highest spheres of thought, provided that he arrived at the same conclusions as were held by those who had never thought in any sphere at all – well, nowadays the man of science and the philosopher would be considerably amused. Yet it is really a very few years since both philosophy and science were subjected to brutal popular control, to authority in fact – the authority of either the general ignorance of the community, or the terror and greed for power of an ecclesiastical or governmental class. Of course, we have to a very great extent got rid of any attempt on the part of the community, or the Church, or the Government, to interfere with the individualism of speculative thought, but the attempt to interfere with the individualism of imaginative art still lingers. In fact, it does more than linger; it is aggressive, offensive, and brutalizing.

In England, the arts that have escaped best are the arts in which the public take no interest. Poetry is an instance of what I mean. We have been able to have fine poetry in England because the public do not read it, and consequently do not influence it. The public like to insult poets because they are individual, but once they have insulted them, they leave them alone. In the case of the novel and the drama, arts in which the public do take an interest, the result of the exercise of popular authority has been absolutely ridiculous. No country produces such badly written fiction, such tedious, common work in the novel form, such silly, vulgar plays as England. It must necessarily be so. The popular standard is of such a character that no artist can get to it. It is at once too easy and too difficult to be a popular novelist. It is too easy, because the requirements of the public as far as plot, style, psychology, treatment of life, and treatment of literature are concerned are within the reach of the very meanest capacity and the most uncultivated mind. It is too difficult, because to meet such requirements the artist would have to do violence to his temperament, would have to write not for the artistic joy of writing, but for the amusement of half-educated people, and so would have to suppress his individualism, forget his culture, annihilate his style, and surrender everything that is valuable in him. In the case of the drama, things are a little better: the theatre-going public like the obvious, it is true, but they do not like the tedious; and burlesque and farcical comedy, the two most popular forms, are distinct forms of art. Delightful work may be produced under burlesque and farcical conditions, and in work of this kind the artist in England is allowed very great freedom. It is when one comes to the higher forms of the drama that the result of popular control is seen. The one thing that the public dislike is novelty. Any attempt to extend the subject-matter of art is extremely distasteful to the public; and yet the vitality and progress of art depend in a large measure on the continual extension of subject-matter. The public dislike novelty because they are afraid of it. It represents to them a mode of Individualism, an assertion on the part of the artist that he selects his own subject, and treats it as he chooses. The public are quite right in their attitude. Art is Individualism, and Individualism is a disturbing and disintegrating force. Therein lies its immense value. For what it seeks to disturb is monotony of type, slavery of custom, tyranny of habit, and the reduction of man to the level of a machine. In Art, the public accept what has been, because they cannot alter it, not because they appreciate it. They swallow their classics whole, and never taste them. They endure them as the inevitable, and as they cannot mar them, they mouth about them. Strangely enough, or not strangely, according to one's own views, this acceptance of the classics does a great deal of harm. The uncritical admiration of the Bible and Shakespeare in England is an instance of what I mean. With regard to the Bible, considerations of ecclesiastical authority enter into the matter, so that I need not dwell upon the point.

But in the case of Shakespeare it is quite obvious that the public really see neither the beauties nor the defects of his plays. If they saw the beauties, they would not object to the development of the drama; and if they saw the defects, they would not object to the development of the drama either. The fact is, the public make use of the classics of a country as a means of checking the progress of Art. They degrade the classics into authorities. They use them as bludgeons for preventing the free expression of Beauty in new forms. They are always asking a writer why he does not write like somebody else, or a painter why he does not paint like somebody else, quite oblivious of the fact that if either of them did anything of the kind he would cease to be an artist. A fresh mode of Beauty is absolutely distasteful to them, and whenever it appears they get so angry and bewildered that they always use two stupid expressions – one is that the work of art is grossly unintelligible; the other, that the work of art is grossly immoral. What they mean by these words seems to me to be this. When they say a work is grossly unintelligible, they mean that the artist has said or made a beautiful thing that is new; when they describe a work as grossly immoral, they mean that the artist has said or made a beautiful thing that is true. The former expression has reference to style; the latter to subject-matter. But they probably use the words very vaguely, as an ordinary mob will use ready-made paving-stones. There is not a single real poet or prose-writer of this century, for instance, on whom the British public have not solemnly conferred diplomas of immorality, and these diplomas practically take the place, with us, of what in France is the formal recognition of an Academy of Letters, and fortunately make the establishment of such an institution quite unnecessary in England. Of course, the public are very reckless in their use of the word. That they should have called Wordsworth an immoral poet, was only to be expected. Wordsworth was a poet. But that they should have called Charles Kingsley an immoral novelist is extraordinary. Kingsley's prose was not of a very fine quality. Still, there is the word, and they use it as best they can. An artist is, of course, not disturbed by it. The true artist is a man who believes absolutely in himself, because he is absolutely himself. But I can fancy that if an artist produced a work of art in England that immediately on its appearance was recognized by the public, through their medium, which is the public Press, as a work that was quite intelligible and highly moral, he would begin seriously to question whether in its creation he had really been himself at all, and consequently whether the work was not quite unworthy of him, and either of a thoroughly second-rate order, or of no artistic value whatsoever.

Perhaps, however, I have wronged the public in limiting them to such words as 'immoral', 'unintelligible', 'exotic', and 'unhealthy'. There is one other word that they use. That word is 'morbid'. They do not use it often. The meaning of the word is so simple that they are afraid of using it. Still, they use it sometimes, and, now and then, one comes across it in popular newspapers. It is, of course, a ridiculous word to apply to a work of art. For what is morbidity but a mood of emotion or a mode of thought that one cannot express? The public are all morbid, because the public can never find expression for anything. The artist is never morbid. He expresses everything. He stands outside his subject, and through its medium produces incomparable and artistic effects. To call an artist morbid because he deals with morbidity as his subject-matter is as silly as if one called Shakespeare mad because he wrote *King Lear*.

On the whole, an artist in England gains something by being attacked. His individuality is intensified. He becomes more completely himself. Of course, the attacks are very gross, very impertinent, and very contemptible. But then no artist expects grace from the vulgar mind, or style from the suburban intellect. Vulgarity and stupidity are two very vivid facts in modern life. One regrets them, naturally. But there they are. They are subjects for study, like everything else. And it is only fair to state, with regard to modern journalists, that they always apologize to one in private for what they have written against one in public.

Within the last few years two other adjectives, it may be mentioned, have been added to the very limited vocabulary of art-abuse that is at the disposal of the public. One is the word 'unhealthy', the other is the word 'exotic'. The latter merely expresses the rage of the momentary mushroom against the immortal, entrancing, and exquisitely lovely orchid. It is a tribute, but a tribute of no importance. The word 'unhealthy', however, admits of analysis. It is a rather interesting word. In fact, it is so interesting that the people who use it do not know what it means.

What does it mean? What is a healthy or an unhealthy work of art? All terms that one applies to a work of art, provided that one applies them rationally, have reference to either its style or its subject, or to both together. From the point of view of style, a healthy work of art is one whose style recognizes the beauty of the material it employs, be that material one of words or of bronze, of colour or of ivory, and uses that beauty as a factor in producing the aesthetic effect. From the point of view of subject, a healthy work of art is one the choice of whose subject is conditioned by the temperament of the artist, and comes directly out of it. In fine, a healthy work of art is one that has both perfection and personality. Of course, form and substance cannot be separated in a work of art; they are always one. But for purposes of analysis, and setting the wholeness of aesthetic impression aside for a moment, we can intellectually so separate them. An unhealthy work of art, on the other hand, is a work whose style is obvious, old-fashioned and common, and whose subject is deliberately chosen, not because the artist has any pleasure in it, but because he thinks that the public will pay him for it. In fact, the popular novel that the public call healthy is always a thoroughly unhealthy production; and what the public call an unhealthy novel is always a beautiful and healthy work of art.

I need hardly say that I am not, for a single moment, complaining that the public and the public Press misuse these words. I do not see how, with their lack of comprehension of what Art is, they could possibly use them in the proper sense. I am merely pointing out the misuse; and as for the origin of the misuse and the meaning that lies behind it all, the explanation is very simple.

It comes from the barbarous conception of authority. It comes from the natural inability of a community corrupted by authority to understand or appreciate Individualism. In a word, it comes from that monstrous and ignorant thing that is called Public Opinion, which, bad and well-meaning as it is when it tries to control action, is infamous and of evil meaning when it tries to control Thought or Art.

Indeed, there is much more to be said in favour of the physical force of the public than there is in favour of the public's opinion. The former may be fine. The latter must be foolish. It is often said that force is no argument. That, however, entirely depends on what one wants to prove. Many of the most important problems of the last few centuries, such as the continuance of personal government in England, or of feudalism in France, have been solved entirely by means of physical force. The very violence of a revolution may make the public grand and splendid for a moment. It was a fatal day when the public discovered that the pen is mightier than the paving-stone, and can be made as offensive as the brickbat. They at once sought for the journalist, found him, developed him, and made him their industrious and well-paid servant. It is greatly to be regretted, for both their sakes. Behind the barricade there may be much that is noble and heroic. But what is there behind the leading-article but prejudice, stupidity, cant and twaddle? And when these four are joined together they make a terrible force, and constitute the new authority.

In the old days men had the rack. Now they have the Press. That is an improvement certainly. But still it is very bad, and wrong, and demoralizing. Somebody – was it Burke? – called journalism the fourth estate. That was true at the time, no doubt. But at the present moment it really is the only estate. It has eaten up the other three. The Lords Temporal say nothing, the Lords Spiritual have nothing to say, and the House of Commons has nothing to say and says it. We are dominated by Journalism. In America the President reigns for four years, and Journalism governs for ever and ever. Fortunately, in America, Journalism has carried its authority to the grossest and most brutal extreme. As a natural consequence it has begun to create a spirit of revolt.

People are amused by it, or disgusted by it, according to their temperaments. But it is no longer the real force it was. It is not seriously treated. In England, Journalism, except in a few well-known instances, not having been carried to such excesses of brutality, is still a great factor, a really remarkable power. The tyranny that it proposes to exercise over people's private lives seems to me to be quite extraordinary. The fact is that the public have an insatiable curiosity to know everything, except what is worth knowing. Journalism, conscious of this, and having trades-man-like habits, supplies their demands. In centuries before ours the public nailed the ears of journalists to the pump. That was quite hideous. In this century journalists have nailed their own ears to the keyhole. That is much worse. And what aggravates the mischief is that the journalists who are most to blame are not the amusing journalists who write for what are called Society papers. The harm is done by the serious, thoughtful, earnest journalists, who solemnly, as they are doing at present, will drag before the eyes of the public some incident in the private life of a great statesman, of a man who is a leader of political thought as he is a creator of political force, and invite the public to discuss the incident, to exercise authority in the matter, to give their views, and not merely to give their views, but to carry them into action, to dictate to the man upon all other points, to dictate to his party, to dictate to his country; in fact, to make themselves ridiculous, offensive, and harmful. The private lives of men and women should not be told to the public. The public have nothing to do with them at all.

In France they manage these things better. There they do not allow the details of the trials that take place in the divorce courts to be published for the amusement or criticism of the public. All that the public are allowed to know is that the divorce has taken place and was granted on petition of one or other or both of the married parties concerned. In France, in fact, they limit the journalist, and allow the artist almost perfect freedom. Here we allow absolute freedom to the journalist and entirely limit the artist. English public opinion, that is to say, tries to constrain and impede and warp the man who makes things that are beautiful in effect, and compels the journalist to retail things that are ugly, or disgusting, or revolting in fact, so that we have the most serious journalists in the world and the most indecent newspapers. It is no exaggeration to talk of compulsion. There are possibly some journalists who take a real pleasure in publishing horrible things, or who, being poor, look to scandals as forming a sort of permanent basis for an income. But there are other journalists, I feel certain, men of education and cultivation, who really dislike publishing these things, who know that it is wrong to do so, and only do it because the unhealthy conditions under which their occupation is carried on oblige them to supply the public with what the public wants, and to compete with other journalists in making that supply as full and satisfying to the gross popular appetite as possible. It is a very degrading position for any body of educated men to be placed in, and I have no doubt that most of them feel it acutely.

However, let us leave what is really a very sordid side of the subject, and return to the question of popular control in the matter of Art, by which I mean Public Opinion dictating to the artist the form which he is to use, the mode in which he is to use it, and the materials with which he is to work. I have pointed out that the arts which have escaped best in England are the arts in which the public have not been interested. They are, however, interested in the drama, and as a certain advance has been made in the drama within the last ten or fifteen years, it is important to point out that this advance is entirely due to a few individual artists refusing to accept the popular want of taste as their standard, and refusing to regard Art as a mere matter of demand and supply. With his marvellous and vivid personality, with a style that has really a true colour-element in it, with his extraordinary power, not over mere mimicry but over imaginative and intellectual creation, Mr Irving, had his sole object been to give the public what they wanted, could have produced the commonest plays in the commonest manner, and made as much success and money as a man could possibly desire. But his object was not that. His object was to realize his own perfection as an artist, under certain conditions and in certain forms of Art. At first he appealed to the few: now he has educated the many. He has created in the public both taste and temperament. The public appreciate his artistic success immensely. I often wonder, however, whether the public understand that that success is entirely due to the fact that he did not accept their standard, but realized his own. With their standard the Lyceum would have been a sort of second-rate booth, as some of the popular theatres in London are at present. Whether they understand it or not, the fact however remains, that taste and temperament have, to a certain extent, been created in the public, and that the public is capable of developing these qualities. The problem then is, why do not the public become more civilized? They have the capacity. What stops them?

The thing that stops them, it must be said again, is their desire to exercise authority over the artists and over works of art. To certain theatres, such as the Lyceum and the Haymarket, the public seem to come in a proper mood. In both of these theatres there have been individual artists, who have succeeded in creating in their audiences – and every theatre in London has its own audience – the temperament to which Art appeals. And what is that temperament? It is the temperament of receptivity. That is all.

If a man approaches a work of art with any desire to exercise authority over it and the artist, he approaches it in such a spirit that he cannot receive any artistic impression from it at all. The work of art is to dominate the spectator: the spectator is not to dominate the work of art. The spectator is to be receptive. He is to be the violin on which the master is to play. And the more completely he can suppress his own silly views, his own foolish prejudices, his own absurd ideas of what Art should be, or should not be, the more likely he is to understand and appreciate the work of art in question. This is, of course, quite obvious in the case of the vulgar theatre-going public of English men and women. But it is equally true of what are called educated people. For an educated person's ideas of Art are drawn naturally from what Art has been, whereas the new work of art is beautiful by being what Art has never been; and to measure it by the standard of the past is to measure it by a standard on the rejection of which its real perfection depends. A temperament capable of receiving, through an imaginative medium, and under imaginative conditions, new and beautiful impressions, is the only temperament that can appreciate a work of art. And true as this is in the case of the appreciation of sculpture and painting, it is still more true of the appreciation of such arts as the drama. For a picture and a statue are not at war with Time. They take no account of its succession. In one moment their unity may be apprehended. In the case of literature it is different. Time must be traversed before the unity of effect is realized. And so, in the drama, there may occur in the first act of the play something whose real artistic value may not be evident to the spectator till the third or fourth act is reached. Is the silly fellow to get angry and call out, and disturb the play, and annoy the artists? No. The honest man is to sit quietly, and know the delightful emotions of wonder, curiosity, and suspense. He is not to go to the play to lose a vulgar temper. He is to go to the play to realize an artistic temperament. He is to go to the play to gain an artistic temperament. He is not the arbiter of the work of art. He is one who is admitted to contemplate the work of art, and, if the work be fine, to forget in its contemplation all the egotism that mars him – the egotism of his ignorance, or the egotism of his information. The point about the drama is hardly, I think, sufficiently recognized. I can quite understand that were *Macbeth* produced for the first time before a modern London audience, many of the people present would strongly and vigorously object to the introduction of the witches in the first act, with their grotesque phrases and their ridiculous words. But when the play is over one realizes that the laughter of the witches in *Macbeth* is as terrible as the laughter of madness in *Lear*, more terrible than the laughter of Iago in the tragedy of the Moor. No spectator of art needs a more perfect mood of receptivity than the spectator of a play. The moment he seeks to exercise authority he becomes the avowed enemy of Art, and of himself. Art does not mind. It is he who suffers.

With the novel it is the same thing. Popular authority and the recognition of popular authority are fatal. Thackeray's *Esmond* is a beautiful work of art because he wrote it to please himself. In his other novels, in *Pendennis*, in *Philip*, in *Vanity Fair* even, at times, he is too conscious of the public, and spoils his work by appealing directly to the sympathies of the public, or by directly mocking at them. A true artist takes no notice whatever of the public. The public are to him non-existent. He has no poppied or honeyed cakes through which to give the monster sleep or sustenance. He leaves that to the popular novelist. One incomparable novelist we have now in England, Mr George Meredith. There are better artists in France, but France has no one whose view of life is so large, so varied, so imaginatively true. There are tellers of stories in Russia who have a more vivid sense of what pain in fiction may be. But to him belongs philosophy in fiction. His people not merely live, but they live in thought. One can see them from myriad points of view. They are suggestive. There is soul in them and around them. They are interpretative and symbolic. And he who made them, those wonderful, quickly moving figures, made them for his own pleasure, and has never asked the public what they wanted, has never cared to know what they wanted, has never allowed the public to dictate to him or influence him in any way, but has gone on intensifying his own personality, and producing his own individual work. At first none came to him. That did not matter. Then the few came to him. That did not change him. The many have come now. He is still the same. He is an incomparable novelist.

With the decorative arts it is not different. The public clung with really pathetic tenacity to what I believe were the direct traditions of the Great Exhibition of international vulgarity, traditions that were so appalling that the houses in which people lived were only fit for blind people to live in. Beautiful things began to be made, beautiful colours came from the dyer's hand, beautiful patterns from the artist's brain, and the use of beautiful things and their value and importance were set forth. The public were really very indignant. They lost their temper. They said silly things. No one minded. No one was a whit the worse. No one accepted the authority of public opinion. And now it is almost impossible to enter any modern house without seeing some recognition of good taste, some recognition of the value of lovely surroundings, some sign of appreciation of beauty. In fact, people's houses are, as a rule, quite charming nowadays. People have been to a very great extent civilized. It is only fair to state, however, that the extraordinary success of the revolution in house-decoration and furniture and the like has not really been due to the majority of the public developing a very fine taste in such matters. It has been chiefly due to the fact that the craftsmen of things so appreciated the pleasure of making what was beautiful, and woke to such a vivid consciousness of the hideousness and vulgarity of what the public had previously wanted, that they simply starved the public out. It would be quite impossible at the present moment to furnish a room as rooms were furnished a few years ago, without going for everything to an auction of second-hand furniture from some third-rate lodging-house. The things are no longer made. However they may object to it, people must nowadays have something charming in their surroundings. Fortunately for them, their assumption of authority in these art-matters came to entire grief.

It is evident, then, that all authority in such things is bad. People sometimes inquire what form of government is most suitable for an artist to live under. To this question there is only one answer. The form of government that is most suitable to the artist is no government at all. Authority over him and his art is ridiculous. It has been stated that under despotism artists have produced lovely work. This is not quite so. Artists have visited despots, not as subjects to be tyrannized over, but as wandering wonder-makers, as fascinating vagrant personalities, to be entertained and charmed and suffered to be at peace, and allowed to create. There is this to be said in favour of the despot, that he, being an individual, may have culture, while the mob, being a monster, has none. One who is an Emperor and King may stoop down to pick up a brush for a painter, but when the democracy stoops down it is merely to throw mud. And yet the democracy have not so far to stoop as the emperor. In fact, when they want to throw mud they have not to stoop at all. But there is no necessity to separate the monarch from the mob; all authority is equally bad.

There are three kinds of despots. There is the despot who tyrannizes over the body. There is the despot who tyrannizes over the soul. There is the despot who tyrannizes over the soul and body alike. The first is called the Prince. The second is called the Pope. The third is called the People. The Prince may be cultivated. Many Princes have been. Yet in the Prince there is danger. One thinks of Dante at the bitter feast in Verona, of Tasso in Ferrara's madman's cell. It is better for the artist not to live with Princes. The Pope may be cultivated. Many Popes have been; the bad Popes have been. The bad Popes loved Beauty, almost as passionately, nay, with as much passion as the good Popes hated Thought. To the wickedness of the Papacy humanity owes much. The goodness of the Papacy owes a terrible debt to humanity. Yet, though the Vatican has kept the rhetoric of its thunders, and lost the rod of its lightning, it is better for the artist not to live with Popes. It was a Pope who said of Cellini to a conclave of Cardinals that common laws and common authority were not made for men such as he; but it was a Pope who thrust Cellini into prison, and kept him there till he sickened with rage, and created unreal visions for himself, and saw the gilded sun enter his room, and grew so enamoured of it that he sought to escape, and crept out from tower to tower, and falling through dizzy air at dawn, maimed himself, and was by a vine-dresser covered with vine leaves, and carried in a cart to one who, loving beautiful things, had care of him. There is danger in Popes. And as for the People, what of them and their authority? Perhaps of them and their authority one has spoken enough. Their authority is a thing blind, deaf, hideous, grotesque, tragic, amusing, serious and obscene. It is impossible for the artist to live with the People. All despots bribe. The People bribe and brutalize. Who told them to exercise authority? They were made to live, to listen, and to love. Someone has done them a great wrong. They have marred themselves by imitation of their superiors. They have taken the sceptre of the Prince. How should they use it? They have taken the triple tiara of the Pope. How should they carry its burden? They are as a clown whose heart is broken. They are as a priest whose soul is not yet born. Let all who love Beauty pity them.

Though they themselves love not Beauty, yet let them pity themselves. Who taught them the trick of tyranny?

There are many other things that one might point out. One might point out how the Renaissance was great, because it sought to solve no social problem, and busied itself not about such things, but suffered the individual to develop freely, beautifully, and naturally, and so had great and individual artists, and great and individual men. One might point out how Louis XIV, by creating the modern state, destroyed the individualism of the artist, and made things monstrous in their monotony of repetition, and contemptible in their conformity to rule, and destroyed throughout all France all those fine freedoms of expression that had made tradition new in beauty, and new modes one with antique form. But the past is of no importance. The present is of no importance. It is with the future that we have to deal. For the past is what man should not have been. The present is what man ought not to be. The future is what artists are.

It will, of course, be said that such a scheme as is set forth here is quite unpractical, and goes against human nature. This is perfectly true. It is unpractical, and it goes against human nature. This is why it is worth carrying out, and that is why one proposes it. For what is a practical scheme? A practical scheme is either a scheme that is already in existence, or a scheme that could be carried out under existing conditions. But it is exactly the existing conditions that one objects to; and any scheme that could accept these conditions is wrong and foolish. The conditions will be done away with, and human nature will change. The only thing that one really knows about human nature is that it changes. Change is the one quality we can predicate of it. The systems that fail are those that rely on the permanency of human nature, and not on its growth and development. The error of Louis XIV was that he thought human nature would always be the same. The result of his error was the French Revolution. It was an admirable result. All the results of the mistakes of governments are quite admirable.

It is to be noted that Individualism does not come to the man with any sickly cant about duty, which merely means doing what other people want because they want it; or any hideous cant about self-sacrifice, which is merely a survival of savage mutilation. In fact, it does not come to a man with any claims upon him at all. It comes naturally and inevitably out of man. It is the point to which all development tends. It is the differentiation to which all organisms grow. It is the perfection that is inherent in every mode of life, and towards which every mode of life quickens. And so Individualism exercises no compulsion over man. On the contrary, it says to man that he should suffer no compulsion to be exercised over him. It does not try to force people to be good. It knows that people are good when they are let alone. Man will develop Individualism out of himself. Man is now so developing Individualism. To ask whether Individualism is practical is like asking whether Evolution is practical. Evolution is the law of life, and there is no evolution except towards individualism. Where this tendency is not expressed, it is a case of artificially arrested growth, or of disease, or of death.

Individualism will also be unselfish and unaffected. It has been pointed out that one of the results of the extraordinary tyranny of authority is that words are absolutely distorted from their proper and simple meaning, and are used to express the obverse of their right signification. What is true about Art is true about Life. A man is called affected, nowadays, if he dresses as he likes to dress. But in doing that he is acting in a perfectly natural manner. Affectation, in such matters, consists in dressing according to the views of one's neighbour, whose views, as they are the view of the majority, will probably be extremely stupid. Or a man is called selfish if he lives in the manner that seems to him most suitable for the full realization of his own personality; if, in fact, the primary aim of his life is self-development. But this is the way in which everyone should live. Selfishness is not living as one wishes to live, it is asking others to live as one wishes to live. And unselfishness is letting other people's lives alone, not interfering with them. Selfishness always aims at creating around it an absolute uniformity of type. Unselfishness recognizes infinite variety of type as a delightful thing, accepts it, acquiesces in it, enjoys it. It is not selfish to think for oneself. A man who does not think for himself does not think at all. It is grossly selfish to require of one's neighbour that he should think in the same way, and hold the same opinions. Why should he? If he can think, he will probably think differently. If he cannot think, it is monstrous to require thought of any kind from him. A red rose is not selfish because it wants to be a red rose. It would be horribly selfish if it wanted all the other flowers in the garden to be both red and roses. Under Individualism people will be quite natural and absolutely unselfish, and will know the meanings of the words, and realize them in their free, beautiful lives. Nor will men be egotistic as they are now. For the egotist is he who makes claims upon others, and the Individualist will not desire to do that. It will not give him pleasure. When man has realized Individualism, he will also realize sympathy and exercise it freely and spontaneously. Up to the present man has hardly cultivated sympathy at all. He has merely sympathy with pain, and sympathy with pain is not the highest form of sympathy. All sympathy is fine, but sympathy with suffering is the least fine mode. It is tainted with egotism. It is apt to become morbid. There is in it a certain element of terror for our own safety. We become afraid that we ourselves might be as the leper or as the blind, and that no man would have care of us. It is curiously limiting, too. One should sympathize with the entirety of life, not with life's sores and maladies merely, but with life's joy and beauty and energy and health and freedom. The wider sympathy is, of course, the more difficult. It requires more unselfishness. Anybody can sympathize with the sufferings of a friend, but it requires a very fine nature – it requires, in fact, that nature of a true Individualist – to sympathize with a friend's success. In the modern stress of competition and struggle for place, such sympathy is naturally rare, and is also very much stifled by the immoral ideal of uniformity of type and conformity to rule which is so prevalent everywhere, and is perhaps most obnoxious in England.

Sympathy with pain there will, of course, always be. It is one of the first instincts of man. The animals which are individual, the higher animals, that is to say, share it with us. But it must be remembered that while sympathy with joy intensifies the sum of joy in the world, sympathy with pain does not really diminish the amount of pain. It may make man better able to endure evil, but the evil remains. Sympathy with consumption does not cure consumption; that is what science does. And when Socialism has solved the problem of poverty, and Science solved the problem of disease, the area of the sentimentalists will be lessened, and the sympathy of man will be large, healthy and spontaneous. Man will have joy in the contemplation of the joyous life of others.

For it is through joy that the Individualism of the future will develop itself. Christ made no attempt to reconstruct society, and consequently the Individualism that he preached to man could be realized only through pain or in solitude. The Ideals that we owe to Christ are the ideals of the man who abandons society entirely, or of the man who resists society absolutely. But man is naturally social. Even the Thebaid became peopled at last. And though the cenobite realizes his personality, it is often an impoverished personality that he so realizes. Upon the other hand, the terrible truth that pain is a mode through which man may realize himself exercises a wonderful fascination over the world. Shallow speakers and shallow thinkers in pulpits and on platforms often talk about the world's worship of pleasure, and whine against it. But it is rarely in the world's history that its ideal has been one of joy and beauty. The worship of pain has far more often dominated the world. Medievalism, with its saints and martyrs, its love of self-torture, its wild passion for wounding itself, its gashing with knives, and its whipping with rods – Medievalism is real Christianity, and the medieval Christ is the real Christ. When the Renaissance dawned upon the world, and brought with it the new ideals of the beauty of life and the joy of living, men could not understand Christ. Even Art shows us that. The painters of the Renaissance drew Christ as a little boy playing with another boy in a palace or a garden, or lying back in his mother's arms, smiling at her, or at a flower, or at a bright bird; or as a noble, stately figure moving nobly through the world; or as a wonderful figure rising in a sort of ecstasy from death to life. Even when they drew him crucified they drew him as a beautiful God on whom evil men had inflicted suffering. But he did not preoccupy them much. What delighted them was to paint the men and women whom they admired, and to show the loveliness of this lovely earth. They painted many religious pictures – in fact they painted far too many, and the monotony of type and motive is wearisome, and was bad for art. It was the result of the authority of the public in art-matters, and is to be deplored. But their soul was not in the subject. Raphael was a great artist when he painted his portrait of the Pope. When he painted his Madonnas and infant Christs, he was not a great artist at all. Christ had no message for the Renaissance, which was wonderful because it brought an ideal at variance with his, and to find the presentation of the real Christ we must go to medieval art. There he is one maimed and marred; one who is not comely to look on, because Beauty is a joy; one who is not in fair raiment, because that may be a joy also: he is a beggar who has a marvellous soul; he is a leper whose soul is divine; he needs neither property nor health; he is a God realizing his perfection through pain.

The evolution of man is slow. The injustice of men is great. It was necessary that pain should be put forward as a mode of self-realization. Even now, in some places in the world, the message of Christ is necessary. No one who lived in modern Russia could possibly realize his perfection except by pain. A few Russian artists have realized themselves in Art; in a fiction that is medieval in character, because its dominant note is the realization of men through suffering. But for those who are not artists, and to whom there is no mode of life but the actual life of fact, pain is the only door to perfection. A Russian who lives happily under the present system of government in Russia must either believe that man has no soul, or that, if he has, it is not worth developing. A Nihilist who rejects all authority because he knows authority to be evil, and welcomes all pain, because through that he realizes his personality, is a real Christian. To him the Christian ideal is a true thing.

And yet, Christ did not revolt against authority. He accepted the imperial authority of the Roman Empire and paid tribute. He endured the ecclesiastical authority of the Jewish Church, and would not repel its violence by any violence of his own. He had, as I said before, no scheme for the reconstruction of society. But the modern world has schemes. It proposes to do away with poverty, and the suffering that it entails. It desires to get rid of pain, and the suffering that pain entails. It trusts to Socialism and to Science as its methods. What it aims at is an Individualism expressing itself through joy. This Individualism will be larger, fuller, lovelier than any Individualism has ever been. Pain is not the ultimate mode of perfection. It is merely provisional and a protest. It has reference to wrong, unhealthy, unjust surroundings. When the wrong, and the disease, and the injustice are removed, it will have no further place. It was a great work, but it is almost over. Its sphere lessens every day.

Nor will man miss it. For what man has sought for is, indeed, neither pain nor pleasure, but simply Life. Man has sought to live intensely, fully, perfectly. When he can do so without exercising restraint on others, or suffering it ever, and his activities are all pleasurable to him, he will be saner, healthier, more civilized, more himself. Pleasure is Nature's test, her sign of approval. When man is happy, he is in harmony with himself and his environment. The new Individualism, for whose service Socialism, whether it wills it or not, is working, will be perfect harmony. It will be what the Greeks sought for, but could not, except in Thought, realize completely because they had slaves, and fed them; it will be what the Renaissance sought for, but could not realize completely except in Art, because they had slaves, and starved them. It will be complete, and through it each man will attain to his perfection. The new Individualism is the new Hellenism.

The Decay of Lying

AN OBSERVATION

A DIALOGUE

Persons: Cyril and Vivian
Scene: The library of a country house
in Nottinghamshire

*

The Decay of Lying

Cyril (*coming in through the open window from the terrace*): My dear Vivian, don't coop yourself up all day in the library. It is a perfectly lovely afternoon. The air is exquisite. There is a mist upon the woods, like the purple bloom upon a plum. Let us go and lie on the grass and smoke cigarettes and enjoy Nature.

Vivian: Enjoy Nature! I am glad to say that I have entirely lost that faculty. People tell us that Art makes us love Nature more than we loved her before; that it reveals her secrets to us; and that after a careful study of Corot and Constable we see things in her that had escaped our observation. My own experience is that the more we study Art, the less we care for Nature. What Art really reveals to us is Nature's lack of design, her curious crudities, her extraordinary monotony, her absolutely unfinished condition. Nature has good intentions, of course, but, as Aristotle once said, she cannot carry them out. When I look at a landscape I cannot help seeing all its defects. It is fortunate for us, however, that Nature is so imperfect, as otherwise we should have no art at all. Art is our spirited protest, our gallant attempt to teach Nature her proper place. As for the infinite variety of Nature, that is a pure myth. It is not to be found in Nature herself. It resides in the imagination, or fancy, or cultivated blindness of the man who looks at her.

Cyril: Well, you need not look at the landscape. You can lie on the grass and smoke and talk.

Vivian: But Nature is so uncomfortable. Grass is hard and lumpy and damp, and full of dreadful black insects. Why, even Morris's poorest workman could make you a more comfortable seat than the whole of Nature can. Nature pales before the furniture of 'the street which from Oxford has borrowed its name', as the poet you love so much once vilely phrased it. I don't complain. If Nature had been comfortable, mankind would never have invented architecture, and I prefer houses to the open air. In a house we all feel of the proper proportions. Everything is subordinated to us, fashioned for our use and our pleasure. Egotism itself, which is so necessary to a proper sense of human dignity, is entirely the result of indoor life. Out of doors one becomes abstract and impersonal. One's individuality absolutely leaves one. And then Nature is so indifferent, so unappreciative. Whenever I am walking in the park here, I always feel that I am no more to her than the cattle that browse on the slope, or the burdock that blooms in the ditch. Nothing is more evident than that Nature hates Mind. Thinking is the most unhealthy thing in the world, and people die of it just as they die of any other disease. Fortunately, in England at any rate, thought is not catching. Our splendid physique as a people is entirely due to our national stupidity. I only hope we shall be able to keep this great historic bulwark of our happiness for many years to come; but I am afraid that we are beginning to be over-educated; at least everybody who is incapable of learning has taken to teaching – that is really what our enthusiasm for education has come to. In the meantime, you had better go back to your wearisome uncomfortable Nature, and leave me to correct my proofs.

Cyril: Writing an article! That is not very consistent after what you have just said.

Vivian: Who wants to be consistent? The dullard and the doctrinaire, the tedious people who carry out their principles to the bitter end of action, to the *reductio ad absurdum* of practice. Not I. Like Emerson, I write over the door of my library the word 'Whim'. Besides, my article is really a most salutary and valuable warning. If it is attended to, there may be a new Renaissance of Art.

Cyril: What is the subject?

Vivian: I intend to call it 'The Decay of Lying: A Protest'.

Cyril: Lying! I should have thought that our politicians kept up that habit.

Vivian: I assure you that they do not. They never rise beyond the level of misrepresentation, and actually condescend to prove, to discuss, to argue. How different from the temper of the true liar, with his frank, fearless statements, his superb irresponsibility, his healthy, natural disdain of proof of any kind! After all, what is a fine lie? Simply that which is its own evidence. If a man is sufficiently unimaginative to produce evidence in support of a lie, he might just as well speak the truth at once. No, the politicians won't do. Something may, perhaps, be urged on behalf of the Bar. The mantle of the Sophist has fallen on its members. Their feigned ardours and unreal rhetoric are delightful. They can make the worse appear the better cause, as though they were fresh from Leontine schools, and have been known to wrest from reluctant juries triumphant verdicts of acquittal for their clients, even when those clients, as often happens, were clearly and unmistakably innocent. But they are briefed by the prosaic, and are not ashamed to appeal to precedent. In spite of their endeavours, the truth will out. Newspapers, even, have degenerated. They may now be absolutely relied upon. One feels it as one wades through their columns. It is always the unreadable that occurs. I am afraid that there is not much to be said in favour of either the lawyer or the journalist. Besides, what I am pleading for is Lying in art. Shall I read you what I have written? It might do you a great deal of good.

Cyril: Certainly, if you give me a cigarette. Thanks. By the way, what magazine do you intend it for?

Vivian: For the *Retrospective Review*. I think I told you that the elect had revived it.

Cyril: Whom do you mean by 'the elect'?

Vivian: Oh, The Tired Hedonists, of course. It is a club to which I belong. We are supposed to wear faded roses in our button-holes when we meet, and to have a sort of cult for Domitian. I am afraid you are not eligible. You are too fond of simple pleasures.

Cyril: I should be black-balled on the ground of animal spirits, I suppose?

Vivian: Probably. Besides, you are a little too old. We don't admit anybody who is of the usual age.

Cyril: Well, I should fancy you are all a good deal bored with each other.

The Decay of Lying

Vivian: We are. That is one of the objects of the club. Now, if you promise not to interrupt too often, I will read you my article.

Cyril: You will find me all attention.

Vivian (*reading in a very clear voice*): 'THE DECAY OF LYING: A PROTEST. – One of the chief causes that can be assigned for the curiously commonplace character of most of the literature of our age is undoubtedly the decay of Lying as an art, a science, and a social pleasure. The ancient historians gave us delightful fiction in the form of fact; the modern novelist presents us with dull facts under the guise of fiction. The Blue-Book is rapidly becoming his ideal both for method and manner. He has his tedious *document humain*, his miserable little *coin de la création*, into which he peers with his microscope. He is to be found at the Librairie Nationale, or at the British Museum, shamelessly reading up his subject. He has not even the courage of other people's ideas, but insists on going directly to life for everything, and ultimately, between encyclopaedias and personal experience, he comes to the ground, having drawn his types from the family circle or from the weekly washerwoman, and having acquired an amount of useful information from which never, even in his most meditative moments, can he thoroughly free himself.

'The loss that results to literature in general from this false ideal of our time can hardly be overestimated. People have a careless way of talking about a "born liar", just as they talk about a "born poet". But in both cases they are wrong. Lying and poetry are arts – arts, as Plato saw, not unconnected with each other – and they require the most careful study, the most disinterested devotion. Indeed, they have their technique, just as the more material arts of painting and sculpture have, their subtle secrets of form and colour, their craft-mysteries, their deliberate artistic methods. As one knows the poet by his fine music, so one can recognize the liar by his rich rhythmic utterance, and in neither case will the casual inspiration of the moment suffice. Here, as elsewhere, practice must precede perfection. But in modern days while the fashion of writing poetry has become far too common, and should, if possible, be discouraged, the fashion of lying has almost fallen into disrepute. Many a young man starts in life with a natural gift for exaggeration which, if nurtured in congenial and sympathetic surroundings, or by the imitation of the best models, might grow into something really great and wonderful. But, as a rule, he comes to nothing. He either falls into careless habits of accuracy –'

Cyril: My dear fellow!

Vivian: Please don't interrupt in the middle of a sentence. 'He either falls into careless habits of accuracy, or takes to frequenting the society of the aged and the well-informed. Both things are equally fatal to his imagination, as indeed they would be fatal to the imagination of anybody, and in a short time he develops a morbid and unhealthy faculty of truth-telling, begins to verify all statements made in his presence, has no hesitation in contradicting people who are much younger than himself, and often ends by writing novels which are so life-like that no one can possibly believe in their probability. This is no isolated instance that we are giving. It is simply one example out of many; and if something cannot be done to check, or at least to modify, our monstrous worship of facts, Art will become sterile, and beauty will pass away from the land.

'Even Mr Robert Louis Stevenson, that delightful master of delicate and fanciful prose, is tainted with this modern vice, for we know positively no other name for it. There is such a thing as robbing a story of its reality by trying to make it too true, and *The Black Arrow* is so inartistic as not to contain a single anachronism to boast of, while the transformation of Dr Jekyll reads dangerously like an experiment out of the *Lancet*. As for Mr Rider Haggard, who really has, or had once, the makings of a perfectly magnificent liar, he is now so afraid of being suspected of genius that when he does tell us anything marvellous, he feels bound to invent a personal reminiscence, and to put it into a footnote as a kind of cowardly corroboration. Nor are our other novelists much better. Mr Henry James writes fiction as if it were a painful duty, and wastes upon mean motives and imperceptible "points of view" his neat literary style, his felicitous phrases, his swift and caustic satire. Mr Hall Caine, it is true, aims at the grandiose, but then he writes at the top of his voice. He is so loud that one cannot hear what he says. Mr James Payn is an adept in the art of concealing what is not worth finding. He hunts down the obvious with the enthusiasm of a short-sighted detective. As one turns over the pages, the suspense of the author becomes almost unbearable. The horses of Mr William Black's phaeton do not soar towards the sun. They merely frighten the sky at evening into violent chromolithographic effects. On seeing them approach, the peasants take refuge in dialect. Mrs Oliphant prattles pleasantly about curates, lawn-tennis parties, domesticity, and other wearisome things. Mr Marion Crawford has immolated himself upon the altar of local colour. He is like the lady in the French comedy who keeps talking about "le beau ciel d'Italie". Besides, he has fallen into the bad habit of uttering moral platitudes. He is always telling us that to be good is to be good, and that to be bad is to be wicked. At times he is almost edifying. *Robert Elsmere* is of course a masterpiece – a masterpiece of the "genre ennuyeux", the one form of literature that the English people seems thoroughly to enjoy. A thoughtful young friend of ours once told us that it reminded him of the sort of conversation that goes on at a meat tea in the house of a serious Nonconformist family, and we can quite believe it. Indeed it is only in England that such a book could be produced. England is the home of lost ideas. As for that great and daily increasing school of novelists for whom the sun always rises in the East-End, the only thing that can be said about them is that they find life crude, and leave it raw.

'In France, though nothing so deliberately tedious as *Robert Elsmere* had been produced, things are not much better. M. Guy de Maupassant, with his keen mordant irony and his hard vivid style, strips life of the few poor rags that still cover her, and shows us foul sore and festering wound. He writes lurid little tragedies in which everybody is ridiculous; bitter comedies at which one cannot laugh for very tears. M. Zola, true to the lofty principle that he lays down in one of his pronunciamientos on literature, "L'homme de génie n'a jamais d'esprit", is determined to show that, if he has not got genius, he can at least be dull. And how well he succeeds! He is not without power. Indeed at times, as in

Germinal, there is something almost epic in his work. But his work is entirely wrong from beginning to end, and wrong not on the ground of morals, but on the ground of art. From any ethical standpoint it is just what it should be. The author is perfectly truthful, and describes things exactly as they happen. What more can any moralist desire? We have no sympathy at all with the moral indignation of our time against M. Zola. It is simply the indignation of Tartuffe on being exposed. But from the standpoint of art, what can be said in favour of the author of *L'Assommoir*, *Nana* and *Pot-Bouille*? Nothing. Mr Ruskin once described the characters in George Eliot's novels as being like the sweepings of a Pentonville omnibus, but M. Zola's characters are much worse. They have their dreary vices, and their drearier virtues. The record of their lives is absolutely without interest. Who cares what happens to them? In literature we require distinction, charm, beauty and imaginative power. We don't want to be harrowed and disgusted with an account of the doings of the lower orders. M. Daudet is better. He has wit, a light touch and an amusing style. But he has lately committed literary suicide. Nobody can possibly care for Delobelle with his "Il faut lutter pour l'art", or for Valmajour with his eternal refrain about the nightingale, or for the poet in *Jack* with his "mots cruels", now that we have learned from *Vingt Ans de ma Vie littéraire* that these characters were taken directly from life. To us they seem to have suddenly lost all their vitality, all the few qualities they ever possessed. The only real people are the people who never existed, and if a novelist is base enough to go to life for his personages he should at least pretend that they are creations, and not boast of them as copies. The justification of a character in a novel is not that other persons are what they are, but that the author is what he is. Otherwise the novel is not a work of art. As for M. Paul Bourget, the master of the *roman psychologique*, he commits the error of imagining that the men and women of modern life are capable of being infinitely analysed for an innumerable series of chapters. In point of fact what is interesting about people in good society – and M. Bourget rarely moves out of the Faubourg St Germain, except to come to London, – is the mask that each one of them wears, not the reality that lies behind the mask. It is a humiliating confession, but we are all of us made out of the same stuff. In Falstaff there is something of Hamlet, in Hamlet there is not a little of Falstaff. The fat knight has his moods of melancholy, and the young prince his moments of coarse humour. Where we differ from each other is purely in accidentals: in dress, manner, tone of voice, religious opinions, personal appearance, tricks of habit and the like. The more one analyses people, the more all reasons for analysis disappear. Sooner or later one comes to that dreadful universal thing called human nature. Indeed, as anyone who has ever worked among the poor knows only too well, the brotherhood of man is no mere poet's dream, it is a most depressing and humiliating reality; and if a writer insists upon analysing the upper classes, he might just as well write of match-girls and costermongers at once.' However, my dear Cyril, I will not detain you any further just here. I quite admit that modern novels have many good points. All I insist on is that, as a class, they are quite unreadable.

Cyril: That is certainly a very grave qualification, but I must say that I think you are rather unfair in some of your strictures. I like *The Deemster*, and *The Daughter of Heth*, and *Le Disciple*, and *Mr Isaacs*, and as for *Robert Elsmere*, I am quite devoted to it. Not that I can look upon it as a serious work. As a statement of the problems that confront the earnest Christian it is ridiculous and antiquated. It is simply Arnold's *Literature and Dogma* with the literature left out. It is as much behind the age as Paley's *Evidences*, or Colenso's method of Biblical exegesis. Nor could anything be less impressive than the unfortunate hero gravely heralding a dawn that rose long ago, and so completely missing its true significance that he proposes to carry on the business of the old firm under the new name. On the other hand, it contains several clever caricatures, and a heap of delightful quotations, and Green's philosophy very pleasantly sugars the somewhat bitter pill of the author's fiction. I also cannot help expressing my surprise that you have said nothing about the two novelists whom you are always reading, Balzac and George Meredith. Surely they are realists, both of them?

The Decay of Lying

Vivian: Ah! Meredith! Who can define him? His style is chaos illumined by flashes of lightning. As a writer he has mastered everything except language: as a novelist he can do everything, except tell a story: as an artist he is everything except articulate. Somebody in Shakespeare – Touchstone, I think – talks about a man who is always breaking his shins over his own wit, and it seems to me that this might serve as the basis for a criticism of Meredith's method. But whatever he is, he is not a realist. Or rather I would say that he is a child of realism who is not on speaking terms with his father. By deliberate choice he has made himself a romanticist. He has refused to bow the knee to Baal, and after all, even if the man's fine spirit did not revolt against the noisy assertions of realism, his style would be quite sufficient of itself to keep life at a respectful distance. By its means he has planted round his garden a hedge full of thorns, and red with wonderful roses. As for Balzac, he was a most remarkable combination of the artistic temperament with the scientific spirit. The latter he bequeathed to his disciples. The former was entirely his own. The difference between such a book as M. Zola's *L'Assommoir* and Balzac's *Illusions Perdues* is the difference between unimaginative realism and imaginative reality. 'All Balzac's characters', said Baudelaire, 'are gifted with the same ardour of life that animated himself. All his fictions are as deeply coloured as dreams. Each mind is a weapon loaded to the muzzle with will. The very scullions have genius.' A steady course of Balzac reduces our living friends to shadows, and our acquaintances to the shadows of shades. His characters have a kind of fervent fiery-coloured existence. They dominate us, and defy scepticism. One of the greatest tragedies of my life is the death of Lucien de Rubempré. It is a grief from which I have never been able completely to rid myself. It haunts me in my moments of pleasure. I remember it when I laugh. But Balzac is no more a realist than Holbein was. He created life, he did not copy it. I admit, however, that he set far too high a value on modernity of form, and that, consequently, there is no book of his that, as an artistic masterpiece, can rank with *Salammbo* or *Esmond*, or *The Cloister and the Hearth*, or the *Vicomte de Bragelonne*.

Cyril: Do you object to modernity of form, then?

Vivian: Yes. It is a huge price to pay for a very poor result. Pure modernity of form is always somewhat vulgarizing. It cannot help being so. The public imagine that, because they are interested in their immediate surroundings, Art should be interested in them also, and should take them as her subject-matter. But the mere fact that they are interested in these things makes them unsuitable subjects for Art. The only beautiful things, as somebody once said, are the things that do not concern us. As long as a thing is useful or necessary to us, or affects us in any way, either for pain or for pleasure, or appeals strongly to our sympathies, or is a vital part of the environment in which we live, it is outside the proper sphere of art. To art's subject-matter we should be more or less indifferent. We should, at any rate, have no preferences, no prejudices, no partisan feeling of any kind. It is exactly because Hecuba is nothing to us that her sorrows are such an admirable motive for a tragedy. I do not know anything in the whole history of literature sadder than the artistic career of Charles Reade. He wrote one beautiful book, *The Cloister and the Hearth*, a book as much above *Romola* as *Romola* is above *Daniel Deronda*, and wasted the rest of his life in a foolish attempt to be modern, to draw public attention to the state of our convict prisons, and the management of our private lunatic asylums. Charles Dickens was depressing enough in all conscience when he tried to arouse our sympathy for the victims of the poor-law administration; but Charles Reade, an artist, a scholar, a man with a true sense of beauty, raging and roaring over the abuses of contemporary life like a common pamphleteer or a sensational journalist, is really a sight for the angels to weep over. Believe me, my dear Cyril, modernity of form and modernity of subject-matter are entirely and absolutely wrong. We have mistaken the common livery of the age for the vesture of the Muses, and spend our days in the sordid streets and hideous suburbs of our vile cities when we should be out on the hillside with Apollo. Certainly we are a degraded race, and have sold our birthright for a mess of facts.

Cyril: There is something in what you say, and there is no doubt that whatever amusement we may find in reading a purely modern novel, we have rarely any artistic pleasure in re-reading it. And this is perhaps the best rough test of what is literature and what is not. If one cannot enjoy reading a book over and over again, there is no use reading it at all. But what do you say about the return to Life and Nature? This is the panacea that is always being recommended to us.

Vivian: I will read you what I say on that subject. The passage comes later on in the article, but I may as well give it to you now:

'The popular cry of our time is "Let us return to Life and Nature; they will recreate Art for us, and send the red blood coursing through her veins; they will shoe her feet with swiftness and make her hand strong". But, alas! we are mistaken in our amiable and well-meaning efforts. Nature is always behind the age. And as for Life, she is the solvent that breaks up Art, the enemy that lays waste her house.'

Cyril: What do you mean by saying that Nature is always behind the age?

Vivian: Well, perhaps that is rather cryptic. What I mean is this. If we take Nature to mean natural simple instinct as opposed to self-conscious culture, the work produced under this influence is always old-fashioned, antiquated, and out of date. One touch of Nature may make the whole world kin, but two touches of Nature will destroy any work of Art. If, on the other hand, we regard Nature as the collection of phenomena external to man, people only discover in her what they bring to her. She has no suggestions of her own. Wordsworth went to the lakes, but he was never a lake poet. He found in stones the sermons he had already hidden there. He went moralizing about the district, but his good work was produced when he returned, not to Nature but to poetry. Poetry gave him 'Laodamia', and the fine sonnets, and the great Ode, such as it is. Nature gave him 'Martha Ray' and 'Peter Bell', and the address to Mr. Wilkinson's spade.

Cyril: I think that view might be questioned. I am rather inclined to believe in 'the impulse from a vernal wood', though of course the artistic value of such an impulse depends entirely on the kind of temperament that receives it, so that the return to

Nature would come to mean simply the advance to a great personality. You would agree with that, I fancy. However, proceed with your article.

Vivian (reading): 'Art begins with abstract decoration, with purely imaginative and pleasurable work dealing with what is unreal and non-existent. This is the first stage. Then Life becomes fascinated with this new wonder, and asks to be admitted into the charmed circle. Art takes life as part of her rough material, recreates it, and refashions it in fresh forms, is absolutely indifferent to fact, invents, imagines, dreams, and keeps between herself and reality the impenetrable barrier of beautiful style, of decorative or ideal treatment. The third stage is when Life gets the upper hand, and drives Art out into the wilderness. This is the true decadence, and it is from this that we are now suffering.

'Take the case of the English drama. At first in the hands of the monks Dramatic Art was abstract, decorative and mythological. Then she enlisted Life in her service, and using some of life's external forms, she created an entirely new race of beings, whose sorrows were more terrible than any sorrow man has ever felt, whose joys were keener than lover's joys, who had the rage of the Titans and the calm of the gods, who had monstrous and marvellous sins, monstrous and marvellous virtues. To them she gave a language different from that of actual use, a language full of resonant music and sweet rhythm, made stately by solemn cadence, or made delicate by fanciful rhyme, jewelled with wonderful words, and enriched with lofty diction. She clothed her children in strange raiment and gave them masks, and at her bidding the antique world rose from its marble tomb. A new Caesar stalked through the streets of risen Rome, and with purple sail and flute-led oars another Cleopatra passed up the river to Antioch. Old myth and legend and dream took shape and substance. History was entirely re-written, and there was hardly one of the dramatists who did not recognize that the object of Art is not simple truth but complex beauty. In this they were perfectly right. Art itself is really a form of exaggeration; and selection, which is the very spirit of art, is nothing more than an intensified mode of over-emphasis.

'But Life soon shattered the perfection of the form. Even in Shakespeare we can see the beginning of the end. It shows itself by the gradual breaking-up of the blank-verse in the later plays, by the predominance given to prose, and by the over-importance assigned to characterization. The passages in Shakespeare – and they are many – where the language is uncouth, vulgar, exaggerated, fantastic, obscene even, are entirely due to Life calling for an echo of her own voice, and rejecting the intervention of beautiful style, through which alone should life be suffered to find expression. Shakespeare is not by any means a flawless artist. He is too fond of going directly to life, and borrowing life's natural utterance. He forgets that when Art surrenders her imaginative medium she surrenders everything. Goethe says, somewhere:

In der Beschränkung zeigt sich erst der Meister,

It is in working within limits that the master reveals himself, and the limitation, the very condition of any art is style. However, we need not linger any longer over Shakespeare's realism. *The Tempest* is the most perfect of palinodes. All that we desired to point out was that the magnificent work of the Elizabethan and Jacobean artists contained within itself the seeds of its own dissolution, and that, if it drew some of its strength from using life as rough material, it drew all its weakness from using life as an artistic method. As the inevitable result of this substitution of an imitative for a creative medium, this surrender of an imaginative form, we have the modern English melodrama. The characters in these plays talk on the stage exactly as they would talk off it; they have neither aspirations nor aspirates; they are taken directly from life and reproduce its vulgarity down to the smallest detail; they present the gait, manner, costume and accent of real people; they would pass unnoticed in a third-class railway carriage. And yet how wearisome the plays are! They do not succeed in producing even that impression of reality at which they aim, and which is their only reason for existing. As a method, realism is a complete failure.

'What is true about the drama and the novel is no less true about those arts that we call the decorative arts. The whole history of these arts in Europe is the record of the struggle between Orientalism, with its frank rejection of imitation, its love of artistic convention, its dislike of the actual representation of any object in Nature, and our own imitative spirit. Wherever the former has been paramount, as in Byzantium, Sicily and Spain, by actual contact or in the rest of Europe by the influence of the Crusades, we have had beautiful and imaginative work in which the visible things of life are transmuted into artistic conventions, and the things that Life has not are invented and fashioned for her delight. But wherever we have returned to Life and Nature, our work has always become vulgar, common and uninteresting. Modern tapestry, with its aerial effects, its elaborate perspective, its broad expanses of waste sky, its faithful and laborious realism, has no beauty whatsoever. The pictorial glass of Germany is absolutely detestable. We are beginning to weave possible carpets in England, but only because we have returned to the method and spirit of the East. Our rugs and carpets of twenty years ago, with their solemn depressing truths, their inane worship of Nature, their sordid reproductions of visible objects, have become, even to the Philistine, a source of laughter. A cultured Mahomedan once remarked to us, "You Christians are so occupied in mis-interpreting the fourth commandment that you have never thought of making an artistic application of the second." He was perfectly right, and the whole truth of the matter is this: The proper school to learn art in is not Life but Art.'

And now let me read you a passage which seems to me to settle the question very completely.

'It was not always thus. We need not say anything about the poets, for they, with the unfortunate exception of Mr Words-worth, have been really faithful to their high mission, and are universally recognized as being absolutely unreliable. But in the works of Herodotus, who, in spite of the shallow and ungenerous attempts of modern sciolists to verify his history, may justly be called the "Father of Lies"; in the published speeches of Cicero and the biographies of Suetonius; in Tacitus at his best; in Pliny's *Natural History*; in Hanno's *Periplus*; in all the early chronicles; in the Lives of the Saints; in Froissart and Sir Thomas Malory; in the travels of Marco Polo; in Olaus Magnus, and Aldrovandus, and Conrad Lycosthenes, with his magnificent *Prodigiorum et Ostentorum Chronicon*; in the autobiography of Benvenuto Cellini; in the memoirs of Casanova; in Defoe's *History of the Plague*; in Boswell's *Life of Johnson*; in Napoleon's despatches, and in the works of our own Carlyle, whose *French Revolution* is one of the most fascinating historical novels ever written, facts are either kept in their proper subordinate position, or else entirely excluded on the general ground of dullness. Now, everything is changed. Facts are not merely finding a footing-place in history, but they are usurping the domain of Fancy, and have invaded the kingdom of Romance. Their chilling touch is over everything. They are vulgarizing mankind. The crude commercialism of America, its materializing spirit, its indifference to the poetical side of things, and its lack of imagination and of high unattainable ideals, are entirely due to that country having adopted for its national hero a man who, according to his own confession, was incapable of telling a lie, and it is not too much to say that the story of George Washington and the cherry-tree has done more harm, and in a shorter space of time, than any other moral tale in the whole of literature.'

Cyril: My dear boy!

Vivian: I assure you it is the case, and the amusing part of the whole thing is that the story of the cherry-tree is an absolute myth. However, you must not think that I am too despondent about the artistic future either of America or of our own country. Listen to this:

'That some change will take place before this century has drawn to its close we have no doubt whatsoever. Bored by the tedious and improving conversation of those who have neither the wit to exaggerate nor the genius to romance, tired of the intelligent person whose reminiscences are always based upon memory, whose statements are invariably limited by probability, and who is at any time liable to be corroborated by the merest Philistine who happens to be present, Society sooner or later must return to its lost leader, the cultured and fascinating liar. Who he was who first, without ever having gone out to the rude chase, told the wandering cavemen at sunset how he had dragged the Megatherium from the purple darkness of its jasper cave, or slain the Mammoth in single combat and brought back its gilded tusks, we cannot tell, and not one of our modern anthropologists, for all their much-boasted science, has had the ordinary courage to tell us. Whatever was his name or race, he certainly was the true founder of social intercourse. For the aim of the liar is simply to charm, to delight, to give pleasure. He is the very basis of civilized society, and without him a dinner-party, even at the mansions of the great, is as dull as a lecture at the Royal Society, or a debate at the Incorporated Authors, or one of Mr Burnand's farcial comedies.

'Nor will he be welcomed by society alone. Art, breaking from the prison-house of realism, will run to greet him, and will kiss his false, beautiful lips, knowing that he alone is in possession of the great secret of all her manifestations, the secret that Truth is entirely and absolutely a matter of style; while Life – poor, probable, uninteresting human life – tired of repeating herself for the benefit of Mr Herbert Spencer, scientific historians, and the compilers of statistics in general, will follow meekly after him, and try to reproduce, in her own simple and untutored way, some of the marvels of which he talks.

'No doubt there will always be critics who, like a certain writer in the *Saturday Review*, will gravely censure the teller of fairy tales for his defective knowledge of natural history, who will measure imaginative work by their own lack of any imaginative faculty, and will hold up their ink-stained hands in horror if some honest gentleman, who has never been farther than the yew-trees of his own garden, pens a fascinating book of travels like Sir John Mandeville, or, like great Raleigh, writes a whole history of the world, without knowing anything whatsoever about the past. To excuse themselves they will try and shelter under the shield of him who made Prospero the magician, and gave him Caliban and Ariel as his servants, who heard the Tritons blowing their horns round the coral reefs of the Enchanted Isle, and the fairies singing to each other in a wood near Athens, who led the phantom kings in dim procession across the misty Scottish heath, and hid

Hecate in a cave with the weird sisters. They will call upon Shakespeare – they always do – and will quote that hackneyed passage forgetting that this unfortunate aphorism about Art holding the mirror up to Nature, is deliberately said by Hamlet in order to convince the bystanders of his absolute insanity in all art-matters.'

Cyril: Ahem! Another cigarette, please.

Vivian: My dear fellow, whatever you may say, it is merely a dramatic utterance, and no more represents Shakespeare's real views upon art than the speeches of Iago represent his real views upon morals. But let me get to the end of the passage:

'Art finds her own perfection within, and not outside of, herself. She is not to be judged by any external standard of resemblance. She is a veil, rather than a mirror. She has flowers that no forests know of, birds that no woodland possesses. She makes and unmakes many worlds, and can draw the moon from heaven with a scarlet thread. Hers are the "forms more real than living man", and hers the great archetypes of which things that have existence are but unfinished copies. Nature has, in her eyes, no laws, no uniformity. She can work miracles at her will, and when she calls monsters from the deep they come. She can bid the almond-tree blossom in winter, and send the snow upon the ripe cornfield. At her word the frost lays its silver finger on the burning mouth of June, and the winged lions creep out from the hollows of the Lydian hills. The dryads peer from the thicket as she passes by, and the brown fauns smile strangely at her when she comes near them. She has hawk-faced gods that worship her, and the centaurs gallop at her side.'

Cyril: I like that. I can see it. Is that the end?

Vivian: No. There is one more passage, but it is purely practical. It simply suggests some methods by which we could revive this lost art of Lying.

Cyril: Well, before you read it to me, I should like to ask you a question. What do you mean by saying that life, 'poor, probable, uninteresting human life', will try to reproduce the marvels of art? I can quite understand your objection to art being treated as a mirror. You think it would reduce genius to the position of a cracked looking-glass. But you don't mean to say that you seriously believe that Life imitates Art, that Life in fact is the mirror, and Art the reality?

Vivian: Certainly I do. Paradox though it may seem – and paradoxes are always dangerous things – it is none the less true that Life imitates art far more than Art imitates life. We have all seen in our own day in England how a certain curious and fascinating type of beauty, invented and emphasized by two imaginative painters, has so influenced Life that whenever one goes to a private view or to an artistic salon one sees, here the mystic eyes of Rossetti's dream, the long ivory throat, the strange square-cut jaw, the loosened shadowy hair that he so ardently loved, there the sweet maidenhood of 'The Golden Stair', the blossom-like mouth and weary loveliness of the 'Laus Amoris', the passion-pale face of Andromeda, the thin hands and lithe beauty of the Vivian in 'Merlin's Dream'. And it has always been so. A great artist invents a type, and Life tries to copy it, to reproduce it in a popular form, like an enterprising publisher. Neither Holbein nor Vandyck found in England what they have given us. They brought their types with them, and Life with her keen imitative faculty set herself to supply the master with models. The Greeks, with their quick artistic instinct, understood this, and set in the bride's chamber the statue of Hermes or of Apollo, that she might bear children as lovely as the works of art that she looked at in her rapture or her pain. They knew that Life gains from art not merely spirituality, depth of thought and feeling, soul-turmoil or soul-peace, but that she can form herself on the very lines and colours of art, and can reproduce the dignity of Pheidias as well as the grace of Praxiteles. Hence came their objection to realism. They disliked it on purely social grounds. They felt that it inevitably makes people ugly, and they were perfectly right. We try to improve the conditions of the race by means of good air, free sunlight, wholesome water, and hideous bare buildings for the better housing of the lower orders. But these things merely produce health, they do not produce beauty. For this, Art is required, and the true disciples of the great artist are not his studio-imitators, but those who become like his works of art, be they plastic as in Greek days, or pictorial as in modern times; in a word, Life is Art's best, Art's only pupil.

As it is with the visible arts, so it is with literature. The most obvious and the vulgarest form in which this is shown is in the case of the silly boys who, after reading the adventures of Jack Sheppard or Dick Turpin, pillage the stalls of unfortunate apple-women, break into sweet-shops at night, and alarm old gentlemen who are returning home from the city by leaping out on them in suburban lanes, with black masks and unloaded revolvers. This interesting phenomenon, which always occurs after the appearance of a new edition of either of the books I have alluded to, is usually attributed to the influence of literature on the imagination. But this is a mistake. The imagination is essentially creative, and always seeks for a new form. The boy-burglar is simply the inevitable result of life's imitative instinct. He is Fact, occupied as Fact usually is, with trying to reproduce Fiction, and what we see in him is repeated on an extended scale throughout the whole of life. Schopenhauer has analysed the pessimism that characterizes modern thought, but Hamlet invented it. The world has become sad because a puppet was once melancholy. The Nihilist, that strange martyr who has no faith, who goes to the stake without enthusiasm, and dies for what he does not believe in, is a purely literary product. He was invented by Tourgénieff, and completed by Dostoieffski. Robespierre came out of the pages of Rousseau as surely as the People's Palace rose out of the *débris* of a novel. Literature always anticipates life. It does not copy it, but moulds it to its purpose. The nineteenth century, as we know it, is largely an invention of Balzac. Our Luciens de Rubempré, our Rastignacs, and De Marsays made their first appearance on the stage of the *Comédie Humaine*. We are merely carrying out, with footnotes and unnecessary additions, the whim or fancy or creative vision of a great novelist. I once asked a lady, who knew Thackeray intimately, whether he had had any model for Becky Sharp. She told me that Becky was an invention, but that the idea of the character had been partly suggested by a governess who lived in the neighbourhood of Kensington Square, and was the companion of a very selfish and rich old woman. I inquired what became of the governess, and she replied that, oddly enough, some years after the appearance of *Vanity Fair*, she ran away with the nephew of the lady with whom she was living, and for a short time made a great splash in society, quite in Mrs Rawdon Crawley's style, and entirely by Mrs Rawdon Crawley's methods. Ultimately she came to grief, disappeared to the Continent, and used to be occasionally seen at Monte Carlo and other gambling places. The noble gentleman from whom the same great sentimentalist drew Colonel Newcome died, a few months after *The Newcomes* had reached a fourth edition, with the word 'Adsum' on his lips. Shortly after Mr Stevenson published his curious psychological story of transformation, a friend of mine, called Mr Hyde, was in the north of London, and being anxious to get to a railway station, took what he thought would be a short cut, lost his way, and found himself in a network of mean, evil-looking streets. Feeling rather nervous he began to walk extremely fast, when suddenly out of an archway ran a child right between his legs. It fell on the pavement, he tripped over it, and trampled upon it. Being, of course, very much frightened and a little hurt, it began to scream, and in a few seconds the whole street was full of rough people who came pouring out of the houses like ants. They surrounded him, and asked him his name. He was just about to give it when he suddenly remembered the opening incident in Mr Stevenson's story. He was so filled with horror at having realized in his own person that terrible and well-written scene, and at having done accidentally, though in fact, what the Mr Hyde of fiction had done with deliberate intent, that he ran away as hard as he could go. He was, however, very closely followed, and finally he took refuge in a surgery, the door of which happened to be open, where he explained to a young assistant, who happened to be there, exactly what had occurred. The humanitarian crowd were induced to go away on his giving them a small sum of money, and as soon as the coast was clear he left. As he passed out, the name on the brass doorplate of the surgery caught his eye. It was 'Jekyll'. At least it should have been.

Here the imitation, as far as it went, was of course accidental.

In the following case the imitation was self-conscious. In the year 1879, just after I had left Oxford, I met at a reception at the house of one of the Foreign Ministers a woman of very curious exotic beauty. We became great friends, and were constantly together. And yet what interested me most in her was not her beauty, but her character, her entire vagueness of character. She seemed to have no personality at all, but simply the possibility of many types. Sometimes she would give herself up entirely to art, turn her drawing-room into a studio, and spend two or three days a week at picture galleries or museums. Then she would take to attending race-meetings, wear the most horsey clothes, and talk about nothing but betting. She abandoned religion for mesmerism, mesmerism for politics, and politics for the melodramatic excitements of philanthropy. In fact, she was a kind of Proteus, and as much a failure in all her transformations as was that wondrous sea-god when Odysseus laid hold of him. One day a serial began in one of the French magazines. At that time I used to read serial stories, and I well remember the shock of surprise I felt when I came to the description of the heroine. She was so like my friend that I brought her the magazine, and she recognized herself in it immediately, and seemed fascinated by the resemblance. I should tell you, by the way, that the story was translated from some dead Russian writer, so that the author had not taken his type from my friend. Well, to put the matter briefly, some months afterwards I was in Venice, and finding the magazine in the reading-room of the hotel, I took it up casually to see what had become of the heroine. It was a most piteous tale, as the girl had ended by running away with a man absolutely inferior to her, not merely in social station, but in character and intellect also. I wrote to my friend that evening about my view on John Bellini, and the admirable ices at Florian's, and the artistic value of gondolas, but added a postscript to the effect that her double in the story had behaved in a very silly manner. I don't know why I added that, but I remember I had a sort of dread over me that she might do the same thing. Before my letter had reached her, she had run away with a man who deserted her in six months. I saw her in 1884 in Paris, where she was living with her mother, and I asked her whether the story had had anything to do with her action. She told me that she had felt an absolutely irresistible impulse to follow the heroine step by step in her strange and fatal progress, and that it was with a feeling of real terror that she had looked forward to the last few chapters of the story. When they appeared, it seemed to her that she was compelled to reproduce them in life, and she did so. It was a most clear example of this imitative instinct of which I was speaking, and an extremely tragic one.

However, I do not wish to dwell any further upon individual instances. Personal experience is a most vicious and limited circle. All that I desire to point out is the general principle that Life imitates Art far more than Art imitates Life, and I feel sure that if you think seriously about it you will find that it is true. Life holds the mirror up to Art, and either reproduces some strange type imagined by painter or sculptor, or realizes in fact what has been dreamed in fiction. Scientifically speaking, the basis of life – the energy of life, as Aristotle would call it – is simply the desire for expression, and Art is always presenting various forms through which the expression can be attained. Life seizes on them and uses them, even if they be to her own hurt. Young men have committed suicide because Rolla did so, have died by their own hand because by his own hand Werther died. Think of what we owe to the imitation of Christ, of what we owe to the imitation of Caesar.

Cyril: The theory is certainly a very curious one, but to make it complete you must show that Nature, no less than Life, is an imitation of Art. Are you prepared to prove that?

Vivian: My dear fellow, I am prepared to prove anything.

Cyril: Nature follows the landscape painter, then, and takes her effects from him?

Vivian: Certainly. Where, if not from the Impressionists, do we get those wonderful brown fogs that come creeping down our streets, blurring the gas-lamps and changing the houses into monstrous shadows? To whom, if not to them and their master, do we owe the lovely silver mists that brood over our river, and turn to faint forms of fading grace curved bridge and swaying barge? The extraordinary change that has taken place in the climate of London during the last ten years is entirely due to a particular school of Art. You smile. Consider the matter from a scientific or a metaphysical point of view, and you will find that I am right. For what is Nature? Nature is no great mother who has borne us. She is our creation. It is in our brain that she quickens to life. Things are because we see them, and what we see, and how we see it, depends on the Arts that have influenced us. To look at a thing is very different from seeing a thing. One does not see anything until one sees its beauty. Then, and then only, does it come into existence. At present, people see fogs, not because there are fogs, but because poets and painters have taught them the mysterious loveliness of such effects. There may have been fogs for centuries in London. I dare say there were. But no one saw them, and so we do not know anything about them. They did not exist till Art had invented them. Now, it must be admitted, fogs are carried to excess. They have become the mere mannerism of a clique, and the exaggerated realism of their method gives dull people bronchitis. Where the cultured catch an effect, the un-cultured catch cold. And so, let us be humane, and invite Art to turn her wonderful eyes elsewhere. She has done so already, indeed. That white quivering sunlight that one sees now in France, with its strange blotches of mauve, and its restless violet shadows, is her latest fancy, and, on the whole, Nature reproduces it quite admirably. Where she used to give us Corots and Daubignys, she gives us now exquisite Monets and entrancing Pissaros. Indeed there are moments, rare, it is true, but still to be observed from time to time, when Nature becomes absolutely modern. Of course she is not always to be relied upon. The fact is that she is in this unfortunate position. Art creates an incomparable and unique effect, and, having done so, passes on to other things. Nature, upon the other hand, forgetting that imitation can be made the sincerest form of insult, keeps on repeating this effect until we all become absolutely wearied of it. Nobody of any real culture, for instance, ever talks nowadays about the beauty of a sunset. Sunsets are quite old-fashioned. They belong to the time when Turner was the last note in art. To admire them is a distinct sign of provincialism of temperament. Upon the other hand they go on. Yesterday evening Mrs Arundel insisted on my going to the window, and looking at the glorious sky, as she called it. Of course I had to look at it. She is one of those absurdly pretty Philistines to whom one can deny nothing. And what was it? It was simply a very second-rate Turner, a Turner of a bad period, with all the painter's worst faults exaggerated and over-emphasized. Of course, I am quite ready to admit that Life very often commits the same error. She produces her false Renés and her sham Vautrins, just as Nature gives us, on one day a doubtful Cuyp, and on another a more than questionable Rousseau. Still, Nature irritates one more when she does things of that kind. It seems so stupid, so obvious, so unnecessary. A false Vautrin might be delightful. A doubtful Cuyp is unbearable. However, I don't want to be too hard on Nature. I wish the Channel, especially at Hastings, did not look quite so often like a Henry Moore, grey pearl with yellow lights, but then, when Art is more varied, Nature will, no doubt, be more varied also. That she imitates Art, I don't think even her worst enemy would deny now. It is the one thing that keeps her in touch with civilized man. But have I proved my theory to your satisfaction?

Cyril: You have proved it to my dissatisfaction, which is better. But even admitting this strange imitative instinct in Life and Nature, surely you would acknowledge that Art expresses the temper of its age, the spirit of its time, the moral and social conditions that surround it, and under whose influence it is produced.

Vivian: Certainly not! Art never expresses anything but itself. This is the principle of my new aesthetics; and it is this, more than that vital connexion between form and substance, on which Mr Pater dwells, that makes basic the type of all the arts. Of course, nations and individuals, with that healthy natural vanity which is the secret of existence, are always under the impression that it is of them that the Muses are talking, always trying to find in the calm dignity of imaginative art some mirror of their own turbid passions, always forgetting that the singer of life is not Apollo but Marsyas. Remote from reality, and with her eyes turned away from the shadows of the cave, Art reveals her own perfection, and the wondering crowd that watches the opening of the marvellous, many-petalled rose fancies that it is its own history that is being told to it, its own spirit that is finding expression in a new form. But it is not so. The highest art rejects the burden of the human spirit, and gains more from a new medium or a fresh material than she does from any enthusiasm for art, or from any lofty passion, or from any great awakening of the human consciousness. She develops purely on her own lines. She is not symbolic of any age. It is the ages that are her symbols.

Even those who hold that Art is representative of time and place and people cannot help admitting that the more imitative an art is, the less it represents to us the spirit of its age. The evil faces of the Roman emperors look out at us from the foul porphyry and spotted jasper in which the realistic artists of the day delighted to work, and we fancy that in those cruel lips and heavy sensual jaws we can find the secret of the ruin of the Empire. But it was not so. The vices of Tiberius could not destroy that supreme civilization, any more than the virtues of the Antonines could save it. It fell for other, for less interesting reasons. The sibyls and prophets of the Sistine may indeed serve to interpret for some that new birth of the emancipated spirit that we call the Renaissance; but what do the drunken boors and bawling peasants of Dutch art tell us about the great soul of Holland? The more abstract, the more ideal an art is, the more it reveals to us the temper of its age. If we wish to understand a nation by means of its art, let us look at its architecture or its music.

Cyril: I quite agree with you there. The spirit of an age may be best expressed in the abstract ideal arts, for the spirit itself is abstract and ideal. Upon the other hand, for the visible aspect of an age, for its looks, as the phrase goes, we must of course go to the arts of imitation.

Vivian: I don't think so. After all, what the imitative arts really give us are merely the various styles of particular artists, or of certain schools of artists. Surely you don't imagine that the people of the Middle Ages bore any resemblance at all to the figures on medieval stained glass, or in medieval stone and wood carving, or on medieval metal-work, or tapestries, or illuminated MSS. They were probably very ordinary-looking people, with nothing grotesque, or remarkable, or fantastic in their appearance. The Middle Ages, as we know them in art, are simply a definite form of style, and there is no reason at all why an artist with this style should not be produced in the nineteenth century. No great artist ever sees things as they really are. If he did, he would cease to be an artist. Take an example from our own day. I know that you are fond of Japanese things. Now, do you really imagine that the Japanese people, as they are presented to us in art, have any existence? If you do, you have never understood Japanese art at all. The Japanese people are the deliberate self-conscious creation of certain individual artists. If you set a picture by Hokusai, or Hokkei, or any of the great native painters, beside a real Japanese gentleman or lady, you will see that there is not the slightest resemblance between them. The actual people who live in Japan are not unlike the general run of English people; that is to say, they are extremely commonplace, and have nothing curious or extraordinary about them. In fact, the whole of Japan is a pure invention. There is no such country, there are no such people. One of our most charming painters went recently to the Land of the Chrysanthemum in the foolish hope of seeing the Japanese. All he saw, all he had the chance of painting, were a few lanterns and some fans. He was quite unable to discover the inhabitants, as his delightful exhibition at Messrs Dowdeswell's Gallery showed only too well. He did not know that the Japanese people are, as I have said, simply a mode of style, an exquisite fancy of art. And so, if you desire to see a Japanese effect, you will not behave like a tourist and go to Tokio. On the contrary, you will stay at home and steep yourself in the work of certain Japanese artists, and then, when you have absorbed the spirit of their style, and caught their imaginative manner of vision, you will go some afternoon and sit in the Park or stroll down Piccadilly, and if you cannot see an absolutely Japanese effect there, you will not see it anywhere. Or, to return again to the past, take as another instance the ancient Greeks. Do you think that Greek art ever tells us what the Greek people were like? Do you believe that the Athenian women were like the stately dignified figures of the Parthenon frieze, or like those marvellous goddesses who sat in the triangular pediments of the same building? If you judge from the art, they certainly were so. But read an authority, like Aristophanes, for instance. You will find that the Athenian ladies laced tightly, wore high-heeled shoes, dyed their hair yellow, painted and rouged their faces, and were exactly like any silly fashionable or fallen creature of our own day. The fact is that we look back on the ages entirely through the medium of art, and art, very fortunately, has never once told us the truth.

Cyril: But modern portraits by English painters, what of them? Surely they are like the people they pretend to represent?

Vivian: Quite so. They are so like them that a hundred years from now no one will believe in them. The only portraits in which one believes are portraits where there is very little of the sitter, and a very great deal of the artist. Holbein's drawings of the men and women of his time impress us with a sense of their absolute reality. But this is simply because Holbein compelled life to accept his conditions, to restrain itself within his limitations, to reproduce his type, and to appear as he wished it to appear. It is style that makes us believe*in a thing – nothing but style. Most of our modern portrait painters are doomed to absolute oblivion. They never paint what they see. They paint what the public sees, and the public never sees anything.

Cyril: Well, after that I think I should like to hear the end of your article.

Vivian: With pleasure. Whether it will do any good I really cannot say. Ours is certainly the dullest and most prosaic century possible. Why, even Sleep has played us false, and has closed up the gates of ivory, and opened the gates of horn. The dreams of the great middle classes of this country, as recorded in Mr Myers's two bulky volumes on the subject, and in the Transactions of the Psychical Society, are the most depressings things I have ever read. There is not even a fine nightmare among them. They are commonplace, sordid and tedious. As for the Church, I cannot conceive anything better for the culture of a country than the presence in it of a body of men whose duty it is to believe in the super-natural, to perform daily miracles, and to keep alive that mytho-poeic faculty which is so essential for the imagination. But in the English Church a man succeeds, not through his capacity for belief, but through his capacity for disbelief. Ours is the only Church where the sceptic stands at the altar, and where St Thomas is regarded as the ideal apostle. Many a worthy clergyman, who passes his life in admirable works of kindly charity, lives and dies unnoticed and unknown; but it is sufficient for some shallow uneducated passman out of either University to get up in his pulpit and express his doubts about Noah's ark, or Balaam's ass, or Jonah and the whale, for half of London to flock to hear him, and to sit open-mouthed in rapt admiration at his superb intellect. The growth of common sense in the English Church is a thing very much to be regretted. It is really a degrading concession to a low form of realism. It is silly, too. It springs from an entire ignorance of psychology. Man can believe the impossible, but man can never believe the improbable. However, I must read the end of my article:

'What we have to do, what at any rate it is our duty to do, is to revive this old art of Lying. Much, of course, may be done, in the way of educating the public, by amateurs in the domestic circle, at literary lunches, and at afternoon teas. But this is merely the light and graceful side of lying, such as was probably heard at Cretan dinner-parties. There are many other forms. Lying for the sake of gaining some immediate personal advantage, for instance – lying with a moral purpose, as it is usually called – though of late it has been rather looked down upon, was ex-tremely popular with the antique world. Athena laughs when Odysseus tells her "his words of sly devising", as Mr William Morris phrases it, and the glory of mendacity illumines the pale brow of the stainless hero of Euripidean tragedy, and sets among the noble women of the past the young bride of one of Horace's most exquisite odes. Later on, what at first had been merely a natural instinct was elevated into a self-conscious science. Elabor-ate rules were laid down for the guidance of mankind, and an important school of literature grew up round the subject. Indeed, when one remembers the excellent philosophical treatise of Sanchez on the whole question, one cannot help regretting that no one has ever thought of publishing a cheap and condensed edition of the works of that great casuist. A short primer, "When to Lie and How", if brought out in an attractive and not too expensive a form, would no doubt command a large sale, and would prove of real practical service to many earnest and deep-thinking people. Lying for the sake of the improvement of the young, which is the basis of home education, still lingers amongst us, and its advantages are so admirably set forth in the early books of Plato's *Republic* that it is unnecessary to dwell upon them here. It is a mode of lying for which all good mothers have peculiar capabilities, but it is capable of still further development, and has been sadly overlooked by the School Board. Lying for the sake of a monthly salary is, of course, well known in Fleet Street, and the profession of a political leader-writer is not without its advantages. But it is said to be a somewhat dull occupation, and it certainly does not lead to much beyond a kind of ostentatious obscurity. The only form of lying that is absolutely beyond reproach is lying for its own sake, and the highest development of this is, as we have already pointed out, Lying in Art. Just as those who do not love Plato more than Truth cannot pass beyond the threshold of the Academe, so those who do not love Beauty more than Truth never know the inmost shrine of Art. The solid, stolid British intellect lies in the desert sands like the Sphinx in Flaubert's marvellous tale, and fantasy, *La Chimère*, dances round it, and calls to it with her false, flute-toned voice. It may not hear her now, but surely some day, when we are all bored to death with the commonplace character of modern fiction, it will hearken to her and try to borrow her wings.

'And when that day dawns, or sunset reddens, how joyous we shall all be! Facts will be regarded as discreditable, Truth will be found mourning over her fetters, and Romance, with her temper of wonder, will return to the land. The very aspect of the world will change to our startled eyes. Out of the sea will rise Behemoth and Leviathan, and sail round the high-pooped galleys, as they do on the delightful maps of those ages when books on geography were actually readable. Dragons will wander about the waste places, and the phoenix will soar from her nest of fire into the air. We shall lay our hands upon the basilisk, and see the jewel in the toad's head. Champing his gilded oats, the Hippogriff will stand in our stalls, and over our heads will float the Blue Bird singing of beautiful and impossible things, of things that are lovely and that never happen, of things that are not and that should be. But before this comes to pass we must cultivate the lost art of Lying.'

Cyril: Then we must entirely cultivate it at once. But in order to avoid making any error I want you to tell me briefly the doctrines of the new aesthetics.

Vivian: Briefly, then, they are these. Art never expresses anything but itself. It has an independent life, just as Thought has, and develops purely on its own lines. It is not necessarily realistic in an age of realism, nor spiritual in an age of faith. So far from being the creation of its time, it is usually in direct opposition to it, and the only history that it preserves for us is the history of its own progress. Sometimes it returns upon its footsteps, and revives some antique form, as happened in the archaistic movement of late Greek Art, and in the pre-Raphaelite movement of our own day. At other times it entirely anticipates its age, and produces in one century work that it takes another century to understand, to appreciate and to enjoy. In no case does it reproduce its age. To pass from the art of a time to the time itself is the great mistake that all historians commit.

The second doctrine is this. All bad art comes from returning to Life and Nature, and elevating them into ideals. Life and Nature may sometimes be used as part of Art's rough material, but before they are of any real service to Art they must be translated into artistic conventions. The moment Art surrenders its imaginative medium it surrenders everything. As a method Realism is a complete failure, and the two things that every artist should avoid are modernity of form and modernity of subject-matter. To us, who live in the nineteenth century, any century is a suitable subject for art except our own. The only beautiful things are the things that do not concern us. It is, to have the pleasure of quoting myself, exactly because Hecuba is nothing to us that her sorrows are so suitable a motive for a tragedy. Besides, it is only the modern that ever becomes old-fashioned. M. Zola sits down to give us a picture of the Second Empire. Who cares for the Second Empire now? It is out of date. Life goes faster than Realism, but Romanticism is always in front of Life.

The third doctrine is that Life imitates Art far more than Art imitates Life. This results not merely from Life's imitative instinct, but from the fact that the self-conscious aim of Life is to find expression, and that Art offers it certain beautiful forms through which it may realize that energy. It is a theory that has never been put forward before, but it is extremely fruitful, and throws an entirely new light upon the history of Art.

It follows, as a corollary from this, that external Nature also imitates Art. The only effects that she can show us are effects that we have already seen through poetry, or in paintings. This is the secret of Nature's charm, as well as the explanation of Nature's weakness.

The final revelation is that Lying, the telling of beautiful untrue things, is the proper aim of Art. But of this I think I have spoken at sufficient length. And now let us go out on the terrace, where 'droops the milk-white peacock like a ghost', while the evening star 'washes the dusk with silver'. At twilight nature becomes a wonderfully suggestive effect, and is not without loveliness, though perhaps its chief use is to illustrate quotations from the poets. Come! We have talked long enough.

De Profundis
[Epistola: in Carcere et Vinculis]

WITH AN INTRODUCTION BY
VYVYAN HOLLAND

INTRODUCTION

In the year 1905 there was published in London a posthumous work by Oscar Wilde, to which was given the title of *De Profundis*. In his preface to the first edition Robert Ross, the author's great friend, wrote: 'The book requires little introduction and scarcely any explanation. I have only to record that it was written by my friend during the last months of his imprisonment, that it was the only work he wrote while in prison, and the last work in prose he ever wrote.'

The 1905 edition of *De Profundis* was composed of extracts from a much longer work, cast in the form of a letter to Lord Alfred Douglas. It was composed of eighty close-written pages, on twenty folio sheets of blue prison paper, stamped at the head of each sheet with the Royal Arms. Wilde was allowed one sheet of this paper at a time; when it was filled it was removed and replaced by another. As will be seen, he never revised the finished document, and it is therefore remarkable that it should flow so smoothly; the original manuscript contains scarcely any alterations.

Wilde's intention was that the completed document should be sent from prison to Robert Ross, with a covering letter containing instructions as to its disposal. Prison rules, however, forbade this, and the covering letter was sent without the manuscript. According to Prison Regulations, nothing written by a prisoner while serving his sentence was allowed to leave the prison, except periodic letters, which were carefully scrutinized and censored by the prison authorities. However, the Governor of Reading Gaol, Major Nelson, handed Wilde his manuscript on the morning of his release, on 19th May 1897. On the same day Wilde left England for the last time: on his arrival at Dieppe he was met by Robert Ross, to whom he handed the document. That was the last he ever had to do with it.

The letter of instructions was written about a month before Wilde's release. This was published *in extenso* in the first collected edition of Wilde's works, published by Methuen & Co. in 1908. The passages chiefly relating to the book are as follows:

'My dear Robbie, – I send you a manuscript separate from this, which I hope will arrive safely. As soon as you have read it, I want you to have it copied for me. There are many reasons why I wish this to be done. One will suffice. I want you to be my literary executor in case of my death, and, to have complete control of my plays, books and papers. . . . Well, if you are my literary executor, you must be in possession of the only document that gives any explanation of my extraordinary behaviour. . . . When you have read the letter, you will see the psychological explanation of a course of conduct that from the outside seems a combination of absolute idiotcy with vulgar bravado. Some day the truth will have to be known – not necessarily in my lifetime . . . but I am not prepared to sit in the grotesque gallery they put me into, for all time; for the simple reason that I inherited from my father and mother a name of high distinction in literature and art, and I cannot for eternity allow that name to be degraded. I do not defend my conduct. I explain it. . . .

'As regards the method of copying. . . . I wish the copy to be done not on tissue paper, but on good paper such as is used for plays, and a wide rubricated margin should be left for corrections. . . . The lady typist might be fed through a lattice in the door, like the Cardinals when they elect a Pope; until she comes out on the balcony and can say to the world: "Habet Mundus Epistolam!" For indeed it is an Encyclical letter, and as the Bulls of the Holy Father are named from their opening words, it may be spoken of as the "Epistola: in Carcere et Vinculis".'

A copy of the manuscript was duly made. Robert Ross would not allow it out of his own hands and dictated it to a typist, who made an original and a carbon copy: the detail is important for the subsequent history of the book. Instead of sending the manuscript itself to Alfred Douglas, Robert Ross kept it in his own possession and sent him the typewritten copy. It was as well that he did so; but then he knew Douglas's character. For, after reading the first few pages, he found it was more than his vanity could stand and he put it down. He subsequently destroyed it, thinking, in one of the fits of naiveté which sometimes assailed him, that it was the only copy in existence and that his act would put an end to an awkward situation.

Some years later, Alfred Douglas quarrelled with Robert Ross. By this time he had discovered that the original manuscript was still in the possession of Robert Ross, and he claimed that, as it was addressed to him, it was his property. No doubt he thought he would be able to get a handsome sum of money for it, as indeed he did from the sale of all the other letters which Wilde wrote to him. Robert Ross, however, settled the matter by sealing up the manuscript and presenting it to the British Museum, with the proviso that it should remain sealed for sixty years, at the end of which time it might be safely presumed that everyone mentioned in it would be dead.

This was in 1909, and there the matter might have rested until 1969. But in 1912 Alfred Douglas took exception to certain passages in a study of Oscar Wilde by Arthur Ransome. Although he was not mentioned by name, he was clearly identifiable by anyone who had any knowledge of the circumstances, and he brought an action for libel against Arthur Ransome, hoping, through him, to be able to damage Robert Ross.

The case was heard in April 1913, before Mr Justice Darling and a special jury, and it lasted for four days. The chief piece of evidence was the letter reposing in the British Museum, which was duly unsealed and produced by the librarian, under subpoena. Large extracts from it were read in open Court and were reported fairly fully in *The Times*. The jury found that the words complained of were libellous but true. A verdict with costs was returned for Arthur Ransome, and the manuscript was returned to the Museum.

As the defence rested mainly upon the prison letter, Alfred Douglas had, of course, to be supplied with another copy of it; and he immediately announced his intention of having it published in America (the British copyright was safe) with his own comments. The carbon copy made in 1897 was still in the possession of Robert Ross. So, in order to circumvent this move, he sent it over by the first boat to New York, where sixteen copies were hurriedly printed by Paul Reynolds, for purposes of copyright. There was not even time for the proofs to be corrected, as the main matter of urgency was to secure copyright before Alfred Douglas could so do.

Paul Reynolds co-operated splendidly and the book was ready within ten days. Of the sixteen copies printed, fifteen came to England, where they were distributed to libraries and to the author's friends. The sixteenth copy was offered for sale in Paul Reynolds's show-room, in accordance with the United States copyright law. It was priced at five hundred dollars, a price meant to discourage the curious. But within a short space of time someone paid the price and took it away; no one ever discovered who the purchaser was. The book as printed was full of errors, misprints, and lacunae, but it was sufficiently accurate for the purpose for which it was intended.

The original (if I may so call it) carbon copy was duly returned to England and, on the death of Robert Ross in 1918, it came into my possession. It is from this copy that the present text is taken. The manuscript itself still reposes in the British Museum: the authorities there have always refused to allow anyone access to it, in spite of the fact that its contents are no longer secret, and therefore the reason for which it was sealed up no longer exists.

In 1936, it was suggested that the time had come to publish the whole letter. Alfred Douglas, who had always objected to having it published, withdrew his objection, realizing that it must be published some time and that it might be better, for his sake, that it should be published in his lifetime. But, when arrangements for its publication were well advanced, he withdrew his consent and the matter had to be shelved. Alfred Douglas died in 1945 and the last objection is thus removed.

In 1908, Robert Ross allowed Dr Max Meyerfeld to translate the work into German, and it was published by the S. Fischer Verlag in Berlin. The title Dr Meyerfeld gave it was the one that Wilde himself had half humorously suggested, namely: *Epistola: in Carcere et Vinculis*. In 1914, Frank Harris published his *Life of*

Oscar Wilde in America. In it he printed extracts from the letter – extracts which were copied from the rather inaccurate *Times* report. Henry Daviel also published parts of it in French. An unauthorized translation from the German into Spanish has appeared, and a ridiculous pirated version has circulated in America, so remote from the original that it might even have been a re-translation into English from the Spanish translation from the German translation!

Be that as it may, this is the first complete and accurate version of the last prose work of Oscar Wilde in English. Through it he hoped that posterity, and even his enemies, might find some sympathy for him. In this tragic document he has, as he himself says, tried to explain his conduct without defending it. Let it rest at that.

VYVYAN HOLLAND

June 1949

Epistola: In Carcere et Vinculis

H.M. PRISON,
READING.

DEAR BOSIE, – After long and fruitless waiting I have determined to write to you myself, as much for your sake as for mine, as I would not like to think that I had passed through two long years of imprisonment without ever having received a single line from you, or any news or message even, except such as gave me pain.

Our ill-fated and most lamentable friendship has ended in ruin and public infamy for me, yet the memory of our ancient affection is often with me, and the thought that loathing, bitterness and contempt should for ever take the place in my heart once held by love is very sad to me: and you yourself will, I think, feel in your heart that to write to me as I lie in the loneliness of prison life is better than to publish my letters without my permission or to dedicate poems to me unasked, though the world will know nothing of whatever words of grief or passion, of remorse or indifference you may choose to send as your answer or your appeal.

I have no doubt that in this letter which I have to write of your life and of mine, of the past and of the future, of sweet things changed to bitterness and of bitter things that may be turned into joy, there will be much that will wound your vanity to the quick. If it prove so, read the letter over and over again till it kills your vanity. If you find in it something of which you feel that you are unjustly accused, remember that one should be thankful that there is any fault of which one can be unjustly accused. If there be in it one single passage that brings tears to your eyes, weep as we weep in prison where the day no less than the night is set apart for tears. It is the only thing that can save you. If you go complaining to your mother, as you did with reference to the scorn of you I displayed in my letter to Robbie, so that she may flatter and soothe you back into self-complacency or conceit, you will be completely lost. If you find one false excuse for yourself you will soon find a hundred, and be just what you were before. Do you still say, as you said to Robbie in your answer, that I 'attribute unworthy motives' to you? Ah! you had no motives in life. You had appetites merely. A motive is an intellectual aim. That you were 'very young' when our friendship began? Your defect was not that you knew so little about life, but that you knew so much. The morning dawn of boyhood with its delicate bloom, its clear pure light, its joy of innocence and expectation you had left far behind. With very swift and running feet you had passed from Romance to Realism. The gutter and the things that live in it had begun to fascinate you. That was the origin of the trouble in which you sought my aid, and I, unwisely according to the wisdom of this world, out of pity and kindness, gave it to you. You must read this letter right through, though each word may become to you as the fire or knife of the surgeon that makes the delicate flesh burn or bleed. Remember that the fool to the eyes of the gods and the fool to the eyes of man are very different. One who is entirely ignorant of the modes of art in its revelation or the mood of thought in its progress, of the pomp of the Latin line or the richer music of the vowelled Greek, of Tuscan sculpture or Elizabethan song, may yet be full of the very sweetest wisdom. The real fool, such as the gods mock or mar, is he who does not know himself. I was such a one too long. You have been such a one too long. Be so no more. Do not be afraid. The supreme vice is shallowness. Everything that is realized is right. Remember also that whatever is misery to you to read, is still greater misery to me to set down. To you the Unseen Powers have been very good. They have permitted you to see the strange and tragic shapes of life as one sees shadows in a crystal. The head of Medusa that turns living men to stone, you have been allowed to look at in a mirror merely. You yourself have walked free among the flowers. From me the beautiful world of colour and motion has been taken away.

I will begin by telling you that I blame myself terribly. As I sit here in this dark cell in convict clothes, a disgraced and ruined man, I blame myself. In the perturbed and fitful nights of anguish, in the long monotonous days of pain, it is myself I blame. I blame myself for allowing an unintellectual friendship, a friendship whose primary aim was not the creation and contemplation of beautiful things, entirely to dominate my life. From the very first there was too wide a gap between us. You had been idle at your school, worse than idle at your university. You did not realize that an artist, and especially such an artist as I am, one, that is to say, the quality of whose work depends on the intensification of personality, requires for the development of his art the companionship of ideas, and intellectual atmosphere, quiet, peace, and solitude. You admired my work when it was finished: you enjoyed the brilliant successes of my first nights, and the brilliant banquets that followed them: you were proud, and quite naturally so, of being the intimate friend of an artist so distinguished: but you could not understand the conditions requisite for the production of artistic work. I am not speaking in phrases of rhetorical exaggeration but in terms of absolute truth to actual fact when I remind you that during the whole time we were together I never wrote one single line. Whether at Torquay, Goring, London, Florence, or elsewhere, my life, as long as you were by my side, was entirely sterile and uncreative. And with but few intervals you were, I regret to say, by my side always.

I remember, for instance, in September 1893, to select merely one instance out of many, taking a set of chambers, purely in order to work undisturbed, as I had broken my contract with John Hare for whom I had promised to write a play and who was pressing me on the subject. During the first week you kept away. We had, not unnaturally indeed, differed on the question of the artistic value of your translation of *Salomé*. So you contented yourself with sending me foolish letters on the subject. In that week I wrote and completed in every detail, as it was ultimately performed, the first act of *An Ideal Husband*. The second week you returned and my work practically had to be given up. I arrived at St James's Place every morning at 11.30 in order to have the opportunity of thinking and writing without the interruption inseparable from my own household, quiet and peaceful as that household was. But the attempt was vain. At 12 o'clock you drove up and stayed smoking cigarettes and chattering till 1.30, when I had to take you out to luncheon at the Café Royal or the Berkeley. Luncheon with its liqueurs lasted usually till 3.30. For an hour you retired to White's. At tea-time you appeared again and stayed till it was time to dress for dinner. You dined with me either at the Savoy or at Tite Street. We did not separate as a rule till after midnight, as supper at Willis's had to wind up the entrancing day. That was my life for those three months, every single day, except during the four days when you went abroad. I then, of course, had to go over to Calais to fetch you back. For one of my nature and temperament it was a position at once grotesque and tragic.

You surely must realize that now. You must see now that your incapacity for being alone: your nature so exigent in its persistent claim on the attention and time of others: your lack of any power of sustained intellectual concentration: the unfortunate accident – for I like to think it was no more – that you had not yet been able to acquire the 'Oxford temper' in intellectual matters, never, I mean, been one who could play gracefully with ideas but had arrived at violence of opinion merely – that all these things, combined with the fact that your desires and your interests were in Life not in Art, were as destructive to your own progress in culture as they were to my work as an artist. When I compare my friendship with you to my friendship with such still younger men as John Gray and Pierre Louys I feel ashamed. My real life, my higher life was with them and such as them.

Of the appalling results of my friendship with you I don't speak at present. I am thinking merely of its quality while it lasted. It was intellectually degrading to me. You had the rudiments of an artistic temperament in its germ. But I met you either too late or too soon, I don't know which. When you were away I was all right. The moment, in the early December of the year to which I have been alluding, I had succeeded in inducing your mother to send you out of England, I collected again the torn and ravelled web of my imagination, got my life back into my own hands, and not merely finished the three remaining acts of *An Ideal Husband* but conceived and had almost completed two other plays of a completely different type, the *Florentine Tragedy* and *La Sainte Courtisane*, when suddenly, unbidden, unwelcome, and under circumstances fatal to my happiness, you returned. The two works left then imperfect I was unable to take up again. The mood that created them I could never recover. You now, having yourself published a volume of verse, will be able to recognize the truth of everything I have said here. Whether you can or not, it remains as a hideous truth in the very heart of our friendship. While you were with me you were the absolute ruin of my art, and in allowing you to stand persistently between Art and myself I give to myself shame and blame in the fullest degree. You couldn't know, you couldn't understand, you couldn't appreciate. I had no right to expect it of you at all. Your interests were merely in your meals and moods. Your desires were simply for amusements, for ordinary or less ordinary pleasures. They were what your temperament needed, or thought it needed for the moment. I should have forbidden you my house and my chambers except when I specially invited you. I blame myself without reserve for my weakness. It was merely weakness. One half-hour with Art was always more to me than a cycle with you. Nothing really at any period of my life was ever of the smallest importance to me compared with Art. But in the case of an artist, weakness is nothing less than a crime, when it is a weakness that paralyses the imagination.

I blame myself for having allowed you to bring me to utter and discreditable financial ruin. I remember one morning in the early October of 1892 sitting in the yellowing woods at Bracknell with your mother. At that time I knew very little of your real nature. I had stayed from a Saturday to Monday with you at Oxford. You had stayed with me at Cromer for ten days and played golf. The conversation turned on you, and your mother began to speak to me about your character. She told me of your two chief faults, your vanity, and your being as she termed it 'all wrong about money'. I have a distinct recollection of how I laughed. I had no idea that the first would bring me to prison and the second to bankruptcy. I thought vanity a sort of graceful flower for a young man to wear: as for extravagance – for I thought she meant no more than extravagance – the virtues of prudence and thrift were not in my own nature or my own race. But before our friendship was one month older I began to see what your mother really meant. Your insistence on a life of reckless profusion, your incessant demands for money, your claim that all your pleasures should be paid for by me whether I was with you or not, brought me after some time into serious monetary difficulties, and what made the extravagance to me at any rate so monotonously uninteresting, as your persistent grasp on my life grew stronger and stronger, was that the money was really spent on little more than the pleasures of eating, drinking, and the like. Now and then it is a joy to have one's table red with wine and roses, but you outstripped all taste and temperance. You demanded without grace and received without thanks. You grew to think that you had a sort of right to live at my expense and in a profuse luxury to which you had never been accustomed, and which for that reason made your appetites all the more keen; and at the end if you lost money gambling in some Algiers Casino you simply telegraphed next morning to me in London to lodge the amount of your losses to your account at your bank, and gave the matter no further thought of any kind.

When I tell you that between the autumn of 1892 and the date of my imprisonment I spent with you and on you more than £5,000 in actual money, irrespective of the bills I incurred, you will have some idea of the sort of life on which you insisted. Do you think I exaggerate? My ordinary expenses with you for any ordinary day in London – for luncheon, dinner, supper, amusements, hansoms, and the rest of it – ranged from £12 to £20, and the week's expenses were naturally in proportion and ranged from £80 to £130. For our three months at Goring my expenses (rent of course included) were £1,340. Step by step with the Bankruptcy Receiver I had to go over every item of my life. It was horrible. 'Plain living and high thinking' was, of course, an ideal you could not at that time have appreciated, but such an extravagance was a disgrace to both of us. One of the most delightful dinners I remember ever having had is one Robbie[1] and I had together in a little Soho café, which cost about as many shillings as my dinners to you used to cost pounds. Out of my dinner with Robbie came the first and best of all my dialogues. Idea, title, treatment, mode, everything was struck out at a 3 franc 50 c. *table d'hôte*. Out of the reckless dinners with you nothing remains but the memory that too much was eaten and too much was drunk. And my yielding to your demands was bad for you. You know that now. It made you grasping often: at times not a little unscrupulous: ungracious always. There was on far too many occasions too little joy or privilege in being your host. You forgot – I will not say the formal courtesy of thanks, for formal courtesies will strain a close friendship – but simply the grace of sweet companionship, the charm of pleasant conversation, that τερπνὸν καλόν as the Greeks called it, and all those gentle humanities that make life lovely, and are an accompaniment to life as music might be, keeping things in tune and filling with melody the harsh or silent places. And though it may seem strange to you that one in the terrible position in which I am situated should find a difference between one disgrace and another, still I frankly admit that the folly of throwing away all this money on you, and letting you squander my fortune to your own hurt as well as to mine, gives to me and in my eyes a note of common profligacy to my bankruptcy and makes me doubly ashamed of it. I was made for other things.

But most of all I blame myself for the entire ethical degradation I allowed you to bring on me. The basis of character is will power, and my will power became absolutely subject to yours. It sounds a grotesque thing to say, but it is none the less true. Those incessant scenes that seemed to be almost physically necessary to you and in which your mind and body grew distorted and you became a thing as terrible to look at as to listen to: that dreadful mania you inherit from your father, the mania for writing revolting and loathsome letters: your entire lack of any control over your emotions, as displayed in your long resentful moods of sullen silence, no less than in your sudden fits of almost epileptic rage:

1. Robert Ross.

all these things in reference to which one of my letters to you, left by you lying about at the Savoy or some other hotel and so produced in Court by your father's Counsel, contained an entreaty not devoid of pathos, had you at that time been able to recognize pathos in its elements or its expression: – these, I say, were the origin and causes of my fatal yielding to you in your daily increasing demands. You wore me out. It was the triumph of the smaller over the bigger nature. It was the case of that tyranny of the weak over the strong which somewhere in one of my plays I describe as being 'the only tyranny that lasts'.

And it was inevitable. In every relation of life with others one has to find some *moyen de vivre*. In your case, one had either to give up to you or to give you up. There was no alternative. Through deep if misplaced affection for you: through great pity for your defects of temper and temperament: through my own proverbial good nature and Celtic laziness: through an artistic aversion from coarse scenes and ugly words: through that incapacity to bear resentment of any kind which at that time characterized me: through my dislike of seeing life made bitter and uncomely by what to me, with my eyes really fixed on other things, seemed to be mere trifles too petty for more than a moment's thought or interest: – through those reasons, simple as they may sound, I gave up to you always. As a natural result, your claims, your efforts at domination, your exactions grew more and more unreasonable. Your meanest motive, your lowest appetite, your most common passion, became to you laws by which the lives of others were to be guided always, and to which, if necessary, they were to be without scruple sacrificed. Knowing that by making a scene you could always have your way, it was but natural that you should proceed, almost unconsciously I have no doubt, to every excess of vulgar violence. At the end you did not know to what you were hurrying, or with what aim in view. Having made your most of my genius, my will power and my fortune, you required, in the blindness of an inexhaustible greed, my entire existence. You took it. At the one supremely and tragically critical moment of all my life, just before my lamentable step of beginning my absurd action, on the one side there was your father attacking me with hideous cards left at my club, on the other side there was you attacking me with no less loathsome letters. The letter I received from you on the morning of the day I let you take me down to the Police Station to apply for the ridiculous warrant for your father's arrest was one of the worst you ever wrote, and for the most shameful reason. Between you both I had lost my head. My judgement forsook me. Terror took its place. I saw no possible escape, I may say frankly, from either of you. Blindly I staggered as an ox to the shambles. I had made a gigantic psychological error. I had always thought that my giving up to you in small things meant nothing: that when a great moment arrived I could myself re-assert my will power in its natural superiority. It was not so. At the great moment my will power completely failed me. In life there is really no great or small thing. All things are of equal value and of equal size. My habit – due to indifference chiefly at first – of giving up to you in everything had become insensibly a real part of my nature. Without my knowing it, it had stereotyped my temperament to one permanent and fatal mood. That is why, in the subtle epilogue to the first edition of his essays, Pater says that 'Failure is to form habits'. When he said it the dull Oxford people thought the phrase a mere wilful inversion of the somewhat wearisome text of Aristotelian Ethics, but there is a wonderful, a terrible truth hidden in it. I had allowed you to sap my strength of character, and to me the formation of a habit had proved to be not failure merely but ruin. Ethically you had been even still more destructive to me than you had been artistically.

The warrant once granted, your will of course directed everything. At the time when I should have been in London taking wise counsel and calmly considering the hideous trap in which I had allowed myself to be caught – the booby trap as your father calls it to the present day – you insisted on my taking you to Monte Carlo, of all revolting places on God's earth, that all day and all night as well you might gamble as long as the Casino remained open. As for me – baccarat having no charms for me – I was left alone outside to myself. You refused to discuss even for five minutes the position to which you and your father had brought me. My business was merely to pay your hotel expenses and your losses. The slightest allusion to the ordeal awaiting me was regarded as a bore. A new brand of champagne that was recommended to us had more interest for you.

On our return to London those of my friends who really desired my welfare implored me to retire abroad, and not to face an impossible trial. You imputed mean motives to them for giving such advice and cowardice to me for listening to it. You forced me to stay to brazen it out, if possible, in the box by absurd and silly perjuries. At the end, of course, I was arrested and your father became the hero of the hour: more indeed than the hero of the hour merely: your family now ranks strangely enough with the Immortals: for with the grotesqueness of effect that is as it were a Gothic element in history, and makes Clio the least serious of all the Muses, your father will always live among the kind pure-minded parents of Sunday school literature; your place is with the infant Samuel; and in the lowest mire of Malebolge I sit between Gilles de Retz and the Marquis de Sade.

Of course, I should have got rid of you. I should have shaken you out of my life as a man shakes from his raiment a thing that has stung him. In the most wonderful of all his plays Aeschylus tells us of the great lord who brings up in his house the lion cub, the λέοντος ἶνιν and loves it because it comes bright-eyed to his call and fawns on him for its food; φαιδρωπὸς ποτὶ χεῖρα σαινων τε γαστρὸς ἀνάγκαις and the thing grows up and shows the nature of its race, ἦθος τὸ πρὸς τοκέων, and destroys the lord and his house and all that he possesses. I feel that I was such a one as he. But my fault was, not that I did not part from you, but that I parted from you far too often. As far as I can make out I ended my friendship with you every three months regularly. And each time that I did so you managed by means of entreaties, telegrams, letters, the interposition of your friends, the interposition of mine, and the like to induce me to allow you back. When at the end of March 1893 you left my house at Torquay I had determined never to speak to you again, or to allow you under any circumstances to be with me, so revolting had been

the scene you made the night before your departure. You wrote
and telegraphed from Bristol to beg me to forgive you and meet
you. Your tutor,[1] who had stayed behind, told me that he thought
that at times you were quite irresponsible for what you said and
did, and that most if not all of the men at Magdalen were of the
same opinion. I consented to meet you and, of course, I forgave
you. On the way up to town you begged me to take you to the
Savoy. That was indeed a fatal visit to me. Three months later,
in June, we were at Goring. Some of your Oxford friends came
to stay from a Saturday to Monday. The morning of the day
they went away you made a scene so dreadful, so distressing that
I told you that we must part. I remember quite well as we stood
on the level croquet ground with the pretty lawn all round us,
pointing out to you that we were spoiling each other's lives, that
you were absolutely ruining mine and that I evidently was not
making you really happy, and that an irrevocable parting and
complete separation was the one wise philosophic thing to do.
You went sullenly after luncheon, leaving one of your most
offensive letters behind with the butler to be handed to me after
your departure. Before three days had elapsed you were tele-
graphing from London to beg to be forgiven and allowed to
return. I had taken the place to please you. I had engaged your
own servants at your request. I was always terribly sorry for the
hideous temper to which you were really a prey. I was fond of
you. So I let you come back and forgave you. Three months
later still, in September, new scenes occurred, the occasion of
them being my pointing out to you the schoolboy faults of your
attempted translation of *Salome*. You must by this time be a fair
enough French scholar to know that the translation was as unworthy of you, as an ordinary Oxonian, as it was of the work it
sought to render. You did not, of course, know it then and, in
one of the violent letters you wrote to me on the point, you said
you were under 'no intellectual obligation of any kind' to me. I
remember that when I read that statement I felt that it was really
the one true thing you had written to me in the whole course of
our friendship. I saw that a less cultivated nature would really

1. Campbell Dodgson.

have suited you much better. I am not saying this in bitterness at all, but simply as a fact of companionship. Ultimately the bond of all companionship, whether in marriage or in friendship, is conversation, and conversation must have a common basis, and between two people of widely different culture the only common basis possible is the lowest level. The trivial in thought and action is charming. I had made it the keystone of a very brilliant philosophy expressed in plays and paradoxes. But the froth and folly of our life grew often very wearisome to me: it was only in the mire that we met: and fascinating, terribly fascinating though the one topic round which your talk invariably centred was, still at the end it became quite monotonous to me. I was often bored to death by it, and accepted it, as I accepted your passion for going to music halls, or your mania for absurd extravagances in eating and drinking, or any other of your to me less attractive characteristics, as a thing, that is to say, that one simply had to put up with, a part of the high price one had to pay for knowing you. When after leaving Goring I went to Dinard for a fortnight you were extremely angry with me for not taking you with me, and, before my departure there, made some very unpleasant scenes on the subject at the Albemarle Hotel, and sent me some equally unpleasant telegrams to a country house where I was staying for a few days. I told you, I remember, that I thought it was your duty to be with your own people for a little, as you had passed the whole season away from them. But in reality, to be perfectly frank with you, I could not under any circumstances have let you be with me. We had been together nearly twelve weeks. I required rest and freedom from the terrible strain of your companionship. It was necessary for me to be a little by myself. It was intellectually necessary. And so I confess I saw in your letter, from which I have quoted, a very good opportunity for ending the fatal friendship that had sprung up between us, and ending it without bitterness, as I had indeed tried to do on that bright June morning at Goring three months before. It was, however, represented to me – I am bound to say candidly by one of my own friends to whom you had gone in your difficulty – that you would be much hurt, perhaps almost humiliated, at having your work sent back to you like a schoolboy's exercise; that I was expecting far too much intellectually from you; and no matter what you wrote or did, you were absolutely and entirely devoted to me. I did not want to be the first to check or discourage you in your beginnings in literature. I knew quite well that no translation, unless one done by a poet, could render the colour and cadence of my work in any adequate measure: devotion seemed to me, seems to me still, a wonderful thing not to be lightly thrown away: so I took the translation and you back. Exactly three months later, after a series of scenes culminating in one more than usually revolting, when you came one Monday evening to my rooms accompanied by two of your friends, I found myself actually flying abroad next morning to escape from you, giving my family some absurd reason for my sudden departure, and leaving a false address with my servant for fear you might follow me by the next train. And I remember that afternoon, as I was in the railway carriage whirling up to Paris, thinking into what an impossible, terrible, utterly wrong state my life had got when I, a man of world-wide reputation, was actually forced to run away from England in order to try to get rid of a friendship that was entirely destructive of everything fine in me either from the intellectual or ethical point of view: the person from whom I was flying being no terrible creature sprung from sewer or mire into modern life with whom I had entangled my days, but you yourself, a young man of my own social rank and position, who had been at my own College at Oxford and was an incessant guest at my house. The usual telegrams of entreating and remorse followed. I disregarded them. Finally you threatened that unless I consented to meet you, you would under no circumstances consent to proceed to Egypt. I had myself, with your knowledge and concurrence, begged your mother to send you to Egypt away from England, as you were wrecking your life in London. I knew that if you did not go it would be a terrible disappointment to her, and for her sake I did meet you, and under the influence of great emotion, which even you cannot have forgotten, I forgave the past; though I said nothing at all about the future. On my return to London next day I remember sitting in my room and sadly and seriously trying to make up my mind whether or not you really were what you seemed to me to be, so full of terrible defects, so utterly ruinous both to yourself and others, so fatal a one to know even or to be with. For a whole week I thought about it, and wondered if, after all, I was not unjust and mistaken in my estimate of you. At the end of the week a letter from your mother was handed in. It expressed to the full every feeling I myself had about you. In it she spoke of your blind exaggerated vanity which made you despise your home, and treat your elder brother – that *candidissima anima* – as 'a Philistine': of your temper which made her afraid to speak to you about your life, the life she felt, she knew, you were leading: about your conduct in money matters, so distressing to her in more ways than one: of the degeneration and change that had taken place in you. She saw, of course, that heredity had burdened you with a terrible legacy, and frankly admitted it, admitted it with terror: he is 'the one of my children who has inherited the fatal Douglas temperament', she wrote of you. At the end she stated that she felt bound to declare that your friendship with me, in her opinion, had so intensified your vanity that it had become the source of all your faults, and earnestly begged me not to meet you abroad. I wrote to her at once in reply, and told her that I agreed entirely with every word she had said. I added much more. I went as far as I could possibly go. I told her that the origin of our friendship was you in your undergraduate days at Oxford coming to beg me to help you in very serious trouble of a very particular character. I told her that your life had been continually in the same manner troubled. The reason of your going to Belgium you had placed to the fault of your companion in that journey, and your mother had reproached me with having introduced you to him. I replaced the fault on the right shoulders, on yours. I assured her at the end that I had not the smallest intention of meeting you abroad and begged her to try to keep you there either as an honorary attaché, if that were possible, or to learn modern languages, if it were not; or for any reason she chose, at least during two or three years and for your sake as well as for mine. In the meantime you were writing to me by every post from

Egypt. I took not the smallest notice of any of your communications. I read them and tore them up. I had quite settled to have no more to do with you. My mind was made up and I gladly devoted myself to the art whose progress I had allowed you to interrupt. At the end of three months, your mother, with that unfortunate weakness of will that characterizes her, and that in the tragedy of my life has been an element no less fatal than your father's violence, actually writes to me herself – I had no doubt of course at your instigation – tells me that you are extremely anxious to hear from me, and in order that I should have no excuse for not communicating with you sends me your address in Athens, which, of course, I knew perfectly well. I confess I was absolutely astounded at her letter. I could not understand how, after what she had written to me in December, and what I in answer had written to her, she could in any way try to repair or renew my unfortunate friendship with you. I acknowledged her letter, of course, and again urged her to try to get you connected with some Embassy abroad, so as to prevent your returning to England, but I did not write to you, or take any more notice of your telegrams than I did before your mother had written to me. Finally you actually telegraphed to my wife begging her to use her influence with me to get me to write to you. Our friendship had always been a source of distress to her: not merely because she had never liked you personally, but because she saw how your continual companionship altered me, and not for the better: still, just as she has always been most gracious and hospitable to you, so she could not bear the idea of my being in any way unkind – for so it seemed to her – to any of my friends. She thought, knew indeed, that it was a thing alien to my character. At her request I did communicate with you. I remember the wording of my telegram quite well. I said that time healed every wound but that for many months to come I would neither write to you nor see you. You started without delay for Paris, sending me passionate telegrams on the road to beg me to see you once, at any rate. I declined. You arrived in Paris late on a Saturday night and found a brief letter from me waiting for you at your hotel stating that I would not see you. Next morning I received in Tite Street a telegram of some ten or eleven pages in length from you. You stated in it that no matter what you had done to me you could not believe that I would absolutely decline to see you: you reminded me that for the sake of seeing me even for one hour you had travelled six days and nights across Europe without stopping once on the way: you made what was, I must admit, a most pathetic appeal and ended with what seemed to me a threat of suicide and one not thinly veiled. You had yourself often told me how many of your race there had been who had stained their hands in their own blood; your uncle certainly, your grandfather possibly, among others in the mad, bad line from which you came. Pity, my old affection for you, regard for your mother to whom your death under such dreadful circumstances would have been a blow almost too great for her to bear, the horror of the idea that so young a life, and one that amidst all its ugly faults had still promise of beauty in it, should come to so revolting an end, merely humanity itself – all these, if excuses be necessary, must serve as my excuse for consenting to accord you one last interview. When I arrived in Paris, your tears breaking out again and again all through the evening, and falling over your cheeks like rain as we sat at dinner first at Voisin's, at supper at Paillard's afterwards: the unfeigned joy you evinced at seeing me, holding my hand whenever you could as though you were a gentle and penitent child: your contrition, so simple and sincere at the moment: made me consent to renew our friendship. Two days after we had returned to London, your father saw you having luncheon with me at the Café Royal, joined my table, drank of my wine, and that afternoon, through a letter addressed to you, began his first attack on me.

It may be strange, but I had once again, I will not say the chance, but the duty of separating from you forced upon me. I need hardly remind you that I refer to your conduct to me at Brighton from 10th to 13th October 1894. Three years is a long time for you to go back. But we who live in prison, and in whose lives there is no event but sorrow, have to measure time by throbs of pain, and the record of bitter moments. We have nothing else to think of. Suffering – curious as it may sound to you – is the means by which we exist, because it is the only means by which we become conscious of existing; and the remembrance of suffering in the past is necessary to us as the warrant, the evidence, of our continued identity. Between myself and the memory of joy lies a gulf no less deep than that between myself and joy in its actuality. Had our life together been as the world fancied it to be, one simply of pleasure, profligacy, and laughter, I would not be able to recall a single passage in it. It is because it was full of moments and days tragic, bitter, sinister in their warnings, dull or dreadful in their monotonous scenes and unseemly violences, that I can see or hear each separate incident in its detail, can indeed see or hear little else. So much in this place do men live by pain that my friendship with you, in the way through which I am forced to remember it, appears to me always as a prelude consonant with those varying modes of anguish which each day I have to realize; nay more, to necessitate them even; as though my life, whatever it had seemed to myself and others, had all the while been a real symphony of sorrow, passing through its rhythmically linked movements to its certain resolution, with that inevitableness that in Art characterizes the treatment of every great theme.

I spoke of your conduct to me on three successive days three years ago, did I not? I was trying to finish my last play at Worthing by myself. The two visits you had paid me had ended. You suddenly appeared a third time bringing with you a companion who you actually proposed should stay in my house. I (you must admit now quite properly) absolutely declined. I entertained you, of course; I had no option in the matter: but elsewhere, and not in my own house. The next day, Monday, your companion returned to the duties of his profession, and you stayed with me. Bored with Worthing, and still more, I have no doubt, with my fruitless efforts to concentrate my attention on my play, the only thing that really interested me at the moment, you insist on being taken to the Grand Hotel at Brighton. The night we arrive you fall ill with that dreadful low fever that is foolishly called the influenza, your second if not your third attack. I need not remind you how I waited on you and tended you, not merely with every luxury of fruit, flowers, presents, books, and the like that money can procure, but with that affection, tenderness and love that whatever you may think is not to be procured for money. Except for an hour's walk in the morning, an hour's drive in the afternoon, I never left the hotel. I got special grapes from London for you as you did not care for those the hotel supplied, invented things to please you, remained either with you or in the room next to yours, sat with you every evening to quiet or amuse you. After four or five days you recover and I take lodgings in order to try to finish my play. You, of course, accompany me. The morning after the day on which we were installed I feel extremely ill. You have to go to London on business, but promise to return in the afternoon. In London you meet a friend, and do not come back to Brighton till late on the next day, by which time I am in a terrible fever, and the doctor finds I have caught the influenza from you. Nothing could have been more uncomfortable for anyone ill than the lodgings turn out to be. My sitting-room is on the first floor, my bedroom on the third. There is no man-servant to wait on one, not even anyone to send out on a message, or to get what the doctor orders. But you are there. I feel no alarm. The next two days you leave me entirely alone without care, without attendance, without anything. It was not a question of grapes, flowers, and charming gifts: it was a question of mere necessaries: I could not even get the milk the doctor had ordered me: lemonade was pronounced an impossibility: and when I begged you to procure a book at the bookseller's, or if they had not got whatever I had fixed on, to choose something else, you never even take the trouble to go there. And when I was left all day without anything to read in consequence, you calmly tell me that you bought me the book and that they promised to send it down, a statement which I found by chance afterwards to have been entirely untrue from beginning to end. All the while you are, of course, living at my expense, driving about, dining at the Grand Hotel, and indeed only appearing in my room for money. On the Saturday night, you having left me completely un-attended and alone since the morning, I asked you to come back after dinner, and sit with me for a little. With irritable voice and ungracious manner you promise to do so. I wait till eleven o'clock and you never appear. I then left a note for you in your room just reminding you of the promise you had made me, and how you had kept it. At three in the morning, unable to sleep, and tortured with thirst, I made my way in the dark and cold, down to the sitting-room in the hopes of finding some water there. I found you. You fell on me with every hideous word an intemperate mood, an undisciplined and untutored nature could suggest. By the terrible alchemy of egotism you converted your remorse into rage. You accused me of selfishness in expecting you to be with me when I was ill; of standing between you and your amusements: of trying to deprive you of your pleasures. You told me, and I know it was quite true, that you had come back at midnight simply in order to change your dress-clothes and go out again to where you hoped new pleasures were awaiting for you, but that by leaving for you a letter in which I had reminded you that you had neglected me the whole day and the whole evening I had really robbed you of your desire for more enjoyments, and diminished your actual capacity for fresh delights. I went back upstairs in disgust and remained sleepless till dawn, nor till long after dawn was I able to get anything to quench the thirst of the fever that was on me. At eleven o'clock you came into my room. In the previous scene I could not help observing that by my letter I had, at any rate, checked you in a night of more than usual excess. In the morning you were quite yourself. I waited naturally to hear what excuses you had to make, and in what way you were going to ask for the forgiveness that you knew in your heart was invariably waiting for you, no matter what you did; your absolute trust that I would always forgive you being the thing in you that I always really liked best, perhaps the best thing in you to like. So far from doing that, you began to repeat the same scene with renewed emphasis and more violent assertion. I told you at length to leave the room: you pretended to do so, but when I lifted up my head from the pillow in which I had buried it, you were still there, and with brutality of laughter and hysteria of rage you moved suddenly towards me. A sense of horror came over me, for what exact reason I could not make out:

but I got out of my bed at once, and bare-footed and just as I was, made my way down the two flights of stairs to the sitting-room, which I did not leave till the owner of the lodgings – whom I had rung for – had assured me that you had left my bedroom, and promised to remain within call in case of necessity. After an interval of an hour, during which time the doctor had come and found me, of course, in a state of absolute nervous prostration, as well as in a worse condition of fever than I had been at the outset, you returned silently for money: took what you could find on the dressing-table and mantelpiece, and left the house with your luggage. Need I tell you what I thought of you during the two lonely wretched days of illness that followed? Is it necessary for me to state that I saw clearly that it would be a dishonour to myself to continue even an acquaintance with such a one as you had showed yourself to be? That I recognized that the ultimate moment had come and recognized it as being really a great relief? And that I knew that for the future my Art and Life would be freer and better and more beautiful in every possible way? Ill as I was, I felt at ease. The fact that the separation was irrevocable gave me peace. By Tuesday the fever had left me: and for the first time I dined downstairs. Tuesday was my birthday. Amongst the telegrams and communications on my table was a letter in your handwriting. I opened it with a sense of sadness on me. I knew that the time had gone by when a pretty phrase, an expression of affection, a word of sorrow would make me take you back. But I was entirely deceived. I had underrated you. The letter you sent to me on my birthday was an elaborate repetition of the two scenes set cunningly and carefully down in black and white! You mocked me with common jests. Your one satisfaction in the whole affair was, you said, that you retired to the Grand Hotel, and entered your luncheon to my account before you left for town. You congratulated me on my prudence in leaving the sickbed, on my sudden flight downstairs. 'It was an ugly moment for you,' you said, 'uglier than you imagine.' Ah! I felt it but too well. What it had really meant I do not know: whether you had with you the pistol you had bought to try to frighten your father with, and that, thinking it to be unloaded, you had once fired off in a public restaurant[1] in my company: whether your hand was moving towards a common dinner knife that by chance was lying on the table between us: whether, forgetting in your rage your low stature and inferior strength, you had thought of some specially personal insult, or attack even, as I lay ill there: I could not tell. I do not know to the present moment. All I know is that a feeling of utter horror had come over me, and that I had felt that unless I left the room at once and got away, you would have done or tried to do something that would have been, even to you, a source of lifelong shame. Only once before in my life had I experienced such a feeling of horror at any human being. It was when in my Library at Tite Street, waving his small hands in the air in epileptic fury, your father, with his bully, or his friend between us, had stood uttering every foul word his foul mind could think of, and screaming the loathsome threats he afterwards with such cunning carried out. In the latter case, he, of course, was the one who had to leave the room first. I drove him out. In your case *I* went. It was not the first time I had been obliged to save you from yourself.

You concluded your letter by saying: 'When you are not on your pedestal you are not interesting. The next time you are ill I will go away at once.' Ah! what coarseness of fibre does that reveal! What an entire lack of imagination! How callous, how common had the temperament by that time become! 'When you are not on your pedestal you are not interesting. The next time you are ill I will go away at once.' How often have those words come back to me in the wretched solitary cell of the various prisons to which I have been sent. I have said them to myself over and over again, and seen in them, I hope unjustly, some of the secret of your strange silence. For you to write this to me, when the very illness and fever from which I was suffering I had caught from tending you, was of course revolting in its coarseness and crudity; but for any human being in the whole wide world to write thus to another would be a sin for which there is no pardon, were there any sin for which there is none.

I confess that when I finished your letter I felt almost polluted,

1. The Berkeley.

as if by associating with one of such a nature I had soiled and shamed my life irretrievably. I had, it is true, done so, but I was not to learn how fully, till just six months later in life. I settled with myself to go back to London on the Friday, and see Sir George Lewis privately and request him to write to your father to state that I had determined never under any circumstances to allow you to enter my house, to sit at my board, to talk to me, walk with me, or anywhere and at any time to be my companion at all. This done I would have written to you just to inform you of the course of action I had adopted; the reasons you would have inevitably have realized yourself. I had everything arranged on Thursday night, when on Friday morning, as I was sitting at breakfast before starting, I happened to open the newspaper and saw in it a telegram stating that your elder brother, the real head of the family, the heir to the title, the pillar of the house, had been found dead in a ditch with his gun lying discharged beside him. The horror of the circumstances of the tragedy, now known to have been an accident, but then stained with a darker suggestion, the pathos of the sudden death of one so loved by all who knew him and almost on the eve, as it were, of his marriage; my idea of what your own sorrow would be, or should be; my consciousness of the misery awaiting your mother at the loss of the one to whom she clung for comfort and joy in life, and who, as she told me once herself, had from the very day of his birth never caused her to shed a single tear; my consciousness of your own isolation, both your other brothers being out of Europe and you consequently the only one to whom your mother and sister could look not merely for companionship in their sorrow but also for those dreary responsibilities of dreadful detail that Death always brings with it; the mere sense of the *lacrimae rerum*, of the tears of which the world is made, and of the sadness of all human things – out of the confluence of these thoughts and emotions crowding into my brain came infinite pity for you and your family. My own griefs and bitterness against you I forgot. What you had been to me in my sickness, I could not be to you in your bereavement. I telegraphed at once to you my deepest sympathy, and in the letter that followed invited you to come to my house as soon as you were able. I felt that to abandon you at that particular moment, and formally through a solicitor, would have been too terrible for you.

On your return to town from the actual scene of the tragedy to which you had been summoned, you came at once to me very sweetly and very simply, in your suit of woe, and with your eyes dim with tears. You sought consolation and help, as a child might seek it. I opened to you my house, my home, my heart. I made your sorrow mine also, that you might have help in bearing it. Never even by one word did I allude to your conduct towards me, to the revolting scenes and the revolting letter. Your grief which was real seemed to me to bring you nearer to me than you had ever been. The flowers you took from me to put on your brother's grave were to be a symbol not merely of the beauty of his life, but of the beauty that in all lives lies dormant and may be brought to light.

The gods are strange. It is not our vices only they make instruments to scourge us. They bring us to ruin through what in us is good, gentle, humane, loving. But for my pity and affection for you and yours, I would not now be weeping in this terrible place.

Of course, I discern in all our relations not Destiny merely, but Doom: Doom that (always) walks swiftly, because she goes to the shedding of blood. Through your father you come of a race, marriage with whom is horrible, friendship fatal, and that lays violent hands either on its own life, or on the lives of others. In every little circumstance in which the ways of our lives met; in every point of great, or seemingly trivial import in which you came to me for pleasure or for help; in the small chances, the slight accidents that look, in their relation to life, to be no more than the dust that dances in a beam, or the leaf that flutters from a tree, Ruin followed like the echo of a bitter cry, or the shadow that hunts with the beast of prey. Our friendship really begins with your begging me in a most pathetic and charming letter to assist you in a position appalling to any one, doubly so to a young man at Oxford: I do so, and ultimately through your using my name as your friend with Sir George Lewis I began to lose his esteem and friendship, a friendship of fifteen years' standing. When I was deprived of his advice and help and regard I was deprived of the one great safeguard of my life.

You send me a very nice poem of the undergraduate school of verse for my approval: I reply by a letter of fantastic literary conceits: I compare you to Hylas, or Hyacinth, Jonquil or Narcisse or some one whom the great God of Poetry favoured, and honoured with his love. The letter is like a passage from one of Shakespeare's sonnets transposed to a minor key. It can be understood only by those who had read the *Symposium* of Plato, or caught the spirit of a certain grave mood made beautiful for us in Greek marbles. It was, let me say frankly, the sort of letter I would, in a happy if wilful moment, have written to any graceful young man of either University who had sent me a poem of his own making, certain that he would have sufficient wit, or culture, to interpret rightly its fantastic phrases. Look at the history of that letter! It passes from you into the hands of a loathsome companion: from him to a gang of blackmailers: copies of it are sent about London to my friends, and to the manager[1] of the theatre where my work is being performed: every construction but the right one is put on it: Society is thrilled with the absurd rumours that I have had to pay a huge sum of money for having written an infamous letter to you: this forms the basis of your father's worst attack: I produce the original letter myself in Court to show what it really is: it is denounced by your father's Counsel as a revolting and insidious attempt to corrupt innocence: ultimately it forms part of a criminal charge: the Crown takes it up: the Judge sums up on it with little learning and much morality: I go to prison for it at last. That is the result of writing you a charming letter.

While I am staying with you at Salisbury you are terribly alarmed at a threatening communication from a former companion of yours: you beg me to see the writer and help you: I do so. The result is ruin for me. I am forced to take everything you have done on my shoulders and answer for it. When, having failed to take your degree, you have to go down from Oxford,

1. Sir Herbert Beerbohm Tree.

you telegraph to me in London to beg me to come to you. I do so at once: you ask me to take you to Goring, as you did not like under the circumstances to go home: at Goring you see a house that charms you: I take it for you: the result from every point of view is ruin for me. One day you come to me and ask me as a personal favour to you, to write something for an Oxford undergraduate magazine, about to be started by some friend of yours of whom I have never heard in all my life, and knew nothing at all about. To please you – what did I not do always to please you? – I sent him a page of paradoxes destined originally for the *Saturday Review*. A few months later I find myself standing in the dock of the Old Bailey on account of the character of the magazine. It forms part of the Crown charge against me. I am called upon to defend your friend's prose and your own verse. The former I cannot palliate: the latter I, loyal to the bitter extreme, to your youthful literature as to your youthful life, do very strongly defend, and will not hear of your being a writer of indecencies. But I go to prison, all the same, for your friend's undergraduate magazine and the 'Love that dares not tell its name.' At Christmas I give you a 'very pretty present' as you described it in your letter of thanks, on which I knew you had set your heart, worth some £40 or £50 at most. When the crash of my life comes and I am ruined, the bailiff who seizes my library, and has it sold, does so to pay for the 'very pretty present'. It was for that the execution was put into my house. At the ultimate and terrible moment when I am taunted, and spurred on by your taunts, to take an action against your father and have him arrested, the last straw to which I clutch in my wretched efforts to escape is the terrible expense. I tell the solicitor in your presence that I have no funds, that I cannot possibly afford the appalling cost, that I have no money at my disposal. What I said was, as you know, perfectly true. On that fatal Friday instead of being in Humphrey's office weakly consenting to my own ruin, I would have been happy and free in France, away from you and your father, unconscious of his loathsome card, and indifferent to your letters, if I had been able to leave the Avondale Hotel. But the hotel people absolutely refused to allow me to go. You had been staying with me for ten days: indeed you ultimately and to my great and, you will admit, rightful indignation, brought a companion of yours to stay with me also: my bill for the ten days was nearly £140. The proprietor said he could not allow my luggage to be removed from the hotel till I had paid the account in full. That is what kept me in London. Had it not been for the hotel bill I would have gone to Paris on Thursday morning.

When I told the solicitor I had no money to face the gigantic expense, you interposed at once. You said that your own family would be only too delighted to pay all the necessary costs: that your father had been an incubus to them all: that they had often discussed the possibility of getting him put into a lunatic asylum so as to keep him out of the way: that he was a daily source of annoyance and distress to your mother and to everyone else: that if only I would come forward to have him shut up I would be regarded by the family as their champion and their benefactor: and that your mother's rich relations themselves would look on it as a real delight to be allowed to pay all costs and expenses that might be incurred in any such effort. The solicitor closed at once, and I was hurried to the Police Court. I had no excuse left for not going. I was forced into it. Of course, your family don't pay the costs, and when I am made bankrupt, it is by your father and for the costs – the meagre balance of them – some £700.[1] At the present moment my wife, estranged from me over the important question whether I should have £3 or £3 10s. a week to live on, is preparing a divorce suit, for which, of course, entirely new evidence and an entirely new trial, to be followed perhaps by more serious proceedings, will be necessary. I, naturally, know nothing of the details. I merely know the name of the witness on whose evidence my wife's solicitors rely. It is your own Oxford servant, whom at your special request I took into my service for our summer at Goring.

But, indeed, I need not go on further into more instances of

1. £700 was the amount of Queensberry's costs in the unsuccessful action. The debts filed amounted to £6,000. Queensberry was the petitioning creditor making Wilde a bankrupt.

the strange doom you seem to have brought on me in all things big or little. It makes me feel sometimes as if you yourself had been merely a puppet worked by some secret and unseen hand to bring terrible events to a terrible issue. But puppets themselves have passions. They will bring a new plot into what they are presenting, and twist the ordered issue of vicissitude to suit some whim or appetite of their own. To be entirely free, and at the same time entirely dominated by law, is the eternal paradox of human life that we realize at every moment: and this, I often think, is the only explanation possible of your nature, if indeed for the profound and terrible mystery of a human soul there is any explanation at all, except one that makes the mystery all the more marvellous still.

Of course, you had your illusions, lived in them indeed, and through the shifting mists and coloured veils saw all things changed. You thought, I remember quite well, that your devoting yourself to me, to the entire exclusion of your family and family life, was a proof of your wonderful appreciation of me and your great affection. No doubt to you it seemed so. But recollect that with me was luxury, high living, unlimited pleasure, money without stint. Your family life bored you. The 'cold cheap wine of Salisbury', to use a phrase of your own making, was distasteful to you. On my side and along with my intellectual attractions were the flesh-pots of Egypt. When you could not find me to be with, the companions whom you chose as substitutes were not flattering.

You thought again that in sending a lawyer's letter to your father to say that, rather than sever your eternal friendship with me, you will give up the allowance of £250 a year which, with, I believe, deductions for your Oxford debts, he was then making you, you were realizing the very chivalry of friendship, touching the noblest note of self-denial. But your surrender of your little allowance did not mean that you were ready to give up even one of your most superfluous luxuries, or most unnecessary extravagances. On the contrary, your appetite for luxurious living was never so keen. My expenses for eight days in Paris for myself, you and your Italian servant were nearly £150: Paillard alone absorbing £85. At the rate at which you wished to live, your entire income for a whole year, if you had taken your meals alone, and had been especially economical in your selection of the cheaper form of pleasures, would hardly have lasted you three weeks. The fact that in what was merely pretence of bravado you had surrendered your allowance, such as it was, gave you at least a plausible reason for your claim to live at my expense: or what you thought a plausible reason: and on many occasions you seriously availed yourself of it, and gave the very fullest expression to it: and the continued drain, principally of course on me, but also to a terrible extent, I know, on your mother, was never so distressing; because in my case, at any rate, never so completely unaccompanied by the smallest word of thanks, or sense of limit.

You thought again that in attacking your own father with dreadful letters, abusive telegrams, and insulting postcards, you were really fighting your mother's battles, coming forward as her champion, and avenging the no doubt terrible wrongs and sufferings of her married life. It was quite an illusion on your part, one of your worst indeed. The way for you to have avenged your mother's wrongs on your father, if you considered it part of a son's duty to do so, was by being a better son to your mother than you had been: by not making her afraid to speak to you on serious things: by not signing bills the payment of which devolved on her: by being gentler to her, and not bringing sorrow into her days. Your brother Francis made great amends to her for what she had suffered, by his sweetness and goodness to her through the brief years of his flower-like life. You should have taken him as your model. You were wrong even in fancying that it would have been an absolute delight and joy to your mother if you had managed through me to get your father put into prison. I feel sure you were wrong. And if you want to know what a woman really feels when her husband and the father of her children is in prison dress, in a prison cell, write to my wife and ask her. She will tell you. *I* also had my illusions. I thought life was going to be a brilliant comedy, and that you were to be one of the graceful figures in it. I found it to be a revolting and repellent tragedy, and that the sinister occasion of the great catastrophe, sinister in its concentration of aim and intensity of narrowed will power, was yourself, stripped of that mask of joy and pleasure by which you, no less than I, had been deceived and led astray.

You can now understand – can you not? – a little of what I am suffering. Some paper, the *Pall Mall Gazette*, I think, describing the dress rehearsal of one of my plays, spoke of you as following me about like my shadow: the memory of our friendship is the shadow that walks with me here: that seems never to leave me: that wakes me up at night to tell me the same story over and over till its wearisome iteration makes all sleep abandon me till dawn: at dawn it begins again: it follows me into the prison yard and makes me talk to myself as I tramp round: each detail that accompanied each dreadful moment I am forced to recall: there is nothing that happened in those ill-starred years that I cannot recreate in that chamber of the brain which is set apart for grief or for despair: every strained note of your voice, every twitch and gesture of your nervous hands, every bitter word, every poisonous phrase comes back to me: I remember the street or river down which we passed: the wall or woodland that surrounded us, at what figure on the dial stood the hands of the clock, which way went the wings of the wind, the shape and colour of the moon.

There is, I know, one answer to all that I have said to you, and that is that you loved me: that all through those two and a half years during which the fates were weaving into one scarlet pattern the threads of our divided lives you really loved me. Yes, I know you did. No matter what your conduct to me was, I always felt that at heart you really did love me. Though I saw quite clearly that my position in the world of Art, the interest that my personality had always excited, my money, the luxury in which I lived, the thousand and one things that went to make up a life so charmingly and so wonderfully improbable as mine was, were, each and all of them, elements that fascinated you and made you cling to me: yet besides all this there was something more, some strange attraction for you: you loved me far better than you loved anyone else. But you, like myself, have had a terrible tragedy in your life, though one of an entirely opposite character to mine. Do you want to learn what it was? It was this. In you hate was always stronger than love. Your hatred of your father was of such stature that it entirely outstripped, overthrew, and overshadowed your love of me. There was no struggle between them at all, or but little: of such dimensions was your hatred and of such monstrous growth. You did not realize that there was no room for both passions in the same soul. They cannot live together in that fair carven house. Love is fed by the imagination, by which we become wiser than we know, better than we feel, nobler than we are: by which we can see life as a whole: by which and by which alone we can understand others in their real as in their ideal relation. Only what is fine, and finely conceived, can feed love. But anything will feed hate. There was not a glass of champagne that you drank, not a rich dish that you ate of in all those years, that did not feed your hate and make it fat. So to gratify it you gambled with my life, as you gambled with my money, carelessly, recklessly, indifferent to the consequence. If you lost, the loss would not, you fancied, be yours. If you won, yours, you knew, would be the exultation and the advantages of victory.

Hate blinds people. You were not aware of that. Love can read the writing on the remotest star; but hate so blinded you that you could see no further than the narrow, walled-in and already lust-withered garden of your common desires. Your terrible lack of imagination, the one really fatal defect of your character, was entirely the result of the hate that lived in you. Subtly, silently, and in secret, hate gnawed at your nature, as the lichen bites at the root of some sallow plant, till you grew to see nothing but the most meagre interests and the most petty aims. That faculty in you which love would have fostered, hate poisoned and paralysed. When your father first began to attack me it was as your private friend, and in a private letter to you. As soon as I had read the letter with its obscene threats and coarse violences I saw at once that there was a terrible danger looming on the horizon of my troubled days: I told you I would not be the cat's-paw between you both in your ancient hatred of each other:

that I in London was naturally much bigger game for him than a Secretary for Foreign Affairs at Homberg; that it would be unfair to me to place me even for a moment in such a position: and that I had something better to do with my life than to have scenes with a man, drunken, déclassé, and half-witted as he was. You would not be made to see this. Hate blinded you. You insisted that the quarrel had really nothing to do with me: that you would not allow your father to dictate to you in your private friendships: that it would be most unfair of me to interfere. You had already, before you saw me on the subject, sent your father a foolish and vulgar telegram as your answer. That, of course, committed you to a foolish and vulgar course of action to follow. The fatal errors of life are not due to man's being unreasonable. An unreasonable moment may be one's finest moment. They are due to man's being logical. There is a wide difference. That telegram conditioned the whole of your subsequent relations with your father, and consequently the whole of my life. And the grotesque thing about it is that it was a telegram of which the commonest street boy would have been ashamed. From pert telegrams to priggish lawyers' letters was a natural progress, and the result of your lawyers' letters to your father was, of course, to urge him on still further. You left him no option but to go on. You forced it on him as a point of honour, or of dishonour rather, that your appeal should have the more effect. So the next time he attacks me no longer in a private letter and as your private friend, but in public and as a public man. I have to expel him from my house. He goes from restaurant to restaurant looking for me, in order to insult me before the whole world, and in such a manner that if I retaliated I would be ruined, and if I did not retaliate I would be ruined also. *Then* surely was the time when *you* should have come forward and said that you would not expose me to such hideous attacks, such infamous persecution, on your account, but would, readily and at once, resign any claim you had to my friendship. You feel that now, I suppose. But it never even occurred to you then. Hate blinded you. All you could think of (besides, of course, writing to him insulting letters and telegrams) was to buy a ridiculous pistol that goes off in the Berkeley under circumstances that create a worse scandal than ever came to *your* ears. Indeed the idea of your being the object of a terrible quarrel between your father and a man of my position seemed to delight you. It, I suppose, very naturally, pleased your vanity and flattered your self-importance. That your father might have had your body which did not interest me, and left me your soul which did not interest him, would have been to you a distressing solution of the question. You scented the chance of a public scandal and flew to it. The prospect of a battle in which you would be safe delighted you. I never remember you in higher spirits than you were for the rest of that season. Your only disappointment seemed to be that nothing actually happened, and that no further meeting or fracas had taken place between us. You consoled yourself by sending him telegrams of such a character that at last the wretched man wrote to you and said that he had given orders to his servants that no telegrams were to be brought to him under any pretence whatsoever. That did not daunt you. You saw the immense opportunities afforded by the open postcard, and availed yourself of them to the full. You hounded him on in the chase still more. I do not suppose he would ever really have given it up. Family instincts were really strong in him. His hatred of you was just as persistent as your hatred of him, and I was the stalking-horse for both of you, and a mode of attack as well as a mode of shelter. His very passion for notoriety was not merely individual but racial. Still, if his interest had flagged for a moment your letters and postcards would soon have quickened it to its ancient flame. They did so. And he naturally went on further still. Having assailed me as a private gentleman and in private, as a public man and in public, he ultimately determines to make his final and great attack on me as an artist, and in the place where my art is being represented. He secures by fraud a seat for the first night of one of my plays, and contrives a plot to interrupt the performance, to make a foul speech about me to the audience, to insult my actors, to throw offensive or indecent missiles at me when I am called before the curtain at the close, utterly in some hideous way to ruin me through my work. By the merest chance, in the brief and accidental sincerity of a more than usually intoxicated mood, he boasts of his intention before others. Information is given to the police, and he is kept out of the theatre. You had your chance then. Then was your opportunity. Don't you realize now that you should have seen it, and come forward and said that you would not have my art, at any rate, ruined for your sake? You knew what my art was to me, the great primal note by which I had revealed, first myself to myself, and then myself to the world; the great passion of my life; the love to which all other loves were as marsh water to red wine; or the glowworm of the marsh to the magic mirror of the moon. Don't you understand now that your lack of imagination was the only really fatal defect of your character? What you had to do was quite simple, and quite clear before you, but hate blinded you, and you could see nothing. I could not apologize to your father for his having insulted me and persecuted me in the most loathsome manner for nearly nine months. I could not get rid of you out of my life. I had tried it again and again. I had gone so far as actually leaving England and going abroad in the hope of escaping from you. It had all been of no use. You were the only person who could have done anything.

The key of the situation rested entirely with yourself. It was the one great opportunity you had of making some slight return to me for all the love and affection and kindness and generosity and care I had shown you. Had you appreciated me even at a tenth of my value as an artist you would have done so. But hate blinded you. The faculty 'by which and by which alone we can understand others in their real, as in their ideal relations' was dead in you. You thought simply of how to get your father into prison. To see him 'in the dock', as you used to say: that was your one idea. The phrase became one of the many *scies* of your daily conversation. One heard it at every meal. Well, you had your desire gratified. Hate granted you every single thing you wished for. It was an indulgent master to you. It is so, indeed, to all who serve it. For two days you sat on a high seat with the Sheriffs, and feasted your eyes with the spectacle of your father standing in the dock of the Central Criminal Court. And on the third day I took his place. What had occurred? In your hideous game of hate together, you had both thrown dice for my soul and you happened to have lost. That was all.

You see that I have to write your life to you and you have to realize it. We have known each other now for more than four years. Half of the time we have been together: the other half I have had to spend in prison as the result of our friendship. Where you will receive this letter, if indeed it ever reaches you, I don't know. Rome, Naples, Paris, Venice, some beautiful city on sea or river, I have no doubt, holds you. You are surrounded, if not with all the useless luxury you had with me, at any rate with everything that is pleasurable to eye, ear and taste. Life is quite lovely to you. And yet, if you are wise, and wish to find life much lovelier still, and in a different manner, you will let the reading of this terrible letter – for such I know it is – prove to you as important a crisis and turning-point of your life as the writing of it is to me. Your pale face used to flush easily with wine or pleasure. If, as you read what is here written, it from time to time becomes scorched as though by a furnace blast, with shame, it will be all the better for you. The supreme vice is shallowness. Whatever is realized is right.

I have now got as far as the house of detention, have I not? After a night passed in the police cells I am sent there in the van. You were most attentive and kind. Almost every afternoon, if not actually every afternoon, till you go abroad you took the trouble to drive up to Holloway to see me. You also wrote very sweet and nice letters. But that it was not your father but you who had put me into prison, that from beginning to end you were the responsible person, that it was through you, for you, and by you that I was there, never for one instant dawned upon you. Even the spectacle of me behind the bars of a wooden cage could not quicken that dead unimaginative nature. You had the sympathy and the sentimentality of the spectator of a rather pathetic play. That you were the true author of the hideous tragedy did not occur to you. I saw that you realized nothing of what you had done. I did not desire to be the one to tell you what your own heart should have told you, what it indeed would have told you if you had not let hate harden it and make it insensate.

Everything must come to one out of one's own nature. There is no use telling a person a thing that he does not feel and can't understand. If I write to you now as I do it is because your own silence and conduct during my long imprisonment have made it necessary. Besides, as things had turned out the blow had fallen upon me alone. That was a source of pleasure to me. I was content for many reasons to suffer, though there was always to my eyes, as I watched you, something not a little contemptible in your complete and wilful blindness. I remember you producing with absolute pride a letter you had published in one of the halfpenny newspapers about me. It was a very prudent, temperate, indeed commonplace production. You appealed to the 'English sense of fair play', or something very dreary of that kind, on behalf of a 'man who was down'. It was the sort of letter you might have written had a painful charge been brought against some respectable person with whom personally you had been quite unacquainted. But you thought it a wonderful letter. You looked on it as a proof of almost quixotic chivalry. I am aware that you wrote other letters to other newspapers that they did not publish. But then they were simply to say that you hated your father. Nobody cared if you did or not. Hate, you had yet to learn, is, intellectually considered, the eternal negation. Considered from the point of view of the emotions it is a form of atrophy, and kills everything but itself. To write to the papers to say that one hates someone is as if one were to write to the papers to say that one had some secret and shameful malady: the fact that the man you hated was your own father, and that the feeling was thoroughly reciprocated, did not make your hate noble or fine in any way. If it showed anything it was simply that it was an hereditary disease.

I remember again, when an execution was put into my house, and my books and furniture were seized and advertised to be sold, and bankruptcy was impending, I naturally wrote to tell you about it. I did not mention that it was to pay for some gifts of mine to you that the bailiffs had entered the house where you had so often dined. I thought, rightly or wrongly, that such news might pain you a little. I merely told you the bare facts. I thought it proper that you should know them. You wrote back from

Boulogne in a strain of almost lyrical exultation. You said that you knew your father was 'hard up for money' and had been obliged to raise £1,500 for the expenses of the trial and that my going bankrupt was really a 'splendid score' off him as he would not then be able to get any of his costs out of me! Do you realize now what hate blinding a person is? Do you recognize now that when I described it as an atrophy destructive of everything but itself, I was scientifically describing a real psychological fact? That all my charming things were to be sold: my Burne-Jones drawings: my Whistler drawings: my Monticelli, my Simeon Solomons: my china: my library with its collection of presentation volumes from almost every poet of my time, from Hugo to Whitman, from Swinburne to Mallarmé, from Morris to Verlaine: with its beautifully bound editions of my father's and mother's works, its wonderful array of college and school prizes: its *éditions de luxe*, and the like: was absolutely nothing to you. You said it was a great bore: that was all. What you really saw in it was the possibility that your father might ultimately lose a few hundred pounds, and that paltry consideration filled you with ecstatic joy. As for the costs of the trial, you may be interested to know that your father openly said in the Orleans Club that if it had cost him £20,000 he would have considered the money thoroughly well spent he had extracted such enjoyment, and delight, and triumph out of it all. The fact that he was able not merely to put me into prison for two years but to take me out for an afternoon and make me a public bankrupt was an extra refinement of pleasure that he had not expected. It was the crowning point of my humiliation and of his complete and perfect victory. Had your father had no claim for his costs on me, you, I know perfectly well, would, as far as words go, at any rate have been most sympathetic about the entire loss of my library, a loss irreparable to a man of letters, the one of all my material losses the most distressing to me. You might even, remembering the sums of money I had lavishly spent on you and how you had lived on me for years, have taken the trouble to buy in some of my books for me. The best all went for less than £150: about as much as I would spend on you in an ordinary week. But the mean, small pleasure of thinking that your father was going to be a few pence out of pocket made you forget all about trying to make me a little return, so slight, so easy, so inexpensive, so obvious, and so enormously welcome to me, had you brought it about. Am I right in saying that hate blinds people? Do you see it now? If you don't, try to see it.

How clearly I saw it then, as now, I need not tell you. But I said to myself: 'At all costs, I must keep love in my heart. If I go into prison without love what will become of my soul?' The letters I wrote to you at that time from Holloway were my effort to keep love as the dominant note of my own nature. I could if I had chosen have torn you to pieces with bitter reproaches. I could have rent you with maledictions. I could have held up a mirror to you, and shown you such an image of yourself that you would not have recognized it as your own till you found it mimicking back your gestures of horror, and then you would have known whose shape it was, and hated it and yourself for ever. More than that indeed. The sins of another were being placed to my account. Had I so chosen, I could on either trial have saved myself at his expense, not from shame indeed, but from imprisonment. Had I cared to show that the Crown witnesses – the three most important – had been carefully coached by your father and his solicitors, not in reticences merely, but in assertions, in the absolute transference deliberate, plotted and rehearsed, of the actions and doings of someone else on to me, I could have had each one of them dismissed from the box by the judge, more summarily than even wretched perjured Atkins was. I could have walked out of Court with my tongue in my cheek, and my hands in my pockets, a free man. The strongest pressure was put upon me to do so. I was earnestly advised, begged, entreated to do so by people whose sole interest was my welfare, and the welfare of my house. But I refused. I did not choose to do so. I have never regretted my decision for a single moment, even in the most bitter periods of my imprisonment. Such a course of action would have been beneath me. Sins of the flesh are nothing. They are maladies for physicians to cure, if they should be cured. Sins of the soul alone are shameful. To have secured my acquittal

by such means would have been a lifelong torture to me. But do
you really think that you were worthy of the love I was showing
you then, or that for a single moment I thought you were? Do
you really think that at any period in our friendship you were
worthy of the love I showed you, or that for a single moment I
thought you were? I knew you were not. But love does not
traffic in a market place, nor use a huckster's scales. Its joy, like
the joy of the intellect, is to feel alive. The aim of love is to
love: no more, and no less. You were my enemy: such an enemy
as no man ever had. I had given you my life: and to gratify the
lowest and most contemptible of all human passions, Hatred and
Vanity and Greed, you had thrown it away. In less than three
years you had entirely ruined me from every point of view. For
my own sake there was nothing for me to do but to love you. I
knew that if I allowed myself to hate you that in the dry desert
of existence over which I had to travel, and am travelling still,
every rock would lose its shadow, every palm tree be withered,
every well of water prove poisoned at its source. Are you beginning now to understand a little? Is your imagination awakening
from the long lethargy in which it has lain? You know already
what hate is. Is it beginning to dawn on you what love is and
what is the nature of love? It is not too late for you to learn,
though to teach it to you I may have had to go to a convict's cell.

After my terrible sentence, when the prison dress was on me,
and the prison house closed, I sat amidst the ruins of my wonderful life, crushed by anguish, bewildered with terror, dazed
through pain. But I would not hate you. Every day I said to
myself: 'I must keep love in my heart to-day, else how shall I
live through the day?' I reminded myself that you meant no evil,
to me at any rate: I set myself to think that you had but drawn a
bow at a venture, and that the arrow had pierced a king between
the joints of his harness. To have weighed you against the smallest
of my sorrows, the meanest of my losses, would have been, I felt,
unfair. I determined I would regard you as one suffering too. I
forced myself to believe that at last the scales had fallen from your
long-blinded eyes. I used to fancy and with pain what your
horror must have been when you contemplated your terrible

handiwork. There were times, even in those dark days, the darkest of all my life, when I actually longed to console you, so sure was I that at last you had realized what you had done.

It did not occur to me then that you could have the supreme vice, shallowness. Indeed it was a real grief to me when I had to let you know that. I was obliged to reserve for my family business my first opportunity of receiving a letter: but my brother-in-law had written to me to say that if I would only write once to my wife she would, for my own sake and for our children's sake, take no action for divorce. I felt my duty was to do so. Setting aside other reasons, I could not bear the idea of being separated from Cyril, that beautiful, loving, lovable child of mine, my friend of all friends, my companion beyond all companions, one single hair of whose little golden head should have been dearer and more valuable to me than, I will not say you from top to toe, but the entire chrysolite of the whole world: was so indeed to me always, though I failed to understand it till too late.

Two weeks after your application, I get news of you. Robert Sherard, that bravest and most chivalrous of all brilliant beings, comes to see me, and among other things tells me that in that ridiculous *Mercure de France*, with its absurd affectation of being the true centre of literary corruption, you are about to publish an article on me with specimens of my letters. He asks me if it really was by my wish. I was greatly taken aback, and much annoyed, and gave orders that the thing was to be stopped at once. You had left my letters lying about for blackmailing companions to steal, for hotel servants to pilfer, for housemaids to sell. That was simply your careless want of appreciation of what I had written to you. But that you should seriously propose to publish selections from the balance was almost incredible to me. And which of my letters were they? I could get no information. That was my first news of you. It displeased me.

The second piece of news followed shortly afterwards. Your father's solicitors had appeared in prison, and served me with a bankruptcy notice for a paltry £700, the amount of their taxed costs. I was adjudged a public insolvent and ordered to be produced in Court. I felt most strongly, and feel still, and will revert to the subject again, that these costs should have been paid by your family. You had taken personally on yourself the responsibility of stating that your family would do so. It was that which had made the solicitor take up the case in the way he did. You were absolutely responsible. Even irrespective of your engagement on your family's behalf you should have felt that as you had brought the whole ruin on me, the least that could have been done was to spare me the additional ignominy of bankruptcy for an absolutely contemptible sum of money, less than half of what I spent on you in three brief summer months at Goring. Of that, however, no more here. I did, through the solicitor's clerk, I fully admit, receive a message from you on the subject, or at any rate in connexion with the occasion. The day he came to receive my depositions and statements, he leant across the table – the prison warder being present – and, having consulted a piece of paper which he pulled from his pocket, said to me in a low voice: 'Prince Fleur de Lys wishes to be remembered to you.' I stared at him. He repeated the message again. I did not know what he meant. 'The gentleman is abroad at present,' he added mysteriously. It all flashed across me, and I remember that, for the first and last time in my entire prison life, I laughed. In that laugh was all the scorn of all the world. Prince Fleur de Lys! I saw – and subsequent events showed me that I rightly saw – that nothing that had happened had made you realize a single thing. You were in your own eyes still the graceful prince of a trivial comedy, not the sombre figure of a tragic show. All that had occurred was as but a feather for the cap that gilds a narrow head, a flower to pink the doublet that hides the heart that hate, and hate alone, can warm, that love, and love alone, finds cold. Prince Fleur de Lys! You were, no doubt, quite right to communicate with me under an assumed name. I myself, at that time, had no name at all. In the great prison where I was then incarcerated, I was merely the figure and letter of a little cell in a long gallery, one of a thousand lifeless numbers, as of a thousand lifeless lives. But surely there were many real names in real history which would have suited you much better, and by which I would have had no difficulty at all in recognizing you at once? I did not look for you behind the spangles of a tinsel vizard suitable only for an amusing masquerade. Ah! had your soul been, as for its own perfection even it should have been, wounded with sorrow, bowed with remorse, and humble with grief, such was not the disguise it would have chosen beneath whose shadow to seek entrance to the House of Pain! The great things of life are what they seem to be, and for that reason, strange as it may sound to you, are often difficult to interpret. But the little things of life are symbols. We receive our bitter lessons most easily through them. Your seemingly casual choice of a feigned name was, and will remain, symbolic. It reveals you.

Six weeks later a third piece of news arrives. I am called out of the hospital ward, where I was lying wretchedly ill, to receive a special message from you through the Governor of the Prison. He reads me out a letter you had addressed to him in which you stated that you proposed to publish an article 'on the case of Mr Oscar Wilde' in the *Mercure de France* (a 'magazine', you added for some extraordinary reason, 'corresponding to the English *Fortnightly Review*') and were anxious to obtain my permission to publish extracts and selections from ... what letters? The letters I had written you from Holloway Prison: the letters that should have been to you things sacred and secret beyond anything in the whole world! These actually were the letters you proposed to publish for the jaded *décadent* to wonder at, for the greedy *feuilletoniste* to chronicle, for the little lions of the *Quartier Latin* to gape and mouth at. Had there been nothing in your own heart to cry out against so vulgar a sacrilege you might at least have remembered the sonnet he wrote who saw with such sorrow and scorn the letters of John Keats sold by public auction in London and have understood at last the real meaning of my lines

> ... I think they love not Art
> Who break the crystal of a poet's heart
> That small and sickly eyes may glare and gloat.

For what was your article to show? That I had been too fond of you? The Paris *gamin* was quite aware of the fact. They all read the newspapers, and most of them write for them. That I was a man of genius? The French understood that, and the peculiar quality of my genius, much better than you did, or could have been expected to do. That along with genius goes often a curious perversity of passion and desire? Admirable: but the subject belongs to Lombroso rather than to you. Besides, the pathological phenomenon in question is found also amongst those who have not genius. That in your war of hate with your father I was at once shield and weapon to each of you? Nay more, that in that hideous hunt for my life, that took place when the war was over, he never could have reached me had not your nets been already about my feet? Quite true: but I am told that Henri Bauer had already done it extremely well. Besides, to corroborate his view, had such been your intention, you did not require to publish my letters: at any rate those written from Holloway Prison.

Will you say, in answer to my questions, that in one of my Holloway letters I had myself asked you to try, as far as you were able, to set me a little right with some small portion of the world? Certainly, I did so. Remember how and why I am here at this very moment. Do you think I am here on account of my relations with the witnesses on my trial? My relations, real or supposed, with people of that kind were matters of no interest either to the Government or to Society. They knew nothing of them and cared less. I am here for having tried to put your father into prison. My attempt failed, of course. My own Counsel threw up their briefs. Your father completely turned the tables on me, and had me in prison, has me there still. That is why there is contempt felt for me. That is why people despise me. That is why I have to serve out every day, every hour, every minute of my dreadful imprisonment. That is why my petitions have been refused.

You were the only person who, and without in any way exposing yourself to scorn or danger or blame, could have given another colour to the whole affair, have put the matter in a different light, have shown to a certain degree how things really stood. I would not, of course, have expected, nor indeed wished you to have stated how and for what purpose you had sought my assistance in your trouble at Oxford: or how, and for what purpose, if you had a purpose at all, you had practically never left my side

for nearly three years. My incessant attempts to break off a friendship that was so ruinous to me as an artist, as a man of position,
as a member of Society even, need not have been chronicled with
the accuracy with which they have been set down here. Nor
would I have desired you to have described the scenes you used
to make with such almost monotonous recurrence: nor to have
reprinted your wonderful series of telegrams to me with their
strange mixture of romance and finance: nor to have quoted from
letters the more revolting or heartless passages as I have been
forced to do. Still, I thought it would have been good, as well for
you as for me, if you had made some protest against your father's
version of our friendship, one no less grotesque than venomous
and as absurd in its inference to you as it was dishonouring in its
reference to me. That version has now actually passed into serious
history: it is quoted, believed, and chronicled: the preacher has
taken it for his text, and the moralist for his barren theme: and I
who appealed to all the ages have had to accept my verdict from
one who is an ape and a buffoon. I have said, and with some
bitterness, I admit, in this letter that such was the irony of things
that your father would live to be the hero of a Sunday school
tract: that you would rank with the infant Samuel: and that my
place would be between Gilles de Retz and the Marquis de Sade.
I dare say it is best so. I have no desire to complain. One of the
many lessons that one learns in prison is, that things are what
they are and will be what they will be. Nor have I any doubt
that the leper of medievalism and the author of *Justine* will prove
better company than *Sandford and Merton*.

But at the time I wrote to you I felt that for both our sakes it
would be a good thing, a proper thing, a right thing, not to accept
that account which your father had put forward through his
Counsel for the edification of a Philistine world, and that is why
I asked you to think out and write something that would be
nearer the truth. It would at least have been better for you than
scribbling to the French papers about the domestic life of your
parents. What did the French care whether or not your parents
had led a happy domestic life? One cannot conceive a subject
more entirely uninteresting to them. What did interest them was

how an artist of my distinction, one who by the school and movement of which he was the incarnation had exercised a marked
influence on the direction of French thought, could, having led
such a life, have brought such an action. Had you proposed for
your article to publish the letters, endless I fear in number, in
which I had spoken to you of the ruin you were bringing on my
life, of the madness of moods of rage that you were allowing to
master you to your own hurt as well as to mine, and of my desire,
nay, my determination to end a friendship so fatal to me in every
way, I could have understood it, though I would not have
allowed such letters to be published: when your father's Counsel
desiring to catch me in a contradiction suddenly produced in
Court a letter of mine, written to you in March 1893, in which I
stated that, rather than endure a repetition of the hideous scenes
you seemed to take such a terrible pleasure in making, I would
readily consent to be 'blackmailed by every renter in London', it
was a very real grief to me that that side of my friendship with you
should inadvertently be revealed to the common gaze: but that
you should have been so slow to see, so lacking in all sensitiveness, and so dull in apprehension of what is rare, delicate and
beautiful, as to propose yourself to publish the letters in which
and through which I was trying to keep alive the very spirit and
soul of love, that it might dwell in my body through the long
years of that body's humiliation, – this was, and still is to me a
source of the very deepest pain, the most poignant disappointment. Why you did so, I fear I know but too well. If hate blinded
your eyes, vanity sewed your eyelids together with threads of
iron. The 'faculty by which, and by which alone, one can understand others in their real as in their ideal relations' your narrow
egotism had blunted, and long disuse had made of no avail. The
imagination was as much in prison as I was. Vanity had barred
up the windows, and the name of the warder was hate.

All this took place in the early part of November of the year
before last. A great river of life flows between me and a date so
distant. Hardly, if at all, can you see across so wide a waste. But
to me it seems to have occurred, I will not say yesterday, but
to-day. Suffering is one very long moment. We cannot divide

it by seasons. We can only record its moods, and chronicle their return. With us time itself does not progress. It revolves. It seems to circle round one centre of pain. The paralysing immobility of a life every circumstance of which is regulated after an unchangeable pattern, so that we eat and drink and lie down and pray, or kneel at least for prayer, according to the inflexible laws of an iron formula: this immobile quality, that makes each dreadful day in the very minutest detail like its brother, seems to communicate itself to those external forces, the very essence of whose existence is ceaseless change. Of seed-time or harvest, of the reapers bending over the corn, or the grape gatherers threading through the vines, of the grass in the orchard made white with broken blossoms or strewn with fallen fruit: of these we know nothing, and can know nothing.

For us there is only one season, the season of sorrow. The very sun and moon seem taken from us. Outside, the day may be blue and gold, but the light that creeps down through the thickly-muffled glass of the small iron-barred window beneath which one sits is grey and niggard. It is always twilight in one's cell, as it is always twilight in one's heart. And in the sphere of thought, no less than in the sphere of time, motion is no more. The thing that you personally have long ago forgotten, or can easily forget, is happening to me now, and will happen to me again to-morrow. Remember this, and you will be able to understand a little of why I am writing, and in this manner writing. . . .

A week later, I am transferred here. Three more months go over and my mother dies. No one knew better than you how deeply I loved and honoured her. Her death was terrible to me; but I, once a lord of language, have no words in which to express my anguish and my shame. Never even in the most perfect days of my development as an artist could I have found words fit to bear so august a burden; or to move with sufficient stateliness of music through the purple pageant of my incommunicable woe. She and my father had bequeathed me a name they had made noble and honoured, not merely in literature, art, archaeology, and science, but in the public history of my own country, in its evolution as a nation. I had disgraced that name eternally. I had made it a low byword among low people. I had dragged it through the very mire. I had given it to brutes that they might make it brutal, and to fools that they might turn it into a synonym for folly. What I suffered then, and still suffer, is not for pen to write or paper to record. My wife, always kind and gentle to me, rather than that I should hear the news from indifferent lips, travelled, ill as she was, all the way from Genoa to England to break to me herself the tidings of so irreparable, so irredeemable, a loss. Messages of sympathy reached me from all who had still affection for me. Even people who had not known me personally, hearing that a new sorrow had broken into my life, wrote to ask that some expression of their condolence should be conveyed to me. . . .

Three months go over. The calendar of my daily conduct and labour that hangs on the outside of my cell door, with my name and sentence written upon it, tells me that it is May.

My friends come to see me again. I enquire, as I always do, after you. I am told that you are in your villa at Naples, and are bringing out a volume of poems. At the close of the interview it is mentioned casually that you are dedicating them to me. The tidings seemed to give me a sort of nausea of life. I said nothing, but silently went back to my cell with contempt and scorn in my heart. How could you dream of dedicating a volume of poems to me without first asking my permission? Dream, do I say? How could you dare do such a thing? Will you give as your answer that in the days of my greatness and fame I had consented to receive the dedication of your early work? Certainly I did so: just as I would have accepted the homage of any other young men beginning the difficult and beautiful art of literature. All homage is delightful to an artist and doubly sweet when youth brings it. Laurel and bay leaf wither when aged hands pluck them. Only youth has a right to crown an artist. That is the real privilege of being young if youth only knew it. But the days of abasement and infamy are different from those of greatness and fame. You had yet to learn that.

Prosperity, pleasure and success, may be rough of grain and common in fibre, but sorrow is the most sensitive of all created things. There is nothing that stirs in the whole world of thought to which sorrow does not vibrate in terrible and exquisite pulsation. The thin beaten-out leaf of tremulous gold that chronicles the direction of forces the eye cannot see is in comparison coarse. It is a wound that bleeds when any hand but that of love touches it, and even then must bleed again, though not in pain.

You could write to the Governor of Wandsworth Prison to ask my permission to publish my letters in the *Mercure de France*, 'corresponding to our English *Fortnightly Review*'. Why not have written to the Governor of the Prison at Reading to ask my permission to dedicate your poems to me, whatever fantastic description you may have chosen to give them? Was it because in the one case the magazine in question had been prohibited by me from publishing letters, the legal copyright of which, as you are, of course, perfectly well aware, was and is vested entirely in me, and in the other you thought that you could enjoy the wilfulness of your own way without my knowing anything about it till it was too late to interfere? The mere fact that I was a man disgraced, ruined and in prison should have made you, if you desired to write my name on the fore-page of your work, beg it of me as a favour, an honour, a privilege: that is the way in which one should approach those who are in distress and sit in shame.

Where there is sorrow there is holy ground. Some day people will realize what that means. They will know nothing of life till they do. Robbie[1] and natures like his can realize it. When I was brought down from my prison to the Court of Bankruptcy, between two policemen, Robbie waited in the long dreary corridor that, before the whole crowd, whom an action so sweet and simple hushed into silence, he might gravely raise his hat to me, as, handcuffed and with bowed head, I passed him by. Men have gone to heaven for smaller things than that. It was in this spirit, and with this mode of love, that the saints knelt down to wash the feet of the poor, or stooped to kiss the leper on the cheek. I have never said one single word to him about what he did. I do not know to the present moment whether he is aware that I was even conscious of his action. It is not a thing for which one can

1. Robert Ross.

render formal thanks in formal words. I store it in the treasure-house of my heart. I keep it there as a secret debt that I am glad to think I can never possibly repay. It is embalmed and kept sweet by the myrrh and cassia of many tears. When wisdom has been profitless to me, philosophy barren, and the proverbs and phrases of those who have sought to give me consolation as dust and ashes in my mouth, the memory of that little, lovely, silent act of love has unsealed for me all the wells of pity: made the desert blossom like a rose, and brought me out of the bitterness of lonely exile into harmony with the wounded, broken, and great heart of the world. When people are able to understand, not merely how beautiful Robbie's action was, but why it meant so much to me, and always will mean so much, then, perhaps, they will realize how and in what spirit they should approach me. . . .

*

The first volume of Poems that in the very springtide of his manhood a young man sends forth to the world should be like a blossom or flower of spring, like the white thorn in the meadow at Magdalen or the cowslips in the Cumnor fields. It should not be burdened by the weight of a terrible and revolting tragedy; a terrible revolting scandal. If I had allowed my name to serve as herald to such a book, it would have been a grave artistic error; it would have brought a wrong atmosphere round the whole work, and in modern art atmosphere counts for so much. Modern life is complex and relative; those are its two distinguishing notes; to render the first we require atmosphere with its subtlety of *nuances*, of suggestion, of strange perspectives; as for the second we require background. That is why sculpture has ceased to be a representative art and why music is a representative art and why literature is, and has been and always will remain the supreme representative art.

I have spoken to you at length on this point in order that you should grasp its full bearings, and understand why I wrote at once to Robbie in terms of such scorn and contempt of you, and absolutely prohibited the dedication, and desired that the words I had written to you should be copied out carefully and sent to you. I felt that at last the time had come when you should be made to see, to recognize, to realize a little what you had done. Blindness may be carried so far that it becomes grotesque, and unimaginative nature, if something be not done to rouse it, will become petrified into absolute insensibility, so that while the body may eat and drink, and have its pleasures, the soul whose house it is, may, like the soul of Branca d'Oria in Dante, be dead absolutely. My letter seems to have arrived not a moment too soon. It fell on you, as far as I can judge, like a thunderbolt. You described yourself, in your answer to Robbie, as being 'deprived of all power of thought and expression'. Indeed apparently you can think of nothing better than to write to your mother to complain. Of course, she with that blindness to your real good that has been her ill-starred fortune and yours, gives you every comfort she can think of, and lulls you back, I suppose, into your former unhappy, unworthy condition; while as far as I am concerned, she lets my friends know that she is 'very much annoyed' at the severity of my remarks about you. Indeed it is not merely to my friends that she conveys her sentiments of annoyance, but also to those – a very much larger number, I need hardly remind you – who are not my friends; and I am informed now, and through channels very kindly disposed to you and yours, that in consequence of this a great deal of the sympathy that, by reason of my distinguished genius and terrible sufferings, had been gradually but surely growing up for me, has been entirely taken away. People say, 'Ah! he first tried to get the kind father put into prison and failed: now he turns around and blames the innocent son for his failure. How right we were to despise him! How worthy of contempt he is!' It seems to me that when my name is mentioned in your mother's presence, if she has no word of sorrow or regret for her share – no slight one – in the ruin of my house, it would be more seemly if she remained silent. And as for you – don't you think now that, instead of writing to her to complain, it would have been better for you, in every way, to have written to me directly, and to have had the courage to say to me whatever you had or fancied you had to say? It is nearly a year ago now since I wrote that letter. You cannot have remained during that entire time 'deprived of all power of thought and expression'. Why did you not write to me? You saw by my letter how deeply wounded, how outraged I was by your whole conduct. More than that: you saw your entire friendship with me set before you at last in its true light, and by a mode not to be mistaken. Often in old days I had told you that you were ruining my life. You had always laughed. When Edwin Levy at the very beginning of our friendship seeing your manner of putting me forward to bear the brunt and annoyance and expense even of that unfortunate Oxford mishap of yours, if we must so term it, in reference to which his advice and help had been sought, warned me for the space of a whole hour against knowing you, you laughed as at Bracknell I described to you my long and impressive interview with him. When I told you how even that unfortunate young man who ultimately stood beside me in the dock had warned me more than once that you would prove far more fatal in bringing me to utter destruction than any even of the common lads whom I was foolish enough to know, you laughed, though not with such sense of amusement. When my more prudent or less well disposed friends either warned me or left me, on account of my friendship with you, you laughed with scorn. You laughed immoderately when, on the occasion of your father writing his first abusive letter to you about me, I told you that I knew I would be the mere cat's-paw of your dreadful quarrel and come to some evil between you. But every single thing happened as I had said it would happen, as far as the result goes. You had no excuse for not seeing how all things had come to pass. Why did you not write to me? Was it cowardice? Was it callousness? What was it? The fact that I was outraged with you and had expressed my sense of the outrage was all the more reason for writing. If you thought my letter just, you should have written. If you thought it in the smallest point unjust, you should have written. I waited for a letter. I felt sure that at last you would see that, if old affection, much protested love, the thousand acts of ill-requited kindness I had showered on you, the thousand unpaid debts of gratitude you owed me: – that if all these were nothing to you, mere duty itself, most barren of all bonds between man and man, should have made you write. You cannot say that you seriously thought I was obliged to receive none but business communications from members of my family. You knew perfectly that every twelve weeks Robbie writes to me a little budget of literary news. Nothing can be more charming than his letters, in their wit, their clever concentrated criticism, their light touch: they are real letters, they are like a person talking to one; they have the quality of a French *causerie intime*: and in his delicate mode of deference to me, appealing at one time to my judgement, at another to my sense of humour, at another to my instinct for beauty or to my culture, and reminding me in a hundred subtle ways that once I was to many an arbiter of style in art; the supreme arbiter to some; he shows how he has the tact of love as well as the tact of literature. His letters have been the messengers between me and that beautiful unreal world of art where once I was King, and would have remained King indeed, had I not let myself be lured into the imperfect world of coarse uncompleted passion, of appetite without distinction, desire without limit, and formless greed. Yet when all is said surely you might have been able to understand or conceive, at any rate that on the ordinary grounds of mere psychological curiosity it would have been more interesting to me to hear from you than to learn that Alfred Austin was trying to bring out a volume of poems; that George Street was writing dramatic criticism for the *Daily Chronicle*; or that by one who cannot speak a panegyric without stammering, Mrs Meynell had been pronounced to be the new Sibyl of style.

Ah! had you been in prison – I will not say through any fault of mine, for that would be a thought too terrible for me to bear – but through fault of your own, error of your own, faith in some unworthy friends, slip in sensual mire, trust misapplied, or love ill bestowed, or none, or all of these – do you think that I would have allowed you to eat your heart away in darkness and solitude without trying in some way, however slight, to help you to bear the bitter burden of your disgrace? Do you think that I would not have let you know that, if you suffered, I was suffering too: that if you wept there were tears in my eyes also: and that if you lay in the house of bondage and were despised of men, I out of my griefs had built a house in which to dwell until your coming, a treasury in which all that man had denied to you would be laid up for your healing, one hundredfold in increase? If bitter necessity, or prudence, to me more bitter still, had prevented my being near you, and robbed me of the joy of your presence, though seen through iron bars and in a shape of shame, I would have written to you in season and out of season in the hope that some mere phrase, some single word, some broken echo even, of love might reach you. If you had refused to receive my letters, I would have written none the less, so that you should have known that at any rate there were always letters awaiting for you. Many have done so to me. Every three months people write to me, or propose to write to me. Their letters and communications are kept. They will be handed to me when I go out of prison. I know they are there. I know the names of the people who have written them. I know that they are full of sympathy, and affection, and kindness. That is sufficient for me. I need know no more. Your silence has been horrible. Nor has it been a silence of weeks and months merely, but of years; of years even as they have to count them who, like yourself, live swiftly in happiness and can hardly catch the gilt feet of the days as they dance by, and are out of breath in a chase after pleasure. It is a silence without excuse; a silence without palliation. I knew you had feet of clay. Who knew better? When I wrote in my aphorisms, that it was simply the feet of clay that made the gold of the image precious,[1] it was of you I was thinking. But it is no gold image with clay feet that you had made for yourself. Out of the very dust of the common highway that the hooves of the horned things pash into mire you have moulded your perfect semblance for me to look at, so that, whatever my secret desire might have been, it would be impossible for me now to have for you any feeling other than that of contempt and scorn. And, on setting aside all other reasons, your indifference, your worldly wisdom, your callousness, your prudence, whatever you may choose to call it, has been made doubly bitter to me by the peculiar circumstances that either accompanied or followed my fall.

1. *Dorian Gray*, ch. xv.

Other miserable men when they are thrown into prison, if they are robbed of the beauty of the world, are at least safe in some measure from the world's most deadly slings, most awful arrows. They can hide in the darkness of their cells and of their very disgrace make a mode of sanctuary. The world having had its will goes its way, and they are left to suffer undisturbed. With me it has been different. Sorrow after sorrow has come beating at the prison doors in search of me; they have opened the gates wide and let them in. Hardly if at all have my friends been suffered to see me. But my enemies have had full access to me always; twice in my public appearances in the Bankruptcy Court; twice again in my public transferences from one prison to another have I been shown under conditions of unspeakable humiliation to the gaze and mockery of men. The messenger of Death had brought me his tidings and gone his way; and in entire solitude and isolated from all that could give me comfort or suggest relief I have had to bear the intolerable burden of misery and remorse, which the memory of my mother placed upon me and places on me still. Hardly has that wound been dulled, not healed, by time, when violent and bitter and harsh letters come to me from my wife's solicitors. I am at once tainted and threatened with poverty. That I can bear. I can school myself to worse than that; but my two children are taken from me by legal procedure. That is, and always will remain to me a source of infinite distress, or infinite pain, of grief without end or limit. That the law should decide and take upon itself to decide that I am one unfit to be with my own children is something quite horrible to me. The disgrace of prison is as nothing compared with it. I envy the other men who tread the yard along with me. I am sure that their children wait for them, look for their coming, will be sweet to them.

The poor are wiser, more charitable, more kind, more sensitive than we are. In their eyes prison is a tragedy in a man's life, a misfortune, a casualty, something that calls for sympathy in others. They speak of one who is in prison as of one who is 'in trouble' simply. It is the phrase they always use, and the expression has the perfect wisdom of love in it. With people of our own rank it is different. With us, prison makes a man a pariah. I, and such as I am, have hardly any right to air and sun. Our presence taints the pleasures of others. We are unwelcome when we reappear. To revisit the glimpses of the moon is not for us. Our very children are taken away. Those lovely links with humanity are broken. We are doomed to be solitary, while our sons still live. We are denied the one thing that might heal us and keep us, that might bring balm to the bruised heart, and peace to the soul in pain.

And to all this has been added the hard small fact that by your actions and by your silence, by what you have done and by what you have left undone, you have made every day of my long imprisonment still more difficult for me to live through. The very bread and water of prison fare you have by your conduct changed. You have rendered the one bitter and the other brackish to me. The sorrow you should have shared you have doubled, the pain you should have sought to lighten you have quickened to anguish. I have no doubt you did not mean to do so. I know that you did not mean to do so. It was simply that 'one really fatal defect in your character, your entire lack of imagination'.

And the end of it all is that I have got to forgive you. I must do so. I don't write this letter to put bitterness into your heart, but to pluck it out of mine. For my own sake I must forgive you. One cannot always keep an adder in one's breast to feed on one, nor rise up every night to sow thorns in the garden of one's soul. It will not be difficult at all for me to do so, if you help me a little. Whatever you did to me in the old days I always readily forgave. It did you no good then. Only one whose life is without stain of any kind can forgive sins. But now when I sit in humiliation and disgrace it is different. My forgiveness should mean a great deal to you now. Some day you will realize it. Whether you do so early or late, soon or not at all, my way is clear before me. I cannot allow you to go through life bearing in your heart the burden of having ruined a man like me. The thought might make you callously indifferent, or morbidly sad. I must take the burden from you and put it on my own shoulders.

I must say to myself that I ruined myself, and that nobody great or small can be ruined except by his own hand. I am quite ready to say so. I am trying to say so, though they may not think it at the present moment. This pitiless indictment I bring without pity against myself. Terrible as was what the world did to me, what I did to myself was far more terrible still.

I was a man who stood in symbolic relations to the art and culture of my age. I had realized this for myself at the very dawn of my manhood, and had forced my age to realize it afterwards. Few men hold such a position in their own lifetime, and have it so acknowledged. It is usually discerned, if discerned at all, by the historian, or the critic, long after both the man and his age have passed away. With me it was different. I felt it myself, and made others feel it. Byron was a symbolic figure, but his relations were to the passion of his age and its weariness of passion. Mine were to something more noble, more permanent, of more vital issue, of larger scope.

The gods had given me almost everything. I had genius, a distinguished name, high social position, brilliancy, intellectual daring; I made art a philosophy and philosophy an art; I altered the minds of men and the colours of things; there was nothing I said or did that did not make people wonder. I took the drama, the most objective form known to art, and made it as personal a mode of expression as the lyric or sonnet; at the same time I widened its range and enriched its characterization. Drama, novel, poem in prose, poem in rhyme, subtle or fantastic dialogue, whatever I touched, I made beautiful in a new mode of beauty: to truth itself I gave what is false no less than what is true as its rightful province, and showed that the false and the true are merely forms of intellectual existence. I treated art as the supreme reality and life as a mere mode of fiction. I awoke the imagination of my century so that it created myth and legend around me. I summed up all systems in a phrase and all existence in an epigram. Along with these things I had things that were different. But I let myself be lured into long spells of senseless and sensual ease. I amused myself with being a *flâneur*, a dandy, a man of fashion. I surrounded myself with the smaller natures and the meaner minds. I became the spendthrift of my own genius, and to waste an eternal youth gave me a curious joy. Tired of being on the heights, I deliberately went to the depths in the search for new sensation. What the paradox was to me in the sphere of thought, perversity became to me in the sphere of passion. Desire, at the end, was a malady, or a madness, or both. I grew careless of the lives of others. I took pleasure where it pleased me, and passed on. I forgot that every little action of the common day makes or unmakes character, and that therefore what one has done in the secret chamber one has some day to cry aloud on the house-tops. I ceased to be lord over myself. I was no longer the captain of my soul, and did not know it. I allowed pleasure to dominate me. I ended in horrible disgrace. There is only one thing for me now, absolute humility.

I have lain in prison for nearly two years. Out of my nature has come wild despair; an abandonment to grief that was piteous even to look at; terrible and impotent rage; bitterness and scorn; anguish that wept aloud; misery that could find no voice; sorrow that was dumb. I have passed through every possible mood of suffering. Better than Wordsworth himself I know what Wordsworth meant when he said –

> Suffering is permanent, obscure, and dark,
> And has the nature of infinity.

But while there were times when I rejoiced in the idea that my sufferings were to be endless, I could not bear them to be without meaning. Now I find hidden somewhere away in my nature something that tells me that nothing in the whole world is meaningless, and suffering least of all. That something hidden away in my nature, like a treasure in a field, is humility.

It is the thing left in me, and the best: the ultimate discovery at which I have arrived, the starting-point for a fresh development. It has come to me right out of myself, so I know that it has come at the proper time. It could not have come before, nor later. Had anyone told me of it, I would have rejected it. Had it been brought to me, I would have refused it. As I found it, I want to keep it. I must do so. It is the one thing that has in it the elements of life, of a new life, a *Vita Nuova* for me. Of all things it is the strangest; one cannot give it away and another may not give it to one. One cannot acquire it except by surrendering everything that one has. It is only when one has lost all things, that one knows that one possesses it.

Now I have realized that it is in me, I see quite clearly what I ought to do; in fact, must do. And when I use such a phrase as that, I need not say that I am not alluding to any external sanction or command. I admit none. I am far more of an individualist than I ever was. Nothing seems to me of the smallest value except what one gets out of oneself. My nature is seeking a fresh mode of self-realization. That is all I am concerned with. And the first thing that I have got to do is to free myself from any possible bitterness of feeling against the world.

I am completely penniless, and absolutely homeless. Yet there are worse things in the world than that. I am quite candid when I say that rather than go out from this prison with bitterness in my heart against the world, I would gladly and readily beg my bread from door to door. If I got nothing from the house of the rich I would get something at the house of the poor. Those who have much are often greedy; those who have little always share. I would not a bit mind sleeping in the cool grass in summer, and when winter came on sheltering myself by the warm close-thatched rick, or under the pent-house of a great barn, provided I had love in my heart. The external things of life seem to me now of no importance at all. You can see to what intensity of individualism I have arrived – or am arriving rather, for the journey is long, and 'where I walk there are thorns'.

Of course I know that to ask alms on the highway is not to be my lot, and that if ever I lie in the cool grass at night-time it will be to write sonnets to the moon. When I go out of prison, Robbie will be waiting for me on the other side of the big iron-studded gate, and he is the symbol, not merely of his own affection, but of the affection of many others besides. I believe I am to have enough to live on for about eighteen months at any rate, so that if I may not write beautiful books, I may at least read beautiful books; and what joy can be greater? After that, I hope to be able to recreate my creative faculty.

But were things different: had I not a friend left in the world; were there not a single house open to me in pity; had I to accept the wallet and ragged cloak of sheer penury: as long as I am free from all resentment, hardness, and scorn, I would be able to face the life with much more calm and confidence than I would were my body in purple and fine linen, and the soul within me sick with hate.

And I really shall have no difficulty. When you really want love you will find it waiting for you.

I need not say that my task does not end there. It would be comparatively easy if it did. There is much more before me. I have hills far steeper to climb, valleys much darker to pass through. And I have to get it all out of myself. Neither religion, morality, nor reason can help me at all.

Morality does not help me. I am a born antinomian. I am one of those who are made for exceptions, not for laws. But while I see that there is nothing wrong in what one does, I see that there is something wrong in what one becomes. It is well to have learned that.

Religion does not help me. The faith that others give to what is unseen, I give to what one can touch, and look at. My gods dwell in temples made with hands; and within the circle of actual experience is my creed made perfect and complete: too complete, it may be, for like many or all of those who have placed their heaven in this earth, I have found in it not merely the beauty of heaven, but the horror of hell also. When I think about religion at all, I feel as if I would like to found an order for those who *cannot* believe: the Confraternity of the Faithless one might call it, where on an altar, on which no taper burned, a priest, in whose heart peace had no dwelling, might celebrate with unblessed bread and a chalice empty of wine. Everything to be true must become a religion. And agnosticism should have its ritual no less than faith. It has sown its martyrs, it should reap its saints, and praise God daily for having hidden Himself from man. But whether it be faith or agnosticism, it must be nothing external to me. Its symbols must be of my own creating. Only that is spiritual which makes its own form. If I may not find its secret within myself, I shall never find it: if I have not got it already, it will never come to me.

Reason does not help me. It tells me that the laws under which I am convicted are wrong and unjust laws, and the system under which I have suffered a wrong and unjust system. But, somehow, I have got to make both of these things just and right to me. And exactly as in Art one is only concerned with what a particular thing is at a particular moment to oneself, so it is also in the ethical evolution of one's character. I have got to make everything that has happened to me good for me. The plank bed, the loath-some food, the hard ropes shredded into oakum till one's finger-tips grow dull with pain, the menial offices with which each day begins and finishes, the harsh orders that routine seems to necessi-tate, the dreadful dress that makes sorrow grotesque to look at, the silence, the solitude, the shame – each and all of these things I had to transform into a spiritual experience. There is not a single degradation of the body which I must not try and make into a spiritualizing of the soul.

I want to get to the point when I shall be able to say quite simply, and without affectation, that the two great turning-points in my life were when my father sent me to Oxford, and when Society sent me to prison. I will not say that prison is the best thing that could have happened to me; for that phrase would savour of too great bitterness towards myself. I would sooner say, or hear it said of me, that I was so typical a child of my age, that in my perversity, and for that perversity's sake, I turned the good things of my life to evil, and the evil things of my life to good.

What is said, however, by myself or by others, matters little. The important thing, the thing that lies before me, the thing that I have to do, if the brief remainder of my days is not to be maimed, marred, and incomplete, is to absorb into my nature all that has been done to me, to make it part of me, to accept it without complaint, fear, or reluctance. The supreme vice is shallowness. Whatever is realized is right.

When first I was put into prison some people advised me to try and forget who I was. It was ruinous advice. It is only by realizing what I am that I have found comfort of any kind. Now

I am advised by others to try on my release to forget that I have ever been in a prison at all. I know that would be equally fatal. It would mean that I would always be haunted by an intolerable sense of disgrace, and that those things that are meant for me as much as for anybody else – the beauty of the sun and moon, the pageant of the seasons, the music of daybreak and the silence of great nights, the rain falling through the leaves, or the dew creeping over the grass and making it silver – would all be tainted for me, and lose their healing power and their power of communicating joy. To regret one's own experiences is to arrest one's own development. To deny one's own experiences is to put a lie into the lips of one's own life. It is no less than a denial of the soul.

For just as the body absorbs things of all kinds, things common and unclean no less than those that the priest or a vision has cleansed, and converts them into swiftness or strength, into the play of beautiful muscles and the moulding of fair flesh, into the curves and colours of the hair, the lids, the eye; so the soul in its turn has its nutritive functions also, and can transform into noble moods of thought and passions of high import what in itself is base, cruel, and degrading; nay, more, may find in these its most august modes of assertion, and can often reveal itself most perfectly through what was intended to desecrate or destroy.

The fact of my having been the common prisoner of a common gaol I must frankly accept, and, curious as it may seem, one of the things I shall have to teach myself is not to be ashamed of it. I must accept it as a punishment, and if one is ashamed of having been punished, one might just as well never have been punished at all. Of course there are many things of which I was convicted that I had not done, but then there are many things of which I was convicted that I had done, and a still greater number of things in my life for which I was never indicted at all. And as the gods are strange, and punish us for what is good and humane in us as much as for what is evil and perverse, I must accept the fact that one is punished for the good as well as for the evil that one does. I have no doubt that it is quite right one should be. It helps one, or should help one, to realize both, and not to be too conceited about either. And if I then am not ashamed of my punishment, as I hope not to be, I shall be able to think, and walk, and live with freedom.

Many men on their release carry their prison about with them into the air, and hide it as a secret disgrace in their hearts, and at length, like poor poisoned things, creep into some hole and die. It is wretched that they should have to do so, and it is wrong, terribly wrong, of Society that it should force them to do so. Society takes upon itself the right to inflict appalling punishment on the individual, but it also has the supreme vice of shallowness, and fails to realize what it has done. When the man's punishment is over, it leaves him to himself; that is to say, it abandons him at the very moment when its highest duty towards him begins. It is really ashamed of its own actions, and shuns those whom it has punished, as people shun a creditor whose debt they cannot pay, or one on whom they have inflicted an irreparable, an irredeemable wrong. I can claim on my side that if I realize what I have suffered, Society should realize what it has inflicted on me; and that there should be no bitterness or hate on either side.

Of course I know that from one point of view things will be made different for me than for others; must indeed, by the very nature of the case, be made so. The poor thieves and outcasts who are imprisoned here with me are in many respects more fortunate than I am. The little way in grey city or green field that saw their sin is small; to find those who know nothing of what they have done they need go no further than a bird might fly between the twilight at dawn and dawn itself: but for me the world is shrivelled to a handsbreadth, and everywhere I turn my name is written on the rocks in lead. For I have come, not from obscurity into the momentary notoriety of crime, but from a sort of eternity of fame to a sort of eternity of infamy, and sometimes seem to myself to have shown, if indeed it required showing, that between the famous and the infamous there is but one step, if as much as one.

Still, in the very fact that people will recognize me wherever I go, and know all about my life, as far as its follies go, I can discern something good for me. It will force on me the necessity of again asserting myself as an artist, and as soon as I possibly can. If I can produce only one beautiful work of art I shall be able to rob malice of its venom, and cowardice of its sneer, and to pluck out the tongue of scorn by the roots.

And if life be, as it surely is, a problem to me, I am no less a problem to life. People must adopt some attitude towards me, and so pass judgement both on themselves and me. I need not say I am not talking of particular individuals. The only people I would care to be with now are artists and people who have suffered: those who know what beauty is, and those who know what sorrow is: nobody else interests me. Nor am I making any demands on life. In all that I have said I am simply concerned with my own mental attitude towards life as a whole; and I feel that not to be ashamed of having been punished is one of the first points I must attain to, for the sake of my own perfection, and because I am so imperfect.

Then I must learn how to be happy. Once I knew it, or thought I knew it, by instinct. It was always springtime once in my heart. My temperament was akin to joy. I filled my life to the very brim with pleasure, as one might fill a cup to the very brim with wine. Now I am approaching life from a completely new standpoint, and even to conceive happiness is often extremely difficult for me. I remember during my first term at Oxford reading in Pater's *Renaissance* – that book which has had such strange influence over my life – how Dante places low in the Inferno those who wilfully live in sadness; and going to the college library and turning to the passage in the *Divine Comedy* where beneath the dreary marsh lie those who were 'sullen in the sweet air', saying for ever and ever through their sighs –

> Tristi fummo
> Nell' aere dolce, che dal sol s'allegra.

I knew the Church condemned *accidia*, but the whole idea seemed to me quite fantastic, just the sort of sin, I fancied, a priest who knew nothing about real life would invent. Nor could I understand how Dante, who says that 'sorrow re-marries us to God', could have been so harsh to those who were enamoured of melancholy, if any such there really were. I had no idea that some day this would become to me one of the greatest temptations of my life.

While I was in Wandsworth Prison I longed to die. It was my one desire. When after two months in the infirmary I was transferred here, and found myself growing gradually better in physical health, I was filled with rage. I determined to commit suicide on the very day on which I left prison. After a time that evil mood passed away, and I made up my mind to live, but to wear gloom as a king wears purple: never to smile again: to turn whatever house I entered into a house of mourning: to make my friends walk slowly in sadness with me: to teach them that melancholy is the true secret of life: to maim them with an alien sorrow: to mar them with my own pain. Now I feel quite differently. I see it would be both ungrateful and unkind of me to pull so long a face that when my friends came to see me they would have to make their faces still longer in order to show their sympathy; or, if I desired to entertain them, to invite them to sit down silently to bitter herbs and funeral baked meats. I must learn how to be cheerful and happy.

The last two occasions on which I was allowed to see my friends here, I tried to be as cheerful as possible, and to show my cheerfulness, in order to make them some slight return for their trouble in coming all the way from town to see me. It is only a slight return, I know, but it is the one, I feel certain, that pleases them most. I saw Robbie for an hour on Saturday week, and I tried to give the fullest possible expression of the delight I really felt at our meeting. And that, in the views and ideas I am here shaping for myself, I am quite right is shown to me by the fact that now for the first time since my imprisonment I have a real desire for life.

There is before me so much to do that I would regard it as a terrible tragedy if I died before I was allowed to complete at any rate a little of it. I see new developments in art and life, each one of which is a fresh mode of perfection. I long to live so that I can explore what is no less than a new world to me. Do you want to know what this new world is? I think you can guess what it is. It is the world in which I have been living. Sorrow, then, and all that it teaches one, is my new world.

I used to live entirely for pleasure. I shunned suffering and sorrow of every kind. I hated both. I resolved to ignore them as far as possible: to treat them, that is to say, as modes of imperfection. They were not part of my scheme of life. They had no place in my philosophy. My mother, who knew life as a whole, used often to quote to me Goethe's lines – written by Carlyle in a book he had given her years ago, and translated by him, I fancy, also:

> Who never ate his bread in sorrow,
>   Who never spent the midnight hours
> Weeping and waiting for the morrow,—
>   He knows you not, ye heavenly powers.

They were the lines which that noble Queen of Prussia, whom Napoleon treated with such coarse brutality, used to quote in her humiliation and exile; they were the lines my mother often quoted in the troubles of her later life. I absolutely declined to accept or admit the enormous truth hidden in them. I could not understand it. I remember quite well how I used to tell her that I did not want to eat my bread in sorrow, or to pass any night weeping and watching for a more bitter dawn.

I had no idea that it was one of the special things that the Fates had in store for me: that for a whole year of my life, indeed, I was to do little else. But so has my portion been meted out to me; and during the last few months I have, after terrible difficulties and struggles, been able to comprehend some of the lessons hidden in the heart of pain. Clergymen and people who use phrases without wisdom sometimes talk of suffering as a mystery. It is really a revelation. One discerns things one never discerned before. One approaches the whole of history from a different standpoint. What one had felt dimly, through instinct, about art, is intellectually and emotionally realized with perfect clearness of vision and absolute intensity of apprehension.

I now see that sorrow, being the supreme emotion of which man is capable, is at once the type and test of all great art. What the artist is always looking for is the mode of existence in which soul and body are one and indivisible: in which the outward is expressive of the inward: in which form reveals. Of such modes of existence there are not a few: youth and the arts preoccupied with youth may serve as a model for us at one moment: at another we may like to think that, in its subtlety and sensitiveness of impression, its suggestion of a spirit dwelling in external things and making its raiment of earth and air, of mist and city alike, and in its morbid sympathy of its moods, and tones, and colours, modern landscape art is realizing for us pictorially what was realized in such plastic perfection by the Greeks. Music, in which all subject is absorbed in expression and cannot be separated from it, is a complex example, and a flower or a child a simple example, of what I mean; but sorrow is the ultimate type both in life and art.

Behind joy and laughter there may be a temperament, coarse, hard and callous. But behind sorrow there is always sorrow. Pain, unlike pleasure, wears no mask. Truth in art is not any correspondence between the essential idea and the accidental existence; it is not the resemblance of shape to shadow, or of the form mirrored in the crystal to the form itself; it is no echo coming from a hollow hill, any more than it is a silver well of water in the valley that shows the moon to the moon and Narcissus to Narcissus. Truth in art is the unity of a thing with itself: the outward rendered expressive of the inward: the soul made incarnate: the body instinct with spirit. For this reason there is no truth comparable to sorrow. There are times when sorrow seems to me to be the only truth. Other things may be illusions of the eye or the appetite, made to blind the one and cloy the other, but out of sorrow have the worlds been built, and at the birth of a child or a star there is pain.

More than this, there is about sorrow an intense, an extraordinary reality. I have said of myself that I was one who stood in symbolic relations to the art and culture of my age. There is not a single wretched man in this wretched place along with me who does not stand in symbolic relation to the very secret of life. For the secret of life is suffering. It is what is hidden behind everything. When we begin to live, what is sweet is so sweet to us, and what is bitter so bitter, that we inevitably direct all our desires towards pleasures, and seek not merely for a 'month or twain to feed on honeycomb', but for all our years to taste no other food, ignorant all the while that we may really be starving the soul.

I remember talking once on this subject to one of the most beautiful personalities I have ever known:[1] a woman, whose sympathy and noble kindness to me, both before and since the tragedy of my imprisonment, have been beyond power and description; one who has really assisted me, though she does not know it, to bear the burden of my troubles more than anyone else in the whole world has, and all through the mere fact of her existence, through her being what she is – partly an ideal and partly an influence: a suggestion of what one might become as well as a real help towards becoming it; a soul that renders the common air sweet, and makes what is spiritual seem as simple and natural as sunlight or the sea: one for whom beauty and sorrow walk hand in hand, and have the same message. On the occasion of which I am thinking I recall distinctly how I said to her that there was enough suffering in one narrow London lane to show that God did not love man, and that wherever there was any sorrow, though but that of a child in some little garden weeping over a fault that it had or had not committed, the whole face of creation was completely marred. I was entirely wrong. She told me so, but I could not believe her. I was not in the sphere in which such belief was to be attained to. Now it seems to me that love of some kind is the only possible explanation of the extraordinary amount of suffering that there is in the world. I cannot conceive of any other explanation. I am convinced that there is no other, and that if the world has indeed, as I have said, been built of sorrow, it has been built by the hands of love, because in no other way could the soul of man, for whom the world was made, reach the full stature of its perfection. Pleasure for the beautiful body, but pain for the beautiful soul.

When I say that I am convinced of these things I speak with too much pride. Far off, like a perfect pearl, one can see the City of God. It is so wonderful that it seems as if a child could reach it in a summer's day. And so a child could. But with me and such

1. Miss Adeline Schuster.

as me it is different. One can realize a thing in a single moment, but one loses it in the long hours that follow with leaden feet. It is so difficult to keep 'heights that the soul is competent to gain'. We think in eternity, but we move slowly through time; and how slowly time goes with us who lie in prison I need not tell again, nor of the weariness and despair that creep back into one's cell, and into the cell of one's heart, with such strange insistence that one has, as it were, to garnish and sweep one's house for their coming, as for an unwelcome guest, or a bitter master, or a slave whose slave it is one's chance or choice to be.

And, though at present my friends may find it a hard thing to believe, it is true none the less, that for them living in freedom and idleness and comfort it is more easy to learn the lessons of humility than it is for me, who begin the day by going down on my knees and washing the floor of my cell. For prison life with its endless privations and restrictions makes one rebellious. The most terrible thing about it is not that it breaks one's heart – hearts are made to be broken – but that it turns one's heart to stone. One some-times feels that it is only with a front of brass and a lip of scorn that one can get through the day at all. And he who is in a state of rebellion cannot receive grace, to use the phrase of which the Church is so fond – so rightly fond, I dare say – for in life as in art the mood of rebellion closes up the channels of the soul, and shuts out the airs of heaven. Yet I must learn these lessons here, if I am to learn them anywhere, and must be filled with joy if my feet are on the right road and my face set towards 'the gate which is called beautiful', though I may fall many times in the mire and often in the mist go astray.

This New Life, as through my love of Dante I like sometimes to call it, is of course no new life at all, but simply the continuance, by means of development and evolution, of my former life. I remember when I was at Oxford saying to one of my friends as we were strolling round Magdalen's narrow bird-haunted walks one morning in the year before I took my degree, that I wanted to eat of the fruit of all the trees in the garden of the world, and that I was going out into the world with that passion in my soul. And so, indeed, I went out, and so I lived. My only mistake was that I confined myself so exclusively to the trees of what seemed to me the sun-lit side of the garden, and shunned the other side for its shadow and its gloom. Failure, disgrace, poverty, sorrow, despair, suffering, tears even, the broken words that come from lips in pain, remorse that makes one walk on thorns, conscience that condemns, self-abasement that punishes, the misery that puts ashes on its head, the anguish that chooses sackcloth for its raiment and into its own drink puts gall: – all these were things of which I was afraid. And as I had determined to know nothing of them, I was forced to taste each of them in turn, to feed on them, to have for a season, indeed, no other food at all.

I don't regret for a single moment having lived for pleasure. I did it to the full, as one should do everything that one does. There was no pleasure I did not experience. I threw the pearl of my soul into a cup of wine. I went down the primrose path to the sound of flutes. I lived on honeycomb. But to have continued the same life would have been wrong because it would have been limiting. I had to pass on. The other half of the garden had its secrets for me also. Of course all this is foreshadowed and pre-figured in my books. Some of it is in *The Happy Prince*, some of it in *The Young King*, notably in the passage where the bishop says to the kneeling boy, 'Is not He who made misery wiser than thou art?' a phrase which when I wrote it seemed to me little more than a phrase; a great deal of it is hidden away in the note of doom that like a purple thread runs through the texture of *Dorian Gray*; in *The Critic as Artist* it is set forth in many colours; in *The Soul of Man* it is written down, and in letters too easy to read; it is one of the refrains whose recurring *motifs* make *Salome* so like a piece of music and bind it together as a ballad; in the prose poem of the man who from the bronze image of the 'Pleasure that liveth for a moment' has to make the image of the 'Sorrow that abideth for ever' it is incarnate. It could not have been otherwise. At every single moment of one's life one is what one is going to be no less than what one has been. Art is a symbol, because man is a symbol.

It is, if I can fully attain to it, the ultimate realization of the ar-tistic life. For the artistic life is simple self-development. Humility in the artist is his frank acceptance of all experiences, just as love in the artist is simply the sense of beauty that reveals to the world its body and its soul. In *Marius the Epicurean* Pater seeks to reconcile the artistic life with the life of religion, in the deep, sweet, and austere sense of the word. But Marius is little more than a spectator: an ideal spectator indeed, and one to whom it is given 'to contemplate the spectacle of life with appropriate emotions', which Wordsworth defines as the poet's true aim; yet a spectator merely, and perhaps a little too much occupied with the comeliness of the benches of the sanctuary to notice that it is the sanctuary of sorrow that he is gazing at.

I see a far more intimate and immediate connexion between the true life of Christ and the true life of the artist; and I take a keen pleasure in the reflexion that long before sorrow had made my days her own and bound me to her wheel I had written in *The Soul of Man* that he who would lead a Christ-like life must be entirely and absolutely himself, and had taken as my types not merely the shepherd on the hillside and the prisoner in his cell, but also the painter to whom the world is a pageant and the poet for whom the world is a song. I remember saying once to André Gide, as we sat together in some Paris café, that while metaphysics had but little real interest for me, and morality absolutely none, there was nothing that either Plato or Christ had said that could not be transferred immediately into the sphere of Art and there find its complete fulfilment.

Nor is it merely that we can discern in Christ that close union of personality with perfection which forms the real distinction between the classical and romantic movement in life, but the very basis of his nature was the same as that of the nature of the artist – an intense and flamelike imagination. He realized in the entire sphere of human relations that imaginative sympathy which in the sphere of Art is the sole secret of creation. He understood the leprosy of the leper, the darkness of the blind, the fierce misery of those who live for pleasure, the strange poverty of the rich. You once wrote to me in trouble, 'When you are not on your pedestal you are not interesting.' How remote were you from what Matthew Arnold calls 'the Secret of Jesus'. Either would have taught you that whatever happens to another happens to oneself, and if you want an inscription to read at dawn and at night-time, and for pleasure or for pain, write up on the walls of your house in letters for the sun to gild and the moon to silver, 'Whatever happens to oneself happens to another'.

Christ's place indeed is with the poets. His whole conception of humanity sprang right out of the imagination and can only be realized by it. What God was to the pantheist, man was to him. He was the first to conceive the divided races as a unity. Before his time there had been gods and men, and, feeling through the mysticism of sympathy that in himself each had been made incarnate, he calls himself the Son of the one or the Son of the other, according to his mood. More than anyone else in history he wakes in us that temper of wonder to which romance always appeals. There is still something to me almost incredible in the idea of a young Galilean peasant imagining that he could bear on his own shoulders the burden of the entire world: all that had already been done and suffered, and all that was yet to be done and suffered: the sins of Nero, of Caesar Borgia, of Alexander VI, and of him who was Emperor of Rome and Priest of the Sun:[1] the sufferings of those whose names are legion and whose dwelling is among the tombs: oppressed nationalities, factory children, thieves, people in prison, outcasts, those who are dumb under oppression and whose silence is heard only of God; and not merely imagining this but actually achieving it, so that at the present moment all who come in contact with his personality, even though they may neither bow to his altar nor kneel before his priest, in some way find that the ugliness of their skin is taken away and the beauty of their sorrow revealed to them.

I had said of Christ that he ranks with the poets. That is true. Shelley and Sophocles are of his company. But his entire life also is the most wonderful of poems. For 'pity and terror' there is nothing in the entire cycle of Greek tragedy to touch it. The absolute purity of the protagonist raises the entire scheme to a height of romantic art from which the sufferings of Thebes and Pelops' line are by their very horror excluded, and shows how

1. Heliogabalus.

wrong Aristotle was when he said in his treatise on the drama that it would be impossible to bear the spectacle of one blameless in pain. Nor in Aeschylus nor Dante, those stern masters of tenderness, in Shakespeare, the most purely human of all the great artists, in the whole of Celtic myth and legend, where the loveliness of the world is shown through a mist of tears, and the life of a man is no more than the life of a flower, is there anything that, for sheer simplicity of pathos wedded and made one with sublimity of tragic effect, can be said to equal or even approach the last act of Christ's passion. The little supper with his companions, one of whom has already sold him for a price; the anguish in the quiet moon-lit garden; the false friend coming close to him so as to betray him with a kiss; the friend who still believed in him, and on whom as on a rock he had hoped to build a house of refuge for Man, denying him as the bird cried to the dawn; his own utter loneliness, his submission, his acceptance of everything; and along with it all such scenes as the high priest of orthodoxy rending his raiment in wrath, and the magistrate of civil justice calling for water in the vain hope of cleansing himself of that stain of innocent blood that makes him the scarlet figure of history; the coronation ceremony of sorrow, one of the most wonderful things in the whole of recorded time; the crucifixion of the Innocent One before the eyes of his mother and of the disciple whom he loved; the soldiers gambling and throwing dice for his clothes; the terrible death by which he gave the world its most eternal symbol; and his final burial in the tomb of the rich man, his body swathed in Egyptian linen with costly spices and perfumes as though he had been a king's son. When one contemplates all this from the point of view of art alone one cannot but be grateful that the supreme office of the Church should be the playing of the tragedy without the shedding of blood: the mystical presentation, by means of dialogue and costume and gesture even, of the Passion of her Lord; and it is always a source of pleasure and awe to me to remember that the ultimate survival of the Greek chorus, lost elsewhere to art, is to be found in the servitor answering the priest at Mass.

Yet the whole life of Christ – so entirely may sorrow and

beauty be made one in their meaning and manifestation – is really an idyll though it ends with the veil of the temple being rent, and the darkness coming over the face of the earth, and the stone rolled to the door of the sepulchre. One always thinks of him as a young bridegroom with his companions, as indeed he somewhere describes himself; as a shepherd straying through a valley with his sheep in search of green meadow or cool stream; as a singer trying to build out of the music the walls of the City of God; or as a lover for whose love the whole world was too small. His miracles seem to me to be as exquisite as the coming of spring, and quite as natural. I see no difficulty at all in believing that such was the charm of his personality that his mere presence could bring peace to souls in anguish, and that those who touched his garments or his hands forgot their pain; or that as he passed by on the highway of life people who had seen nothing of life's mystery saw it clearly, and others who had been deaf to every voice but that of pleasure heard for the first time the voice of love and found it as 'musical as Apollo's lute'; or that evil passions fled at his approach, and men whose dull unimaginative lives had been but a mode of death rose as it were from the grave when he called them; or that when he taught on the hillside the multitude forgot their hunger and thirst and the cares of this world, and that to his friends who listened to him as he sat at meat the coarse food seemed delicate, and the water had the taste of good wine, and the whole house became full of the odour and sweetness of nard.

Renan in his *Vie de Jésus* – the gracious fifth gospel, the gospel according to St Thomas, one might call it – says somewhere that Christ's great achievement was that he made himself as much loved after his death as he had been during his lifetime. And certainly, if his place is among the poets, he is the leader of all the lovers. He saw that love was the first secret of the world for which the wise men had been looking, and that it was only through love that one could approach either the heart of the leper or the feet of God.

And above all, Christ is the most supreme of individualists. Humility, like the artistic acceptance of all experiences, is merely a mode of manifestation. It is man's soul that Christ is always looking for. He calls it 'God's Kingdom', and finds it in every one. He compares it to little things, to a tiny seed, to a handful of leaven, to a pearl. That is because one realizes one's soul only by getting rid of all alien passions, all acquired culture, and all external possessions, be they good or evil.

I bore up against everything with some stubbornness of will and much rebellion of nature, till I had absolutely nothing left in the world but one thing. I had lost my name, my position, my happiness, my freedom, my wealth. I was a prisoner and a pauper. But I still had my children left. Suddenly they were taken away from me by the law. It was a blow so appalling that I did not know what to do, so I flung myself on my knees, and bowed my head, and wept, and said, 'The body of a child is as the body of the Lord: I am not worthy of either.' That moment seemed to save me. I saw then that the only thing for me was to accept everything. Since then – curious as it will no doubt sound – I have been happier. It was of course my soul in its ultimate essence that I had reached. In many ways I had been its enemy, but I found it waiting for me as a friend. When one comes in contact with the soul it makes one simple as a child, as Christ said one should be.

It is tragic how few people ever 'possess their souls' before they die. 'Nothing is more rare in any man,' says Emerson, 'than an act of his own.' It is quite true. Most people are other people. Their thoughts are someone else's opinions, their lives a mimicry, their passions a quotation. Christ was not merely the supreme individualist, but he was the first individualist in history. People have tried to make him out an ordinary philanthropist, or ranked him as an altruist with the unscientific and sentimental. But he was really neither one nor the other. Pity he has, of course, for the poor, for those who are shut up in prisons, for the lowly, for the wretched; but he has far more pity for the rich, for the hard hedonists, for those who waste their freedom in becoming slaves to things, for those who wear soft raiment and live in kings' houses. Riches and pleasure seemed to him to be really greater tragedies than poverty or sorrow. And as for altruism, who knew better than he that it is vocation not volition that determines us, and that one cannot gather grapes of thorns or figs from thistles?

To live for others as a definite self-conscious aim was not his creed. It was not the basis of his creed. When he says, 'Forgive your enemies,' it is not for the sake of the enemy, but for one's own sake that he says so, and because love is more beautiful than hate. In his own entreaty to the young man, 'Sell all that thou hast and give to the poor,' it is not of the state of the poor that he is thinking, but of the soul of the young man, the soul that wealth was marring. In his view of life he is one with the artist who knows that by the inevitable law of self-perfection, the poet must sing, and the sculptor think in bronze, and the painter make the world a mirror for his moods, as surely and as certainly as the hawthorn must blossom in spring, and the corn turn to gold at harvest-time, and the moon in her ordered wanderings change from shield to sickle, and from sickle to shield.

But while Christ did not say to men, 'Live for others', he pointed out that there was no difference at all between the lives of others and one's own life. By this means he gave to man an extended, a Titan personality. Since his coming the history of each separate individual is, or can be made, the history of the world. Of course, culture has intensified the personality of man. Art has made us myriad-minded. Those who have the artistic temperament go into exile with Dante and learn how salt is the bread of others, and how steep their stairs; they catch for a moment the serenity and calm of Goethe, and yet know but too well that Baudelaire cried to God –

> O Seigneur, donnez-moi la force et le courage
> De contempler mon corps et mon cœur sans dégoût.

Out of Shakespeare's sonnets they draw, to their own hurt it may be, the secret of his love and make it their own; they look with new eyes on modern life, because they have listened to one of Chopin's nocturnes, or handled Greek things, or read the story of the passion of some dead man for some dead woman whose hair was like threads of fine gold, and whose mouth was as a pomegranate. But the sympathy of the artistic temperament is necessarily with what has found expression. In words or in colours, in music or in marble, behind the painted masks of an Aeschylean play, or through some Sicilian shepherds' pierced and jointed reeds, the man and his message must have been revealed.

To the artist, expression is the only mode under which he can conceive life at all. To him what is dumb is dead. But to Christ it was not so. With a width and wonder of imagination that fills one almost with awe, he took the entire world of the inarticulate, the voiceless world of pain, as his kingdom, and made of himself its external mouthpiece. Those of whom I have spoken, who are dumb under oppression and 'whose silence is heard only of God', he chose as his brothers. He sought to become eyes to the blind, ears to the deaf, and a cry in the lips of those whose tongues had been tied. His desire was to be to the myriads who had found no utterance a very trumpet through which they might call to heaven. And feeling, with the artistic nature of one to whom suffering and sorrow were modes through which he could realize his conception of the beautiful, that an idea is of no value till it becomes incarnate and is made an image, he made of himself the image of the Man of Sorrows, and as such has fascinated and dominated art as no Greek god ever succeeded in doing.

For the Greek gods, in spite of the white and red of their fair fleet limbs, were not really what they appeared to be. The curved brow of Apollo was like the sun's disc over a hill at dawn, and his feet were as the wings of the morning, but he himself had been cruel to Marsyas and had made Niobe childless. In the steel shields of Athena's eyes there had been no pity for Arachne; the pomp and peacocks of Hera were all that was really noble about her; and the Father of the Gods himself had been too fond of the daughters of men. The two most deeply suggestive figures of Greek mythology were, for religion, Demeter, an earth goddess, not one of the Olympians, and for art, Dionysos, the son of a mortal woman to whom the moment of his birth had proved also the moment of her death.

But Life itself from its lowliest and most humble sphere produced one far more marvellous than the mother of Proserpina or the son of Semele. Out of the Carpenter's shop at Nazareth had come a personality infinitely greater than any made by myth and legend, and one, strangely enough, destined to reveal to the world the mystical meaning of wine and the real beauties of the lilies of the field as none, either on Cithaeron or at Enna, had ever done.

The song of Isaiah, 'He is despised and rejected of men, a man of sorrows and acquainted with grief: and we hid as it were our faces from him,' had seemed to him to prefigure himself, and in him the prophecy was fulfilled. We must not be afraid of such a phrase. Every single work of art is the fulfilment of a prophecy: for every work of art is the conversion of an idea into an image. Every single human being should be the fulfilment of a prophecy: for every human being should be the realization of some ideal, either in the mind of God or in the mind of man. Christ found the type and fixed it, and the dream of a Virgilian poet, either at Jerusalem or at Babylon, became in the long progress of the centuries incarnate in him for whom the world was 'waiting'. 'His visage was marred more than any man's, and his form was more than the sons of men,' are among the signs noted by Isaiah as distinguishing the new ideal, and as soon as art understood what was meant it opened like a flower at the presence of one in whom truth in art was set forth as it had never been before. For is not truth in art, as I have said, 'that in which the outward is expressive of the inward; in which the soul is made flesh and the body instinct with spirit in which form reveals.'

To me one of the things in history the most to be regretted is that the Christ's own renaissance which has produced the Cathedral at Chartres, the Arthurian cycle of legends, the life of St Francis of Assisi, the art of Giotto, and Dante's *Divine Comedy*, was not allowed to develop on its own lines, but was interrupted and spoiled by the dreary classical Renaissance that gave us Petrarch, and Raphael's frescoes, and Palladian architecture, and formal French tragedy, and St Paul's Cathedral, and Pope's poetry, and everything that is made from without and by dead rules, and does not spring from within through some spirit informing it. But wherever there is a romantic movement in art there somehow, and under some form, is Christ, or the soul of Christ. He is in *Romeo and Juliet*, in the *Winter's Tale*, in Provençal poetry, in the *Ancient Mariner*, in *La Belle Dame sans merci*, and in Chatterton's *Ballad of Charity*.

We owe to him the most diverse things and people. Hugo's *Les Misérables*, Baudelaire's *Fleurs du Mal*, the note of pity in Russian novels, Verlaine and Verlaine's poems, the stained glass and tapestries and the quattrocento work of Burne-Jones and Morris, belong to him no less than the tower of Giotto, Lancelot and Guinevere, Tannhäuser, the troubled romantic marbles of Michael Angelo, pointed architecture, and the love of children and flowers – for both of which, indeed, in classical art there was but little place, hardly enough for them to grow or play in, but which, from the twelfth century down to our own day, have been continually making their appearances in art, under various modes and at various times, coming fitfully and wilfully, as children, as flowers, are apt to do: spring always seeming to one as if the flowers had been in hiding, and only came out into the sun because they were afraid that grown-up people would grow tired of looking for them and give up the search; and the life of a child being no more than an April day on which there is both rain and sun for the narcissus.

It is the imaginative quality of Christ's own nature that makes him this palpitating centre of romance. The strange figures of poetic drama and ballad are made by the imagination of others, but out of his own imagination entirely did Jesus of Nazareth create himself. The cry of Isaiah had really no more to do with his coming than the song of the nightingale has to do with the rising of the moon – no more, though perhaps no less. He was the denial as well as the affirmation of prophecy. For every expectation that he fulfilled there was another that he destroyed. 'In all beauty', says Bacon, 'there is some strangeness of proportion,' and of those who are born of the spirit – of those, that is to say, who like himself are dynamic forces – Christ says that they are like the wind that 'bloweth where it listeth, and no man can tell whence it cometh and whither it goeth'. This is why he is so fascinating to artists. He has all the colour elements of life; mystery, strangeness, pathos, suggestion, ecstasy, love. He appeals to the temper of wonder, and creates that mood in which alone he can be understood.

And to me it is a joy to remember that if he is 'of imagination all compact', the world itself is of the same substance. I said in *Dorian Gray* that the great sins of the world take place in the brain: but it is in the brain that everything takes place. We know now that we do not see with the eyes or hear with the ears. They are really channels for the transmission, adequate or inadequate, of sense impressions. It is in the brain that the poppy is red, that the apple is odorous, that the skylark sings.

Of late I have been studying with diligence the four prose poems about Christ. At Christmas I managed to get hold of a Greek Testament, and every morning, after I had cleaned my cell and polished my tins, I read a little of the Gospels, a dozen verses taken by chance anywhere. It is a delightful way of opening the day. Everyone, even in a turbulent, ill-disciplined life, should do the same. Endless repetition, in and out of season, has spoiled for us the freshness, the naïveté, the simple romantic charm of the Gospels. We hear them read far too often and far too badly, and all repetition is anti-spiritual. When one returns to the Greek, it is like going into a garden of lilies out of some narrow and dark house.

And to me, the pleasure is doubled by the reflexion that it is extremely probable that we have the actual terms, the *ipsissima verba*, used by Christ. It was always supposed that Christ talked in Aramaic. Even Renan thought so. But now we know that the Galilean peasants, like the Irish peasants of our own day, were bilingual, and that Greek was the ordinary language of intercourse all over Palestine, as indeed all over the Eastern world. I never liked the idea that we knew of Christ's own words only through a translation of a translation. It is a delight to me to think that as far as his conversation was concerned, Charmides might have listened to him, and Socrates reasoned with him, and Plato understood him: that he really said ἐγώ εἰμι ὁ ποιμὴν ὁ καλός, that when he thought of the lilies of the field and how they neither toil nor spin, his absolute expression was καταμάθετε τὰ κρίνα τοῦ ἀγροῦ πῶς αὐξάνει· οὐ κοπιᾷ οὐδὲ νήθει, and that his last word when he cried out 'my life has been completed, has reached its fulfilment, has been perfected', was exactly as St John tells us it was: τετέλεσται – no more.

While in reading the Gospels – particularly that of St John himself, or whatever early Gnostic took his name and mantle – I see the continual assertion of the imagination as the basis of all spiritual and material life, I see also that to Christ imagination was simply a form of love, and that to him love was lord in the fullest meaning of the phrase. Some six weeks ago I was allowed by the doctor to have white bread to eat instead of the coarse black or brown bread of ordinary prison fare. It is a great delicacy. It will sound strange that dry bread could possibly be a delicacy to anyone. To me it is so much so that at the close of each meal I carefully eat whatever crumbs may be left on my tin plate, or have fallen on the rough towel that one uses as a cloth so as not to soil one's table; and I do so not from hunger – I get now quite sufficient food – but simply in order that nothing should be wasted of what is given to me. So one should look on love.

Christ, like all fascinating personalities, had the power of not merely saying beautiful things himself, but of making other people say beautiful things to him; and I love the story St Mark tells us about the Greek woman, who, when as a trial of her faith he said to her that he could not give her the bread of the children of Israel, answered him that the little dogs – (κυνάρια, 'little dogs' it should be rendered) – who are under the table eat of the crumbs that the children let fall. Most people live for love and admiration. But it is by love and admiration that we should live. If any love is shown us we should recognize that we are quite unworthy of it. Nobody is worthy to be loved. The fact that God loves man shows us that in the divine order of ideal things it is written that eternal love is to be given to what is eternally unworthy. Or if that phrase seems to be a bitter one to bear, let us say that every one is worthy of love, except him who thinks that he is. Love is a sacrament that should be taken kneeling, and *Domine, non sum dignus* should be on the lips and in the hearts of those who receive it.

If ever I write again, in the sense of producing artistic work, there are just two subjects on which and through which I desire to express myself: one is 'Christ as the precursor of the romantic movement in life': the other is 'The artistic life considered in its relation to conduct'. The first is, of course, intensely fascinating, for I see in Christ not merely the essentials of the supreme romantic type, but all the accidents, the wilfulnesses even, of the romantic temperament also. He was the first person who ever said to people that they should live 'flower-like lives'. He fixed the phrase. He took children as the type of what people should try to become. He held them up as examples to their elders, which I myself have always thought the chief use of children, if what is perfect should have a use. Dante describes the soul of a man as coming from the hand of God 'weeping and laughing like a little child', and Christ also saw that the soul of each one should be *a guisa di fanciulla che piangendo e ridendo pargoleggia.* He felt that life was changeful, fluid, active, and that to allow it to be stereotyped into any form was death. He saw that people should not be too serious over material, common interests; that to be unpractical was to be a great thing: that one should not bother too much over affairs. The birds didn't, why should man? He is charming when he says, 'Take no thought for the morrow; is not the soul more than meat? is not the body more than raiment?' A Greek might have used the latter phrase. It is full of Greek feeling. But only Christ could have said both, and so summed up life perfectly for us.

His morality is all sympathy, just what morality should be. If the only thing that he ever said had been, 'Her sins are forgiven her because she loved much', it would have been worth while dying to have said it. His justice is all poetical justice, exactly what justice should be. The beggar goes to heaven because he has been unhappy. I cannot conceive a better reason for his being sent there. The people who work for an hour in the vineyard in the cool of the evening receive just as much reward as those who have toiled there all day long in the hot sun. Why shouldn't they? Probably no one deserved anything. Or perhaps they were a different kind of people. Christ had no patience with the dull lifeless mechanical systems that treat people as if they were things, and so treat everybody alike: for him there were no laws: there were exceptions merely, as if anybody, or anything, for that matter, was like aught else in the world!

That which is the very keynote of romantic art was to him the proper basis of natural life. He saw no other basis. And when they brought him one taken in the very act of sin and showed him her sentence written in the law, and asked him what was to be done, he wrote with his finger on the ground as though he did not hear them, and finally when they pressed him again, looked up and said, 'Let him of you who has never sinned be the first to throw the stone at her.' It was worth while living to have said that.

Like all poetical natures he loved ignorant people. He knew that in the soul of one who is ignorant there is always room for a great idea. But he could not stand stupid people, especially those who are made stupid by education: people who are full of opinions not one of which they even understand, a peculiarly modern type, summed up by Christ when he describes it as the type of one who has the key of knowledge, cannot use it himself, and does not allow other people to use it, though it may be made to open the gate of God's Kingdom. His chief war was against the Philistines. That is the war every child of light has to wage. Philistinism was the note of the age and community in which he lived. In their heavy inaccessibility to ideas, their dull respectability, their tedious orthodoxy, their worship of vulgar success, their entire preoccupation with the gross materialistic side of life, and their ridiculous estimate of themselves and their importance, the Jews of Jerusalem in Christ's day were the exact counterpart of the British Philistine of our own. Christ mocked at the 'whited sepulchre' of respectability, and fixed that phrase for ever. He treated worldly success as a thing absolutely to be despised. He saw nothing in it at all. He looked on wealth as an encumbrance to a man. He would not hear of life being sacrificed to any system of thought or morals. He pointed out that forms and ceremonies were made for man, not man for forms and ceremonies. He took sabbatarianism as a type of the things that should be set at nought. The cold philanthropies, the ostentatious public charities, the tedious formalisms so dear to the middle-class mind, he exposed with utter and relentless scorn. To us, what is termed orthodoxy is merely a facile unintelligent acquiescence; but to them, and in their hands, it was a terrible and paralysing tyranny. Christ swept it aside. He showed that the spirit alone was of value. He took a keen pleasure in pointing out to them that though they were always reading the law and the prophets, they had not really the smallest idea of what either of them meant. In opposition to their tithing of each separate day into the fixed routine of prescribed duties, as they tithe mint and rue, he preached the enormous importance of living completely for the moment.

Those whom he saved from their sins are saved simply for beautiful moments in their lives. Mary Magdalen, when she sees Christ, breaks the rich vase of alabaster that one of her seven lovers had given her, and spills the odorous spices over his tired dusty feet, and for that one moment's sake sits for ever with Ruth and Beatrice in the tresses of the snow-white rose of Paradise. All that Christ says to us by the way of a little warning is that every moment should be beautiful, that the soul should always be ready for the coming of the bridegroom, always waiting for the voice of the lover, Philistinism being simply that side of man's nature that is not illumined by the imagination. He sees all the lovely influences of life as modes of light: the imagination itself is the world of light. The world is made by it, and yet the world cannot understand it: that is because the imagination is simply a manifestation of love, and it is love and the capacity for it that distinguishes one human being from another.

But it is when he deals with a sinner that Christ is most romantic, in the sense of most real. The world had always loved the saint as being the nearest possible approach to the perfection of God. Christ, through some divine instinct in him, seems to have always loved the sinner as being the nearest possible approach to the perfection of man. His primary desire was not to reform people, any more than his primary desire was to relieve suffering. To turn an interesting thief into a tedious honest man was not his aim. He would have thought little of the Prisoners' Aid Society and other modern movements of the kind. The conversion of a publican into a Pharisee would not have seemed to him a great achievement. But in a manner not yet understood of the world he regarded sin and suffering as being in themselves beautiful holy things and modes of perfection.

It seems a very dangerous idea. It is – all great ideas are dangerous. That it was Christ's creed admits of no doubt. That it is the true creed I don't doubt myself.

Of course the sinner must repent. But why? Simply because otherwise he would be unable to realize what he had done. The moment of repentance is the moment of initiation. More than that: it is the means by which one alters one's past. The Greeks thought that impossible. They often say in their Gnomic aphorisms, 'Even the Gods cannot alter the past.' Christ showed that the commonest sinner could do it, that it was the one thing he could do. Christ, had he been asked, would have said – I feel quite certain about it – that the moment the prodigal son fell on his knees and wept, he made his having wasted his substance with harlots, his swineherding and hungering for the husks they ate, beautiful and holy moments in his life. It is difficult for most people to grasp the idea. I dare say one has to go to prison to understand it. If so, it may be worth while going to prison.

There is something so unique about Christ. Of course, just as there are false dawns before the dawn itself, and winter days so full of sudden sunlight that they will cheat the wise crocus into squandering its gold before its time, and make some foolish bird call to its mate to build on barren boughs, so there were Christians before Christ. For that we should be grateful. The unfortunate thing is that there have been none since. I make one exception, St Francis of Assisi. But then God had given him at his birth the soul of a poet, as he himself when quite young had in mystical marriage taken poverty as his bride: and with the soul of a poet and the body of a beggar he found the way to perfection not difficult. He understood Christ and so he became like him. We do not require the Liber Conformitatum to teach us that the life of St Francis was the true *Imitatio Christi*, a poem compared to which the book of that name is merely prose.

Indeed, that is the charm about Christ, when all is said: he is just like a work of art. He does not really teach one anything, but by being brought into his presence one becomes something. And everybody is predestined to his presence. Once at least in his life each man walks with Christ to Emmaus.

As regards the other subject, the Relation of the Artistic Life to Conduct, it will no doubt seem strange to you that I should select it. People point to Reading Gaol and say, 'That is where the artistic life leads a man.' Well, it might lead to worse places. The more mechanical people to whom life is a shrewd speculation depending on a careful calculation of ways and means, always know where they are going, and go there. They start with the ideal desire of being the parish beadle, and in whatever sphere they are placed they succeed in being the parish beadle and no more. A man whose desire to to be something separate from himself, to be a member of Parliament, or a successful grocer, or a prominent solicitor, or a judge, or something equally tedious, invariably succeeds in being what he wants to be. That is his punishment. Those who want a mask have to wear it.

But with the dynamic forces of life, and those in whom those dynamic forces become incarnate, it is difficult. People whose desire is solely for self-realization never know where they are going. They can't know. In one sense of the word it is of course necessary, as the Greek oracle said, to know oneself: that is the first achievement of knowledge. But to recognize that the soul of a man is unknowable, is the ultimate achievement of wisdom. The final mystery is oneself. When one has weighed the sun in the balance, and measured the steps of the moon, and mapped out the seven heavens star by star, there still remains oneself. Who can calculate the orbit of his own soul? When the son went out to look for his father's assets, he did not know that a man of God was waiting for him with the very chrism of coronation, and that his own soul was already the soul of a king.

I hope to live long enough and to produce work of such a character that I shall be able at the end of my days to say, 'Yes! this is just where the artistic life leads a man!' Two of the most perfect lives I have come across in my own experience are the lives of Verlaine and of Prince Kropotkin: both of them men who have passed years in prison: the first, the one Christian poet since Dante; the other, a man with a soul of that beautiful white Christ which seems coming out of Russia. And for the last seven or eight months, in spite of a succession of great troubles reaching me from the outside world almost without intermission, I have been placed in direct contact with a new spirit working in this prison through man and things, that has helped me beyond any possibility of expression in words: so that while for the first year of my imprisonment I did nothing else, and can remember doing nothing else, but wring my hands in impotent despair, and say, 'What an ending, what an appalling ending!' now I try to say to myself, and sometimes when I am not torturing myself do really and sincerely say, 'What a beginning, what a wonderful beginning!' It may really be so. It may become so. If it does I shall owe much to this new personality that has altered every man's life in this place.

You may realize it when I say that had I been released last May, as I tried to be, I would have left this place loathing it and every official in it with a bitterness of hatred that would have poisoned my life. I have had a year longer of imprisonment, but humanity has been in the prison along with us all, and now when I go out I shall always remember great kindnesses that I have received here from almost everybody, and on the day of my release I shall give many thanks to many people, and ask to be remembered by them in turn.

The prison style is absolutely and entirely wrong. I would give anything to be able to alter it when I go out. I intend to try. But there is nothing in the world so wrong but that the spirit of humanity, which is the spirit of love, the spirit of the Christ who is not in churches, may make it, if not right, at least possible to be borne without too much bitterness of heart.

I know also that much is waiting for me outside that is very delightful, from what St Francis of Assisi calls 'my brother the wind, and my sister the rain', lovely things both of them, down to the shop-windows and sunsets of great cities. If I made a list of all that still remains to me, I don't know where I should stop: for, indeed, God made the world just as much for me as for anyone else. Perhaps I may go out with something that I had not got before. I need not tell you that to me reformations in morals are as meaningless and vulgar as Reformations in theology. But while to propose to be a better man is a piece of unscientific cant, to have become a deeper man is the privilege of those who have suffered. And such I think I have become.

If after I am free a friend of mine gave a feast, and did not invite me to it, I should not mind a bit. I can be perfectly happy by myself. With freedom, flowers, books, and the moon, who could not be perfectly happy? Besides, feasts are not for me any more. I have given too many to care about them. That side of life is over for me, very fortunately, I dare say. But if after I am free a friend of mine had a sorrow and refused to allow me to share it, I should feel it most bitterly. If he shut the doors of the house of mourning against me, I would come back again and again and beg to be admitted, so that I might share in what I was entitled to share in. If he thought me unworthy, unfit to weep with him, I should feel it as the most poignant humiliation, as the most terrible mode in which disgrace could be inflicted on me. But that could not be. I have a right to share in sorrow, and he who can look at the loveliness of the world and share its sorrow, and realize something of the wonder of both, is in immediate contact with divine things, and has got as near to God's secret as anyone can get.

Perhaps there may come into my art also, no less than into my life, a still deeper note, one of greater unity of passion, and directness of impulse. Not width but intensity is the true aim of modern art. We are no longer in art concerned with the type. It is with the exception that we have to do. I cannot put my sufferings into any form they took, I need hardly say. Art only begins where Imitation ends, but something must come into my work, of fuller memory of words perhaps, of richer cadences, of more curious effects, of simpler architectural order, of some aesthetic quality at any rate.

When Marsyas was 'torn from the scabbard of his limbs' – *della vagina della membra sue*, to use one of Dante's most terrible Tacitean phrases – he had no more song, the Greek said. Apollo had been victor. The lyre had vanquished the reed. But perhaps the Greeks were mistaken. I hear in much modern art the cry of Marsyas. It is bitter in Baudelaire, sweet and plaintive in Lamartine, mystic in Verlaine. It is in the deferred resolutions of Chopin's music. It is in the discontent that haunts Burne-Jones's women.

Even Matthew Arnold, whose song of Callicles tells of 'the triumph of the sweet persuasive lyre', and the 'famous final victory', in such a clear note of lyrical beauty, has not a little of it; in the troubled undertone of doubt and distress that haunts his verses, neither Goethe nor Wordsworth could help him, though he followed each in turn, and when he seeks to mourn for *Thyrsis* or to sing of the *Scholar Gipsy*, it is the reed that he has to take for the rendering of his strain. But whether or not the Phrygian Faun was silent, I cannot be. Expression is as necessary to me as leaf and blossoms are to the black branches of the trees that show themselves above the prison walls and are so restless in the wind. Between my art and the world there is now a wide gulf, but between art and myself there is none. I hope at least that there is none.

To each of us different fates are meted out. My lot has been one of public infamy, of long imprisonment, of misery, of ruin, of disgrace, but I am not worthy of it – not yet, at any rate. I remember that I used to say that I thought I could bear a real tragedy if it came to me with purple pall and a mask of noble sorrow, but that the dreadful thing about modernity was that it put tragedy into the raiment of comedy, so that the great realities seemed commonplace or grotesque or lacking in style. It is quite true about modernity. It has probably always been true about actual life. It is said that all martyrdoms seemed mean to the looker-on. The nineteenth century is no exception to the rule.

Everything about my tragedy has been hideous, mean, repellent, lacking in style; our very dress makes us grotesque. We are the zanies of sorrow. We are clowns whose hearts are broken. We are specially designed to appeal to the sense of humour. On 13th November 1895, I was brought down here from London. From two o'clock till half-past two on that day I had to stand on the centre platform of Clapham Junction in convict dress, and handcuffed, for the world to look at. I had been taken out of the hospital ward without a moment's notice being given to me. Of all possible objects I was the most grotesque. When people saw me they laughed. Each train as it came up swelled the audience. Nothing could exceed their amusement. That was, of course, before they knew who I was. As soon as they had been informed they laughed still more. For half an hour I stood there in the grey November rain surrounded by a jeering mob.

For a year after that was done to me I wept every day at the same hour and for the same space of time. That is not such a tragic thing as possibly it sounds to you. To those who are in prison tears are part of every day's experience. A day in prison on which one does not weep is a day on which one's heart is hard, not a day on which one's heart is happy.

Well, now I am really beginning to feel more regret for the people who laughed than for myself. Of course when they saw me I was not on my pedestal, I was in the pillory. But it is a very unimaginative nature that only cares for people on their pedestals. A pedestal may be a very unreal thing. A pillory is a terrific reality. They should have known also how to interpret sorrow better. I have said that behind sorrow there is always sorrow. It were wiser still to say that behind sorrow there is always a soul. And to mock at a soul in pain is a dreadful thing. In the strangely simple economy of the world people only get what they give, and to those who have not enough imagination to penetrate the mere outward shell of things, and feel pity, what pity can be given save that of scorn?

I write this account of the mode of my being transferred here simply that it should be realized how hard it has been for me to get anything out of my punishment but bitterness and despair. I have, however, to do it, and now and then I have moments of submission and acceptance. All the spring may be hidden in the single bud, and the low ground nest of the lark may hold the joy that is to herald the feet of many rose-red dawns. So perhaps whatever beauty of life still remains to me is contained in some moment of surrender, abasement, and humiliation. I can, at any rate, merely proceed on the lines of my own development, and, accepting all that has happened to me, make myself worthy of it.

People used to say of me that I was too individualistic. I must be far more of an individualist than ever I was. I must get far more out of myself than ever I got, and ask for less of the world than ever I asked. Indeed, my ruin came not from too great individualism of life, but from too little. The one disgraceful, unpardonable, and to all time contemptible action of my life was to allow myself to appeal to Society for help and protection. To have made such an appeal would have been from the individualist point of view bad enough, but what excuse can there ever be put forward for having made it? Of course once I had put into motion the forces of Society, Society turned on me and said, 'Have you been living all this time in defiance of my laws, and do you now appeal to those laws for protection? You shall have those laws exercised to the full. You shall abide by what you have appealed to.' The result is I am in gaol. Certainly no man ever fell so ignobly, and by such ignoble instruments, as I did. I say in *Dorian Gray* somewhere that 'A man cannot be too careful in the choice of his enemies.' I little thought that it was by a pariah I was to be made a pariah myself.

The Philistine element in life is not the failure to understand art. Charming people, such as fishermen, shepherds, ploughboys, peasants and the like, know nothing about art, and are the very salt of the earth. He is the Philistine who upholds and aids the heavy, cumbrous, blind, mechanical forces of Society, and who does not recognize dynamic force when he meets it either in a man or a movement.

People thought it dreadful of me to have entertained at dinner the evil things of life, and to have found pleasure in their company. But then, from the point of view through which I, as an artist in life, approach them they were delightfully suggestive and stimulating. It was like feasting with panthers; the danger was half the excitement. I used to feel as a snake-charmer must feel when he lures the cobra to stir from the painted cloth or reed basket that holds it and makes it spread its hood at his bidding and sway to and fro in the air as a plant sways restfully in a stream. They were to me the brightest of gilded snakes, their poison was part of their perfection. I did not know that when they were to strike at me it was to be at another's piping and at another's pay. I don't feel at all ashamed at having known them, they were intensely interesting; what I do feel ashamed of is the horrible Philistine atmosphere into which I was brought. My business as an artist was with Ariel, I set myself to wrestle with Caliban. Instead of making beautiful coloured musical things such as *Salome* and the *Florentine Tragedy* and *La Sainte Courtisane*, I forced myself to send long lawyer's letters and was constrained to appeal to the very things against which I had always protested. Clibborn and Atkins were wonderful in their infamous war against life. To entertain them was an astounding adventure; Dumas *père*, Cellini, Goya, Edgar Allan Poe, or Baudelaire would have done just the same. What is loathsome to me is the memory of interminable visits paid by me to the solicitor Humphreys, when in the ghastly glare of a bleak room I would sit with a serious face telling serious lies to a bald man till I really groaned and yawned with ennui. There is where I found myself, right in the centre of Philistia, away from everything that was beautiful or brilliant or wonderful or daring. I had come forward as the champion of respectability in conduct, of puritanism in life, and of morality in art. *Voilà ou mènent les mauvais chemins.*

And the curious thing to me is that you should have tried to imitate your father in his chief characteristics. I cannot understand why he was to you an exemplar, where he should have been a warning, except that whenever there is hatred between two people there is bond or brotherhood of some kind. I suppose that, by some strange law of the antipathy of similars, you loathed each other, not because in so many points you were so different but because in some you were so like. In June 1893, when you left Oxford, without a degree and with debts, petty in themselves, but considerable to a man of your father's income, your father wrote you a very vulgar, violent and abusive letter. The letter you sent him in reply was in every way worse, and of course far less excusable, and consequently you were extremely proud of it. I remember quite well your saying to me with your most conceited air that you could beat your father 'at his own trade'. Quite true. But what a trade! What a competition! You used to laugh and sneer at your father for retiring from your cousin's house where he was living in order to write filthy letters to him from a neighbouring hotel. You used to do just the same to me. You constantly lunched with me at some public restaurant, sulked or made a scene during luncheon, and then retired to White's Club and wrote me a letter of the very foulest character. The only difference between you and your father was that after you had dispatched your letter to me by special messenger, you would arrive yourself at my rooms some hours later not to apologize, but to know if I had ordered dinner at the Savoy, and if not, why not. Sometimes you would actually arrive before the offensive letter had been read. I remember on one occasion you had asked me to invite to luncheon at the Café Royal two of your friends, one of whom I had never seen in my life. I did so, and at your special request ordered beforehand a specially luxurious luncheon to be prepared. The chef, I remember, was sent for, and particular instructions given about the wines. Instead of coming to luncheon you sent me at the Café an abusive letter timed so as to reach me after we had been waiting half an hour for you. I read the first line, and saw what it was, and putting the letter in my pocket explained to your friends that you were suddenly taken ill, and that the rest of the letter referred to your symptoms. In point of fact I did not read the letter till I was dressing for dinner at Tite Street that evening. As I was in the middle of its mire, wondering with infinite sadness how you could write letters that were really like the froth and foam on the lips of an epileptic, my servant came in to tell me that you were in the hall and very anxious to see me for five minutes. I at once sent down and asked you to come up. You arrived, looking, I admit, very frightened and pale, to beg my advice and assistance, as you had been told that a man from Lumley, the solicitor, had been enquiring for you at Cadogan Place, and you were afraid that your Oxford trouble or some new danger was threatening you. I consoled you, and told you, what proved to be the case, that it was merely a tradesman's bill probably, and let you stay to dinner and pass your evening with me. You never mentioned a single word about your hideous letter, nor did I. I treated it simply as an unhappy symptom of an unhappy temperament. The subject was never alluded to. To write to me a loathsome letter at 2.30 and fly to me for help and sympathy at 7.15 the same afternoon, was a perfectly ordinary occurrence in your life. You went quite beyond your father in such habits, as you did in others. When his revolting letters to you were read in open Court he naturally felt ashamed and pretended to weep. Had your letters to him been read by his own Counsel still more horror and repugnance would have been felt by everyone. Nor was it merely in style that you beat him at 'his own trade', but in the mode of attack you distanced him completely. You availed yourself of the public telegram, and the open postcard. I think you might have left such modes of annoyance to people like Alfred Wood whose sole source of income it is. Don't you? What was a profession to him and his class was a pleasure to you, and a very evil one. Nor have you ever given up your horrible habit of writing offensive letters, after all that has happened to me through them and for them. You still regard it as one of your accomplishments, and you exercise it on my friends, or those who have been kind to me in prison like Robert Sherard and others. That is disgraceful of you. When Robert Sherard heard from me that I did not wish you to publish any article on me in the *Mercure de France*, with or without letters, you should have been grateful to him for having ascertained my wishes on the point, and for having saved you from inflicting, without intending it, more pain on me than you had already done. You must remember that a patronizing and Philistine letter about 'fair play' for a 'man who is down' is all right for an English newspaper. It carries on the old traditions of English journalism in regard to its attitude towards artists. But in France such a tone would have exposed me to ridicule and you to contempt. I could not have allowed any article till I had known its aim, temper, mode of approach and the like. In art, good intentions are not of the smallest value. All bad art is the result of good intentions.

Nor is Robert Sherard the only one of my friends to whom you have addressed acrimonious and bitter letters because they sought that my wishes and my feelings should be consulted in matters concerning myself, the publication of articles on me, the dedication of your verses, the surrender of my letters and presents, and such like. You have annoyed or sought to annoy others also.

Does it ever occur to you what an awful position I would have been in if for the last two years, during my appalling sentence, I had been dependent on you as a friend? Do you ever think of that? Do you ever feel any gratitude to those who by kindness without stint, devotion without limit, cheerfulness and joy in giving have lightened my black burden for me, have visited me again and again, have written to me beautiful and sympathetic letters, have managed my affairs for me, arranged my future life, and stood by me in the teeth of obloquy, taunt and open sneer, or insult even? I owe everything to them. The very books in my cell are paid for by Robbie out of his pocket-money; from the same source are to come clothes for me when I am released. I am not ashamed of taking a thing that is given in love and affection; I am proud of it. Yes, I think of my friends, such as More Adey, Robbie, Robert Sherard, Frank Harris, Arthur Clifton, and what they have been to me, in giving me help, affection, and sympathy. I think of every single person who has been kind to me in my prison life down to the warder who gives me a 'Good-morning' and a 'Good-night' (not one of his prescribed duties) down to the common policemen who, in their homely, rough way strove to comfort me on my journeys to and from the Bankruptcy Court under conditions of terrible mental distress – down to the poor thief who recognizing me as we tramped round the yard at Wandsworth, whispered to me in the hoarse prison voice men get from long and compulsory silence: 'I am sorry for you; it is harder for the likes of you than it is for the likes of us.' I suppose that has never dawned on you. And yet – if you had any imagination in you – you would know that there is not one, not one of them all, I say, the very mire from whose shoes you should not be proud to kneel down and clean.

Have you not imagination enough to see what a fearful tragedy it was for me to have come across your family? What a tragedy it would have been for anyone at all, who had a great position, and great name, anything of importance to lose? There is hardly one of the elders of your family – with the exception of Percy, who is a really good fellow – who did not in some way contribute to my ruin.

I have spoken of your mother to you with some bitterness, and I strongly advise you to let her see this letter, for your own sake chiefly. If it is painful for her to read such an indictment against one of her sons, let her remember that my mother, who intellectually ranks with Elizabeth Barrett Browning, and historically with Madame Roland, died broken-hearted because the son of whose genius and art she had been proud, and whom she had regarded always as a worthy continuer of a distinguished name, had been condemned to the treadmill for two years. You will ask me in what way your mother contributed to my destruction. I will tell you. Just as you strove to shift on me all your immoral responsibilities, so your mother strove to shift on me all her moral responsibilities with regard to you. Instead of speaking directly to you about your life, as a mother should, she always wrote privately to me with earnest, frightened entreaties not to let you know that she was writing to me. You see the position in which I was placed between you and your mother. It was one as false, as absurd, and as tragic as the one in which I was placed between you and your father. In August 1892 and on the 8th day of November of the same year I had two long interviews with your mother about you. On both occasions I asked her why she did not speak directly to you herself. On both occasions she gave me the same answer: 'I am afraid to: he gets so angry when he is spoken to.' The first time I knew you so slightly that I did not understand what she meant. The second time I knew you so well that I understood perfectly. (During the interval you had had an attack of jaundice and been ordered by the doctor to go for a week to Bournemouth, and had induced me to accompany you as you hated being alone.) But the first duty of a mother is not to be afraid of speaking seriously to her son. Had your mother spoken seriously to you about the trouble she saw you were in in July 1892, and made you confide in her, it would have been much better and much happier ultimately for both of you. All the underhand and secret communications with me were wrong. What was the use of your mother sending me endless little notes, marked 'Private' on the envelope, begging me not to ask you so often to dinner, and not to give you any money, each note ending with an earnest postscript: 'On no account let Alfred know that I have written to you'? What good could come of such a correspondence? Did you ever wait to be asked to dinner? Never. You took all your meals as a matter of course with me. If I remonstrated you always had one observation: 'If I don't dine with you, where am I to dine? You don't suppose that I am going to dine at home.' It was unanswerable. And if I absolutely refused to let you dine with me, you always threatened that you would do something foolish, and always did it. What possible result could there be from letters such as your mother used to send me, except that which did occur, a foolish and fatal shifting of the moral responsibility on to my shoulders? Of the various details in which your mother's weakness and lack of courage proved so ruinous to herself, to you and to me, I don't want to speak any more; but surely, when she heard of your father coming down to my house to make a loathsome scene and create a public scandal, she might then have seen that a serious crisis was impending, and taken some steps to try to avoid it? But all she could think of doing was to send down plausible George Wyndham with his pliant tongue to propose to me – what? That I should gradually 'drop you'. As if it had been possible for me to 'gradually' drop you! I had tried to end our friendship in every possible way, going so far as actually to leave England and give a false address abroad in the hopes of breaking at one blow a bond that had become irksome, hateful and ruinous to me. Do you think that I *could* have 'gradually' dropped you? Do you think that would have satisfied your father? You knew it would not. What your father wanted, indeed, was not the cessation of our friendship, but a public scandal. That is what he was striving for. His name had not been in the papers for years. He saw the opportunity of appearing before the British public in an entirely new character, that of an affectionate father. His sense of humour was roused. Had I severed my friendship with you it would have been a terrible disappointment to him, and the small notoriety of a second divorce suit, however revolting its detail and origin, would have proved but little consolation to him. For what he was aiming at was popularity, and to pose as the champion of purity, as it is termed, is in the present condition of the British public the surest mode of becoming for once a heroic figure. Of this public I have said in one of my plays, that if it is Caliban for one half of the year, it is Tartuffe for the other: and your father, in whom both characters may be said to have become incarnate, was in this way marked out as the proper representative of Puritanism in its aggressive and most characteristic form. No 'gradual' dropping of you would have been of avail, even had it been practicable. Don't you feel now that the only thing for your mother to have done was to have asked me to come to see her, and had you and your brother present, and said definitely that the friendship must absolutely cease? She would have found in me her warmest seconder, and with Drumlanrig and myself in the room she need not have been afraid of speaking to you. She did not do so. She was afraid of her responsibilities, and tried to shift them on to me. One letter she did certainly write to me. It was a brief one to ask me not to send the lawyer's letter to your father warning him to desist. She was quite right. It was ridiculous my consulting lawyers and seeking their protection. But she nullified any effect her letter might have produced by her usual postscript: 'On no account let Alfred know that I have written to you.' You were entranced at the idea of my sending lawyers' letters to your father, as well as yourself. It was your suggestion. I could not tell you that your mother was strongly against the idea, for she had bound me with the most solemn promises never to tell you about her letters to me, and I foolishly kept my promise to her. Don't you see that it was wrong of her not to speak directly to you? That all the backstairs interviews with me, and the area-gate correspondence were wrong? Nobody can shift his responsibilities on to anyone else. They always return ultimately to the proper owner. Your one idea of life, your one philosophy, if you are to be credited with a philosophy, was that whatever you did was to be paid for by someone else: I don't mean merely in the financial sense – that was simply the practical application of your philosophy to everyday life – but in the broadest, fullest sense of transferred responsibility. You made that your creed. It was very successful as far as it went. You forced me into taking action because you knew that your father would not attack your life or yourself in any way and that I would defend both to the utmost, and take on my own shoulders whatever would be thrust on me. You were quite right. Your father and I, each from different motives, of course, did exactly as you counted on our doing. But somehow, in spite of everything, you have not really escaped. The 'infant Samuel theory', as for brevity's sake one may term it, is all very well as far as the general world knows. It may be a good deal scorned in London, and a little sneered at in Oxford, but that is merely because there are a few people who know you in each place, and because in each place you left traces of your passage. Outside of a small set in those two cities, the world looks on you as the good man who was very nearly tempted into wrongdoing by the wicked and immoral artist, but was rescued just in time by his kind and loving father. It sounds all right. And yet, you know you have not escaped. I am not referring to a silly question asked by a silly juryman which was, of course, treated with contempt by the Crown and Judge. No one cared about that. I am referring perhaps principally to yourself. In your own eyes, and some day, you will have to think of your conduct; you are not, cannot be, quite satisfied at the way in which things have turned out. Secretly you must think of yourself with a good deal of shame. A brazen face is a capital thing to show to the world, but now and then when you are alone, and have no audience, you have, I suppose, to take the mask off for breathing purposes. Else, indeed, you would be stifled.

And in the same manner your mother must at times regret that she tried to shift her grave responsibilities on to someone else, who already had enough of a burden to carry. She occupied the position of both parents to you. Did she really fulfil the duties of either? If I bore with your bad temper and your rudeness and your scenes, she might have borne with them too. When last I saw my wife – fourteen months ago now – I told her that she would have to be to Cyril a father as well as a mother. I told her everything about your mother's code of dealing with you in every detail as I have set it down in this letter, only, of course, far more fully. I told her the reasons of the endless notes with 'Private'

on the envelope that used to come to Tite Street from your
mother, so constantly that my wife used to laugh and say we must
be collaborating in a society novel or something of the kind. I
implored her not to be to Cyril what your mother was to you. I
told her that she should bring him up so that if he shed innocent
blood he would come and tell her, that she might cleanse his
hands for him first, and then teach him how by penance or
expiation to cleanse his soul afterwards. I told her that if she was
frightened of facing the responsibility of the life of another,
though her own child, she should get a guardian to help her.
That she has, I am glad to say, done. She has chosen Adrian Hope,
a man of high birth and culture and fine character, her own cousin,
whom you met once at Tite Street, and with him Cyril and
Vyvyan have a good chance of a beautiful future. Your mother,
if she was afraid of talking seriously to you, should have chosen
someone among her own relatives to whom you might have
listened. But she should not have been afraid. She should have had
it out with you and faced it. At any rate, look at the result. Is
she satisfied and pleased?

I know she puts the blame on me. I hear of it, not from people
who know you, but from people who do not know you, and
do not desire to know you. I hear of it often. She talks of the
influence of an elder over a younger man, for instance. It is one
of her favourite attitudes towards the question, as it is always a
successful appeal to popular prejudice and ignorance. I need not
ask you what influence I had over you. You know I had none.
It was one of your frequent boasts that I had none, and the only
one, indeed, that was well founded. What was there, as a mere
matter of fact, in you that I could influence? Your brain? It was
undeveloped. Your imagination? It was dead. Your heart? It was
not yet born. Of all the people who have ever crossed my life,
you were the one, and the only one, I was unable in any way to
influence in any direction. When I lay ill and helpless in fever
caught from tending on you I had not sufficient influence over
you to induce you to get me even a cup of milk to drink, or to
see that I had the ordinary necessities of a sickroom, or to take
the trouble to drive a couple of hundred yards to a bookseller to

get me a book at my own expense. When I was actually engaged in writing, and penning comedies that were to beat Congreve for brilliancy, and Dumas *fils* for philosophy, and I suppose everybody else for every other quality, I had not sufficient influence with you to get you to leave me undisturbed as an artist should be left. Wherever my writing room was, it was to you an ordinary lounge, a place to smoke and drink hock and seltzer in, and chatter about absurdities. The 'influence of an elder over a younger man' is an excellent theory till it comes to my ears. Then it becomes grotesque. When it comes to your ears, I suppose you smile – to yourself you are certainly entitled to do so. I hear also much of what she says about money. She states, and with perfect justice, that she was ceaseless in her entreaties to me not to supply you with money. I admit it. Her letters were endless, and the postscript 'Pray do not let Alfred know that I have written to you' appears in them all. But it was no pleasure to me to have to pay for every single thing for you from your morning shave to your midnight hansom. It was a horrible bore. I used to complain to you again and again about it. I used to tell you – you remember, don't you? – how I loathed your regarding me as a 'useful' person, because the artist, like art itself, is of his very essence quite useless. You used to get very angry when I said it to you. The truth always made you angry. Truth, indeed, is a thing which is most painful to listen to and most painful to utter. But it did not make you alter your views or your mode of life. Every day I had to pay for every single thing you did all day long. Only a person of absurd good nature or of indescribable folly would have done so. I unfortunately was a complete combination of both. When I used to suggest that your mother should supply you with the money you wanted, you always had a very pretty and graceful answer. You said that the income allowed her by your father – some £1,500 a year, I believe – was quite inadequate to the wants of a lady of her position, and that you would not go to her for more money than you were already getting. You were quite right about her income being one absolutely unsuitable to a lady of her position and tastes, but you should not have made that an excuse for living in luxury on me: it should on the contrary have been a suggestion to you for economy in your own life. The fact is that you were, and are I suppose still, a typical sentimentalist. For a sentimentalist is simply one who desires to have the luxury of an emotion without paying for it. To propose to spare your mother's pocket was beautiful. To do so at my expense was ugly.

I think that if you look back to your attitude towards your mother's income, and your attitude towards my income, you will not feel proud of yourself, and perhaps you may some day, if you don't show your mother this letter, explain to her that your living on me was a matter in which my wishes were not consulted for a moment. It was simply a peculiar and, to me personally, most distressing form that your devotion to me took. To make yourself dependent on me for the smallest as well as for the largest sums, lent you in your own eyes all the charm of childhood, and in the insisting on my paying for every one of your pleasures you thought that you had found the secret of eternal youth. I confess that it pains me when I hear of your mother's remarks about me, and I am sure that on reflexion you will agree with me that if she has no word of regret or sorrow for the ruin your race has brought on me it would be better if she remained silent. Of course, there is no reason she should see any portion of this letter that refers to any mental development I have been going through, or to any point of departure I hope to attain to. It would not be interesting to her. But the parts concerned purely with your life I should show her if I were you.

If I were you, in fact, I would not care about being loved on false pretences. There is no reason why a man should show his life to the world. The world does not understand things. But with people whose affection one desires to have it is different.

A great friend of mine – a friend of ten years' standing – came to see me some time ago, and told me that he did not believe a single word of what was said against me, and wished me to know that he considered me quite innocent, and the victim of a hideous plot. I burst into tears at what he said, and told him that while there was much amongst the definite charges that was quite untrue and transferred to me by revolting malice, still that my life had been full of perverse pleasures, and that unless he accepted that as a fact about me and realized it to the full I could not possibly be friends with him any more, or ever be in his company. It was a terrible shock to him, but we are friends, and I have not got his friendship on false pretences. I have said to you to speak the truth is a painful thing. To be forced to tell lies is much worse.

I remember that as I was sitting in the dock on the occasion of my last trial listening to Lockwood's appalling denunciation of me – like a thing out of Tacitus, like a passage in Dante, like one of Savonarola's indictments of the Popes of Rome – and being sickened with horror at what I heard, suddenly it occurred to me, *How splendid it would be, if I was saying all this about myself.* I saw then at once that what is said of a man is nothing. The point is, who says it. A man's very highest moment is, I have no doubt at all, when he kneels in the dust, and beats his breast, and tells all the sins of his life. So with you. You would be much happier if you let your mother know a little at any rate of your life from yourself. I told her a good deal about it in December 1893, but of course I was forced into reticences and generalities. It did not seem to give her any more courage in her relations with you. On the contrary, she avoided looking at the truth more persistently than ever. If you told her yourself it would be different. My words may perhaps be often too bitter to you, but the facts you cannot deny. Things were as I have said they were, and if you have read this letter carefully as you should have done you have met yourself face to face.

I have now written, and at great length, to you in order that you should realize what you were to me before my imprisonment, during those three years' fatal friendship; what you have been to me during my imprisonment, already within two moons of its completion almost; and what I hope to be to myself and to others when my imprisonment is over. I cannot reconstruct my letter or rewrite it. You must take it as it stands, blotted in many places with tears, in some with the signs of passion or pain, and make it out as best you can, blots, corrections, and all. As for the corrections and errata, I have made them in order that my words should be an absolute expression of my thoughts, and err neither through surplusage nor through being inadequate. Language requires to be tuned, like a violin: and just as too many or too few vibrations in the voice of the singer or the trembling of the string will make the note false, so too much or too little in words will spoil the message. As it stands, at any rate, my letter has its definite meaning behind every phrase. There is in it nothing of rhetoric. Whenever there is erasion or substitution, however slight, however elaborate, it is because I am seeking to render my real impression, to find for my mood its exact equivalent. Whatever is first in feeling comes away last in form.

I will admit that it is a severe letter. I have not spared you. Indeed you may say that, after admitting that to weigh you against the smallest of my sorrows, the meanest of my losses would be really unfair to you, I have actually done so, and made scruple by scruple the most careful assay of your nature. That is true. But you must remember that you put yourself in the scales.

You must remember that, if when matched with one mere moment of my imprisonment the balance in which you lie kicks the beam. Vanity made you choose the balance, and Vanity made you cling to it. *There* was the one great psychological error of our friendship, its entire want of proportion. You forced your way into a life too large for you, one whose orbit transcended your power of vision no less than your power of cyclic motion, one whose thoughts, passions and actions were of intense import, of wide interest, and fraught, too heavily indeed, with wonderful or awful consequences. Your little life of little whims and moods was admirable in its own little sphere. It was admirable at Oxford, where the worst that could happen to you was a reprimand from the Dean or a lecture from the President, and where the highest excitement was Magdalen becoming head of the river, and the lighting of a bonfire in the Quad as a celebration of the august event. It should have continued in its own sphere after you left Oxford. In yourself you were all right. You were a very complete specimen of a very modern type. It was simply in reference to me that you were wrong. Your reckless extravagance was a crime. Youth is always extravagant. It was your forcing me to pay for your extravagances that was disgraceful. Your desire to have a friend with whom you could pass your time from morning to night was charming. It was almost idyllic. But the friend you fastened on should not have been a man of letters, an artist, one to whom your continual presence was utterly destructive of all beautiful work as it was actually paralysing to the creative faculty. There was no harm in your seriously considering that the most perfect way of passing an evening was to have a champagne dinner at the Savoy, a box at a music hall to follow, and a champagne supper at Willis's as a *bonne bouche* for the end. Heaps of delightful young men in London are of the same opinion. It is not even an eccentricity. It is a qualification for becoming a member of White's. But you had no right to require of me that I should become the purveyor of such pleasures for you. It showed your lack of any real appreciation of my genius. Your quarrel with your father, again, whatever one may think about its character, should obviously have remained a question entirely between the two of you. It should have been carried on in a back yard. Such quarrels I believe usually are. Your mistake was in insisting on its being played as a tragi-comedy on a high stage in history, with the whole world as an audience, and myself as the prize for the victor in the contemptible contest. The fact that your father loathed you, and that you loathed your father, was not a matter of any interest to the English public. Such feelings are very common in English domestic life, and should be confined to the place they characterize: the home. Away from the home circle they are quite out of place. To translate them is an offence. Family life is not to be treated as a red flag to be flaunted in the streets, or a horn to be blown hoarsely on the housetop. You took domesticity out of its proper sphere, just as you took yourself out of your proper sphere. And those who quit their proper sphere change their surroundings merely, not their natures. They do not acquire the thoughts or passions appropriate to the sphere they enter. It is not in their power to do so.

Emotional forces, as I say somewhere in *Intentions*, are as limited in extent and duration as the forces of physical energy. The little cup that is made to hold so much can hold so much and no more, though all the purple vats of Burgundy be filled with wine to the brim, and the treaders stand knee-deep in the gathered grapes of the stony vineyards of Spain. There is no error more common than that of thinking that those who are the causes or occasions of great tragedies share in the feelings suitable to the tragic mood: no error more fatal than expecting it of them. The martyr in his 'shirt of flame' may be looking on the face of God, but to him who is piling the faggots or loosening the logs for the blast the whole scene is no more than the slaying of an ox is to the butcher, or the felling of a tree to the charcoal burner in the forest, or the fall of a flower to one who is mowing down the grass with a scythe. Great passions are for the great of soul, and great events can be seen only by those who are on a level with them. We think we can have our emotions for nothing. We cannot. Even the finest and the most self-sacrificing emotions have to be paid for. Strangely enough, that is what makes them fine. The intellectual and emotional life of ordinary people is a very contemptible affair. Just as they borrow their ideas from a sort of circulating library of thought – the *Zeitgeist* of an age that has no soul and send them back soiled at the end of each week – so they always try to get their emotions on credit, or refuse to pay the bill when it comes in. We must pass out of that conception of life; as soon as we have to pay for an emotion we shall know its quality and be the better for such knowledge. Remember that the sentimentalist is always a cynic at heart. Indeed sentimentality is merely the bankholiday of cynicism. And delightful as cynicism is from its intellectual side, now that it has left the tub for the club, it never can be more than the perfect philosophy for a man who has no soul. It has its social value; and to an artist all modes of expression are interesting, but in itself it is a poor affair, for to the true cynic nothing is ever revealed.

*

I know of nothing in all drama more incomparable from the point of view of art, nothing more suggestive in its subtlety of observation, than Shakespeare's drawing of Rosencrantz and Guildenstern. They are Hamlet's college friends. They have been his companions. They bring with them memories of pleasant days together. At the moment when they come across him in the play he is staggering under the weight of a burden intolerable to one of his temperament. The dead have come armed out of the grave to impose on him a mission at once too great and too mean for him. He is a dreamer, and he is called upon to act. He has the nature of the poet, and he is asked to grapple with the common complexity of cause and effect, with life in its practical realization, of which he knows nothing, not with life in its ideal essence, of which he knows so much. He has no conception of what to do, and his folly is to feign folly. Brutus used madness as a cloak to conceal the sword of his purpose, the dagger of his will, but the Hamlet madness is a mere mask for the hiding of weakness. In the making of fancies and jests he sees a chance of delay. He keeps playing with action as an artist plays with a theory. He makes himself the spy of his proper actions, and listening to his own words knows them to be but 'words, words, words'. Instead of trying to be the hero of his own history, he seeks to be the spectator of his own tragedy. He disbelieves in everything, including himself, and yet his doubt helps him not, as it comes not from scepticism but from a divided will.

Of all this Guildenstern and Rosencrantz realize nothing. They bow and smirk and smile, and what the one says the other echoes with sickliest intonation. When, at last, by means of the play within the play, and the puppets in their dalliance, Hamlet 'catches the conscience' of the King, and drives the wretched man in terror from his throne, Guildenstern and Rosencrantz see no more in his conduct than a rather painful breach of Court etiquette. That is as far as they can attain to in 'the contemplation of the spectacle of life with appropriate emotions'. They are close to his very secret and know nothing of it. Nor would there be any use in telling them. They are the little cups that can hold so much and no more. Towards the close it is suggested that, caught in a cunning springe set for another, they have met, or may meet, with a violent and sudden death. But a tragic ending of this kind, though touched by Hamlet's humour with something of the surprise and justice of comedy, is really not for such as they. They never die. Horatio, who in order to 'report Hamlet and his cause aright to the unsatisfied',

> Absents him from felicity a while,
> And in this harsh world draws his breath in pain,

dies, though not before an audience, and leaves no brother. But Guildenstern and Rosencrantz are as immortal as Angelo and Tartuffe, and should rank with them. They are what modern life has contributed to the antique ideal of friendship. He who writes a new *De Amicitia* must find a niche for them, and praise them in Tuscan prose. They are types fixed for all time. To censure them would show 'a lack of appreciation'. They are merely out of their sphere: that is all. In sublimity of soul there is no contagion. High thoughts and high emotions are by their very existence isolated. What Ophelia herself could not understand was not to be realized by 'Guildenstern and gentle Rosencrantz', by 'Rosencrantz and the gentle Guildenstern'. Of course, I do not propose to compare you. There is a wide difference between you. What with them was chance, with you was choice. Deliberately and by me uninvited you thrust yourself into my sphere, usurped there a place for which you had neither right nor qualifications, and having by curious persistence and by the rendering of your very presence a part of each separate day, succeeded in absorbing my entire life and could do no better with that life than break it in pieces. Strange as it may sound to you it was but natural that you should do so. If one gives to a child a toy too wonderful for its little mind, or too beautiful for its but half awakened eyes, it breaks the toy if it is wilful; if it is listless it lets it fall and goes its way to its own companions. So it was with you. Having got hold of my life, you did not know what to do with it. You couldn't have known. It was too wonderful a thing to be in your grasp. You should have let it slip from your hands and gone back to your own companions at their play. But unfortunately you were wilful, and so you broke it. That, when everything is said, is perhaps the ultimate secret of all that has happened. For secrets are always smaller than their manifestations. By the displacement of an atom a world may be shaken. And that I may not spare myself any more than you I will add this: that dangerous to me as my meeting with you was, it was rendered fatal to me by the particular moment in which we met. For you were at that time of life when all that one does is no more than the sowing of the seed, and I was at that time of life when all that one does is no less than the reaping of the harvest.

There are some few things more about which I must write to you. The first is about my bankruptcy. I heard some days ago, with great disappointment I admit, that it is too late now for your family to pay your father off, that it would be illegal, and that I must remain in my present painful position for some considerable time to come. It is bitter to me because I am assured on legal authority that I cannot even publish a book without the permission of the Receiver, to whom all the accounts must be submitted. I cannot enter into a contract with the manager of a theatre, or produce a play without the receipts passing to your father and my few other creditors. I think that even you will admit now that the scheme of 'scoring off' your father by allowing him to make me a bankrupt has not really been the brilliant all-round success you imagined it was going to turn out to be.

It has been so to me at any rate, and my feelings of pain and humiliation at my pauperism should have been consulted rather than your own sense of humour, however caustic or unexpected. In point of actual fact, in permitting my bankruptcy, as in urging me on to the original trial, you really were playing right into your father's hands, and doing just what he wanted.

Alone, and unassisted, he would from the very outset have been powerless. In you – though you did not mean to hold such a horrible office – he has always found his chief ally.

I am told by More Adey in his letter that last summer you really did express on more than one occasion your desire to repay me 'a little of what I spent' on you. As I said to him in my answer, unfortunately I spent on you my art, my life, my name, my place in history: and if your family had all the marvellous things in the world at their command, or what the world holds as marvellous, genius, beauty, wealth, high position and the like, and laid them all at my feet, it would not repay me for one tithe of the smallest things that have been taken from me, or one tear of the least tears that I have shed. However, of course, everything one does has to be paid for. Even to the bankrupt it is so.

You seem to be under the impression that bankruptcy is a convenient means by which a man can avoid paying his debts, a 'score off his creditors' in fact. It is quite the other way.

It is the method by which a man's creditors 'score off' him, if we are to continue your favourite phrase, and by which the law, by the confiscation of all his property, forces him to pay every one of his debts, and if he fails to do so leaves him as penniless as the commonest mendicant who stands in an archway or creeps down a road, holding out his hand for the alms for which, in England, at any rate, he is afraid to ask. The law has taken from me not merely all that I have, my books, furniture, pictures, my copyright in my published works, my copyright in my plays, everything in fact from *The Happy Prince* and *Lady Windermere's Fan* down to the stair carpets and door-scraper of my house, but also all that I am ever going to have. My interest in my marriage settlement, for instance, was sold.

Fortunately, I was able to buy it in through my friends. Otherwise, in case my wife died, my two children during my lifetime would be as penniless as myself. My interest in our Irish estate, entailed on me by my own father, will, I suppose, have to go next.

I feel very bitterly about it being sold, but I must submit.

Your father's seven hundred pence, – or pounds is it? – stand in the way, and must be refunded. Even when I am stripped of all I have, and am ever to have, and am granted a discharge as a hopeless insolvent, I have still got to pay my debts. The Savoy dinners – the clear turtle soup; the luscious ortolans wrapped in their crinkled Sicilian vine-leaves, the heavy amber-coloured, indeed almost amber-scented champagne – Dagonet, 1880, I think was your favourite wine – all have still to be paid for. The suppers at Willis's, the special *cuvées* of Perrier-Jouet reserved always for us, the wonderful *pâtés* procured directly from Strasburg, the marvellous *fine champagne* served always at the bottom of great bell-shaped glasses that its bouquet might be the better savoured by the true epicures of what was really exquisite in life – these cannot be left unpaid, as bad debts of a dishonest client. Even the dainty sleeve-links – four heart-shaped moonstones of silver mist girdled by alternate ruby and diamond for their setting – that I designed and had made at Henry Lewis's as a special little present to you, to celebrate the success of my second comedy – these even – though I believe you sold them for a song a few months afterwards – have to be paid for. I cannot leave the jeweller out of pocket for the presents I gave you, no matter what you did with them. So, even if I get my discharge, you see I have still my debts to pay.

And what is true of a bankrupt is true of everyone else in life. For every single thing that is done someone has to pay. Even you yourself – with all your desire for absolute freedom from all duties, your insistence on having everything supplied to you by others, your attempts to reject any claim on your affection, or regard, or gratitude – even you will have some day to reflect seriously on what you have done, and try, however unavailingly, to make some attempt at atonement. The fact that you will not be able really to do so will be part of your punishment. You can't wash your hands of all responsibility, and propose, with a shrug or a smile, to pass on to a new friend and a freshly spread feast. You can't treat all that you have brought upon me as a sentimental reminiscence to be served up occasionally with the cigarettes and liqueurs, a picturesque background to a modern life of pleasure like an old tapestry hung in a common inn. It may for the moment have the charm of a new sauce or a fresh vintage, but the scraps of a banquet grow stale, and the dregs of a bottle are bitter. Either to-day, or to-morrow, or some day you have to realize it. Otherwise you may die without having done so, and then what a mean, starved, unimaginative life you would have had. In my letter to More I have suggested one point of view from which you had better approach the subject as soon as possible. He will tell you what it is. To understand it you will have to cultivate your imagination. Remember that imagination is the quality that enables one to see things and people in their real as in their ideal relations. If you cannot realize it by yourself, talk to others on the subject. I have had to look at my past face to face. Look at your past face to face. Sit down quietly and consider it. The supreme vice is shallowness. Whatever is realized is right. Talk to your brother about it. Indeed, the proper person to talk to is Percy. Let him read this letter, and know all the circumstances of our friendship. When things are clearly put before him, no judgement is better. Had we told him the truth what a lot would have been saved to me of suffering and disgrace! You remember that I proposed to do so the night you arrived in London from Algiers. You absolutely refused. So when he came in after dinner we had to play the comedy of your father being an insane man subject to absurd and unaccountable delusions. It was a capital comedy while it lasted, none the less so because Percy took it all quite seriously. Unfortunately it ended in a very revolting manner. The subject on which I write now is one of its results, and if it be a trouble to you, pray do not forget that it is the deepest of my humiliations, and one I must go through. I have no option. You have none either.

The second thing about which I have to speak to you is with regard to the conditions, circumstances, and place of our meeting when my term of imprisonment is over. From extracts from your letter to Robbie written in the early summer of last year, I understand that you have sealed up in two packages my letters and my presents to you – such at least as remain of either – and are anxious to hand them personally to me. It is, of course, necessary that they should be given up. You did not understand why I wrote beautiful letters to you, any more than you understood why I gave you beautiful presents. You failed to see that the former were not meant to be published any more than the latter were meant to be pawned. Besides, they belong to a side of life that is long over, to a friendship that somehow you were unable to appreciate at its proper value. You must look back with wonder now to the days when you had my entire life in your hands. I too look back to them with wonder and with other, with far different, emotions.

Of course to one so modern as I am, *enfant de mon siècle*, merely to look at the world will be always lovely. I tremble with pleasure when I think that on the very day of my leaving prison both the laburnum and the lilac will be blooming in the gardens, and that I shall see the wind stir into restless beauty the swaying gold of the one, and make the other toss the pale purple of its plumes so that all the air shall be Arabia for me. Linnaeus fell on his knees and wept for joy when he saw for the first time the long heath of some English upland made yellow with the tawny aromatic blossoms of the common furze; and I know that for me, to whom flowers are part of desire, there are tears waiting in the petals of some rose. It has always been so with me from my boyhood. There is not a single colour hidden away in the chalice of a flower, or the curve of a shell, to which, by some subtle sympathy with the very soul of things, my nature does not answer. Like Gautier, I have always been one of those *pour qui le monde visible existe*.

Still, I am conscious now that behind all this beauty, satisfying though it may be, there is some spirit hidden of which the painted forms and shapes are but modes of manifestation, and it is with this spirit that I desire to become in harmony. I have grown tired of the articulate utterances of men and things. The Mystical in Art, the Mystical in Life, the Mystical in Nature – this is what I am looking for. It is absolutely necessary for me to find it somewhere.

I have a strange longing for the great simple primeval things, such as the sea, to me no less of a mother than the Earth. It seems to me that we all look at Nature too much, and live with her too little. I discern great sanity in the Greek attitude. They never chattered about sunsets, or discussed whether the shadows on the grass were really mauve or not. But they saw that the sea was for the swimmer, and the sand for the feet of the runner. They loved the trees for the shadow that they cast, and the forest for its silence at noon. The vineyard-dresser wreathed his hair with ivy that he might keep off the rays of the sun as he stooped over the young shoots, and for the artist and the athlete, the two types that Greece gave us, they plaited with garlands the leaves of the bitter laurel and of the wild parsley, which else had been of no service to men.

We call ours a utilitarian age, and we do not know the uses of any single thing. We have forgotten that water can cleanse, and fire purify, and that the Earth is mother to us all. As a consequence our art is of the moon and plays with shadows, while Greek art is of the sun and deals directly with things. I feel sure that in elemental forces there is purification, and I want to go back to them and live in their presence.

All trials are trials for one's life, just as all sentences are sentences of death; and three times have I been tried. The first time I left the box to be arrested, the second time to be led back to the house of detention, the third time to pass into a prison for two years. Society, as we have constituted it, will have no place for me, has none to offer; but Nature, whose sweet rains fall on unjust and just alike, will have clefts in the rocks where I may hide, and secret valleys in whose silence I may weep undisturbed. She will hang the night with stars so that I may walk abroad in the darkness without stumbling, and send the wind over my footprints so that none may track me to my hurt: she will cleanse me in great waters, and with bitter herbs make me whole.

I am to be released, if all goes well with me, towards the end of May, and hope to go at once to some little seaside village abroad with Robbie and More.

The sea, as Euripides says in one of his plays about Iphigeneia, washes away the stains and wounds of the world.

At the end of a month, when the June roses are in all their wanton opulence, I will, if I feel able, arrange through Robbie to meet you in some quiet foreign town like Bruges, where grey houses and green canals and cool still ways had a charm for me years ago. For the moment you will have to change your name. The little title of which you were so vain, – and indeed it made your name sound like the name of a flower! – you will have to surrender, if you wish to see me; just as my name once so musical in the mouth of Fame will have to be abandoned by me in turn. How narrow and mean, and inadequate to its burdens is this century of ours: it can give to success its palace of porphyry, but for sorrow and shame it does not keep even a wattled house in which they may dwell: all it can do for me is to bid me alter my name into some other name, where even medievalism would have given me the cowl of a monk or the face of the leper behind which I might be at peace.

I hope that our meeting will be what a meeting between you and me should be, after everything that has occurred. In old days there was always a wide chasm between us, the chasm of achieved art and acquired culture; there is a still wider chasm between us now, the chasm of sorrow: but to humility there is nothing that is impossible, and to love all things are easy.

As regards your letter to me in answer to this, it may be long or as short as you choose. Address the envelope to 'The Governor, H.M. Prison, Reading'. Inside, in another, and an open envelope, place your own letter to me: if your paper is very thin do not write on both sides, as it makes it hard for others to read. I have written to you with perfect freedom. You can write to me with the same. What I must know from you is why you have never made any attempt to write to me since the August of the year before last, more especially after, in the May of last year, eleven months ago now, you knew and admitted to others that you knew how you made me suffer, and how I realized it.

I waited month after month to hear from you. Even if I had not been waiting but had shut the doors against you, you should have remembered that no one can possibly shut the doors against love for ever. The unjust judge in the Gospels rises up at length to give a just decision because justice comes knocking daily at his door; and at night time the friend in whose heart there is no real friendship yields at length to his friend 'because of his importunity'. There is no prison in any world into which love cannot force an entrance. If you did not understand that, you did not understand anything about love at all. Then, let me know all about your article on me for the *Mercure de France*. I know something of it. You had better quote from it. It is set up in type. Also, let me know the exact terms of your dedication of your poems. If it is in prose, quote the prose; if in verse, quote the verse. I have no doubt that there will be beauty in it. Write to me with full frankness, about yourself: about your life: your friends: your occupations: your books. Tell me about your volume and its reception. Whatever you have to say for yourself, say it without fear. Don't write what you don't mean: that is all. If anything in your letter is false or counterfeit I shall detect it by the ring at once.

It is not for nothing, or to no purpose, that in my lifelong cult of literature I have made myself

> Miser of sound and syllable, no less
> Than Midas of his coinage.[1]

Remember also that I have yet to know you. Perhaps we have yet to know each other. For yourself, I have but this last thing to say. Do not be afraid of the past. If people tell you that it is irrevocable, do not believe them. The past, the present and the future are but one moment in the sight of God, in whose sight we should try to live. Time and space, succession and extension, are merely accidental conditions of thought. The imagination can transcend them, and more in a free sphere of ideal existences. Things, also, are in their essence what we choose to make them. A thing is, according to the mode in which one looks at it. 'Where others', says Blake, 'see but the dawn coming over the hill, I see the sons of God shouting for joy.' What seemed to the world and to myself my future I lost irretrievably when I let myself be taunted into taking the action against your father: I had, I dare say, lost it in reality long before that. What lies before me is my past. I have got to make myself look on that with different eyes, to make the world look on it with different eyes, to make God look on it with different eyes. This I cannot do by ignoring it, or slighting it, or praising it, or denying it. It is only to be done fully by accepting it as an inevitable part of the evolution of my life and character: by bowing my head to everything that I have suffered. How far I am away from the true temper of soul, this letter in its changing uncertain moods, its scorn and bitterness, its aspirations and its failures to realize those aspirations, shows you quite clearly. But do not forget in what a terrible school I am sitting at my task. And incomplete, imperfect, as I am, yet from me you may have still much to gain. You came to me to learn the

1. Keats.

pleasure of life and the pleasure of art. Perhaps I am chosen to teach you something much more wonderful – the meaning of sorrow and its beauty.

Your affectionate friend,

OSCAR WILDE

Poems

SONNET TO LIBERTY

NOT that I love thy children, whose dull eyes
See nothing save their own unlovely woe,
Whose minds know nothing, nothing care to know, –
But that the roar of thy Democracies,
Thy reigns of Terror, thy great Anarchies,
Mirror my wildest passions like the sea
And give my rage a brother —! Liberty!
For this sake only do thy dissonant cries
Delight my discreet soul, else might all kings
By bloody knout or treacherous cannonades
Rob nations of their rights inviolate
And I remain unmoved – and yet, and yet,
These Christs that die upon the barricades,
God knows it I am with them, in some things.

REQUIESCAT

Tread lightly, she is near
    Under the snow,
Speak gently, she can hear
    The daisies grow.

All her bright golden hair
    Tarnished with rust,
She that was young and fair
    Fallen to dust.

Lily-like, white as snow,
    She hardly knew
She was a woman, so
    Sweetly she grew.

Coffin-board, heavy stone,
    Lie on her breast,
I vex my heart alone,
    She is at rest.

Peace, Peace, she cannot hear
    Lyre or sonnet,
All my life's buried here,
    Heap earth upon it.

AVIGNON

AVE MARIA GRATIA PLENA

WAS this His coming! I had hoped to see
   A scene of wondrous glory, as was told
   Of some great God who in a rain of gold
Broke open bars and fell on Danae:
Or a dread vision as when Semele
   Sickening for love and unappeased desire
   Prayed to see God's clear body, and the fire
Caught her white limbs and slew her utterly:
With such glad dreams I sought this holy place,
   And now with wondering eyes and heart I stand
   Before this supreme mystery of Love:
A kneeling girl with passionless pale face,
   An angel with a lily in his hand,
   And over both with outstretched wings the Dove.

FLORENCE

SONNET

ON HEARING THE DIES IRAE SUNG IN
THE SISTINE CHAPEL

NAY, Lord, not thus! white lilies in the spring,
  Sad olive-groves, or silver-breasted dove,
  Teach me more clearly of Thy life and love
Than terrors of red flame and thundering.
The empurpled vines dear memories of Thee bring:
  A bird at evening flying to its nest
  Tells me of One who had no place of rest:
I think it is of Thee the sparrows sing.
Come rather on some autumn afternoon,
  When red and brown are burnished on the leaves,
  And the fields echo to the gleaner's song,
Come when the splendid fulness of the moon
  Looks down upon the rows of golden sheaves,
  And reap Thy harvest: we have waited long.

MAGDALEN WALKS

THE little white clouds are racing over the sky,
  And the fields are strewn with the gold of the flower of March,
  The daffodil breaks under foot, and the tasselled larch
Sways and swings as the thrush goes hurrying by.

A delicate odour is borne on the wings of the morning breeze,
  The odour of leaves and of grass, and of newly upturned earth,
  The birds are singing for joy of the Spring's glad birth,
Hopping from branch to branch on the rocking trees.

And all the woods are alive with the murmur and sound of Spring,
  And the rose-bud breaks into pink on the climbing briar,
  And the crocus-bed is a quivering moon of fire
Girdled round with the belt of an amethyst ring.

And the plane to the pine-trees is whispering some tale of love
  Till it rustles with laughter and tosses its mantle of green,
  And the gloom of the wych-elm's hollow is lit with the iris
    sheen
Of the burnished rainbow throat and the silver breast of a dove.

See! the lark starts up from his bed in the meadow there,
  Breaking the gossamer threads and the nets of dew,
  And flashing adown the river, a flame of blue!
The kingfisher flies like an arrow, and wounds the air.

THE GRAVE OF SHELLEY

LIKE burnt-out torches by a sick man's bed
  Gaunt cypress-trees stand round the sun-bleached stone;
  Here doth the little night-owl make her throne,
And the slight lizard show his jewelled head.
And, where the chaliced poppies flame to red,
  In the still chamber of yon pyramid
  Surely some Old-World Sphinx lurks darkly hid,
Grim warder of this pleasaunce of the dead.

Ah! sweet indeed to rest within the womb
  Of Earth, great mother of eternal sleep,
But sweeter far for thee a restless tomb
  In the blue cavern of an echoing deep,
Or where the tall ships founder in the gloom
  Against the rocks of some wave-shattered steep.

ROME

FABIEN DEI FRANCHI

TO MY FRIEND HENRY IRVING

THE silent room, the heavy creeping shade,
  The dead that travel fast, the opening door,
  The murdered brother rising through the floor,
The ghost's white fingers on thy shoulders laid,
And then the lonely duel in the glade,
  The broken swords, the stifled scream, the gore,
  Thy grand revengeful eyes when all is o'er, –
These things are well enough, – but thou wert made
  For more august creation! frenzied Lear
  Should at thy bidding wander on the heath
  With the shrill fool to mock him, Romeo
For thee should lure his love, and desperate fear
Pluck Richard's recreant dagger from its sheath –
  Thou trumpet set for Shakespeare's lips to blow!

PORTIA

[TO ELLEN TERRY]

I MARVEL not Bassanio was so bold
 To peril all he had upon the lead,
 Or that proud Aragon bent low his head
Or that Morocco's fiery heart grew cold:
For in that gorgeous dress of beaten gold
 Which is more golden than the golden sun
 No woman Veronese looked upon
Was half so fair as thou whom I behold.
Yet fairer when with wisdom as your shield
 The sober-suited lawyer's gown you donned,
And would not let the laws of Venice yield
 Antonio's heart to that accursed Jew –
 O Portia! take my heart: it is thy due:
I think I will not quarrel with the Bond.

ΓΛΥΚΥΠΙΚΡΟΣ ΕΡΩΣ

S WEET, I blame you not, for mine the fault was, had I not been
made of common clay
I had climbed the higher heights unclimbed yet, seen the fuller
air, the larger day.

From the wildness of my wasted passion I had struck a better,
clearer song,
Lit some lighter light of freer freedom, battled with some Hydra-
headed wrong.

Had my lips been smitten into music by the kisses that but made
them bleed,
You had walked with Bice and the angels on that verdant and
enamelled mead.

I had trod the road which Dante treading saw the suns of seven
circles shine,
Ay! perchance had seen the heavens opening, as they opened to
the Florentine.

And the mighty nations would have crowned me, who am crown-
less now and without name,
And some orient dawn had found me kneeling on the threshold
of the House of Fame.

I had sat within that marble circle where the oldest bard is as the
young,
And the pipe is ever dropping honey, and the lyre's strings are
ever strung.

Keats had lifted up his hymenaeal curls from out the poppy-
seeded wine,
With ambrosial mouth had kissed my forehead, clasped the hand
of noble love in mine.

And at springtide, when the apple-blossoms brush the burnished
    bosom of the dove,
Two young lovers lying in an orchard would have read the story
    of our love.

Would have read the legend of my passion, known the bitter
    secret of my heart,
Kissed as we have kissed, but never parted as we two are fated
    now to part.

For the crimson flower of our life is eaten by the cankerworm of
    truth,
And no hand can gather up the fallen withered petals of the rose
    of youth.

Yet I am not sorry that I loved you – ah! what else had I a boy
    to do, –
For the hungry teeth of time devour, and the silent-footed years
    pursue.

Rudderless, we drift athwart a tempest, and when once the storm
    of youth is past,
Without lyre, without lute or chorus, Death the silent pilot comes
    at last.

And within the grave there is no pleasure, for the blindworm
    battens on the root,
And Desire shudders into ashes, and the tree of Passion bears no
    fruit.

Ah! what else had I to do but love you, God's own mother was
    less dear to me,
And less dear the Cytheraean rising like an argent lily from the
    sea.

I have made my choice, have lived my poems, and, though youth
    is gone in wasted days,
I have found the lover's crown of myrtle better than the poet's
    crown of bays.

TO MY WIFE

WITH A COPY OF MY POEMS

I CAN write no stately proem
   As a prelude to my lay;
From a poet to a poem
   I would dare to say.

For if of these fallen petals
   One to you seem fair,
Love will waft it till it settles
   On your hair.

And when wind and winter harden
   All the loveless land,
It will whisper of the garden,
   You will understand.

FROM 'THE SPHINX'

Away to Egypt! Have no fear. Only one God has ever died.
Only one God has let His side be wounded by a soldier's spear.

But these, thy lovers, are not dead. Still by the hundred-cubit
    gate
Dog-faced Anubis sits in state with lotus-lilies for thy head.

Still from his chair of porphyry gaunt Memnon strains his lidless
    eyes
Across the empty land, and cries each yellow morning unto thee.

And Nilus with his broken horn lies in his black and oozy bed
And till thy coming will not spread his waters on the withering
    corn.

Your lovers are not dead, I know. They will rise up and hear your
    voice
And clash their cymbals and rejoice and run to kiss your mouth!
    And so,

Set wings upon your argosies! Set horses to your ebon car!
Back to your Nile! Or if you are grown sick of dead divinities

Follow some roving lion's spoor across the copper-coloured
    plain,
Reach out and hale him by the mane and bid him be your
    paramour!

Couch by his side upon the grass and set your white teeth in his
    throat

And when you hear his dying note lash your long flanks of
polished brass

And take a tiger for your mate, whose amber sides are flecked
with black,
And ride upon his gilded back in triumph through the Theban
gate,

And toy with him in amorous jests, and when he turns, and snarls,
and gnaws,
O smite him with your jasper claws! and bruise him with your
agate breasts!

The Ballad of Reading Gaol

THE BALLAD OF READING GAOL

I

He did not wear his scarlet coat,
  For blood and wine are red,
And blood and wine were on his hands
  When they found him with the dead,
The poor dead woman whom he loved,
  And murdered in her bed.

He walked amongst the Trial Men
  In a suit of shabby grey;
A cricket cap was on his head,
  And his step seemed light and gay;
But I never saw a man who looked
  So wistfully at the day.

I never saw a man who looked
  With such a wistful eye
Upon that little tent of blue
  Which prisoners call the sky,
And at every drifting cloud that went
  With sails of silver by.

I walked, with other souls in pain,
  Within another ring,
And was wondering if the man had done
  A great or little thing,
When a voice behind me whispered low,
  '*That fellow's got to swing.*'

Dear Christ! the very prison walls
  Suddenly seemed to reel,

And the sky above my head became
   Like a casque of scorching steel;
And, though I was a soul in pain,
   My pain I could not feel.

I only knew what hunted thought
   Quickened his step, and why
He looked upon the garish day
   With such a wistful eye;
The man had killed the thing he loved,
   And so he had to die.

*

Yet each man kills the thing he loves,
   By each let this be heard,
Some do it with a bitter look,
   Some with a flattering word.
The coward does it with a kiss,
   The brave man with a sword!

Some kill their love when they are young,
   And some when they are old;
Some strangle with the hands of Lust,
   Some with the hands of Gold:
The kindest use a knife, because
   The dead so soon grow cold.

Some love too little, some too long,
   Some sell, and others buy;
Some do the deed with many tears,
   And some without a sigh:
For each man kills the thing he loves,
   Yet each man does not die.

He does not die a death of shame
   On a day of dark disgrace,

Nor have a noose about his neck,
    Nor a cloth upon his face,
Nor drop feet foremost through the floor
    Into an empty space.

He does not sit with silent men
    Who watch him night and day;
Who watch him when he tries to weep,
    And when he tries to pray;
Who watch him lest himself should rob
    The prison of its prey.

He does not wake at dawn to see
    Dread figures throng his room,
The shivering Chaplain robed in white,
    The Sheriff stern with gloom,
And the Governor all in shiny black,
    With the yellow face of Doom.

He does not rise in piteous haste
    To put on convict-clothes,
While some coarse-mouthed Doctor gloats, and notes
    Each new and nerve-twitched pose,
Fingering a watch whose little ticks
    Are like horrible hammer-blows.

He does not feel that sickening thirst
    That sands one's throat, before
The hangman with his gardener's gloves
    Comes through the padded door,
And binds one with three leathern thongs,
    That the throat may thirst no more.

He does not bend his head to hear
    The Burial Office read,
Nor, while the anguish of his soul
    Tells him he is not dead,

Cross his own coffin, as he moves
   Into the hideous shed.

He does not stare upon the air
   Through a little roof of glass:
He does not pray with lips of clay
   For his agony to pass;
Nor feel upon his shuddering cheek
   The kiss of Caiaphas.

2

SIX weeks the guardsman walked the yard,
   In the suit of shabby grey:
His cricket cap was on his head,
   And his step seemed light and gay,
But I never saw a man who looked
   So wistfully at the day.

I never saw a man who looked
   With such a wistful eye
Upon that little tent of blue
   Which prisoners call the sky,
And at every wandering cloud that trailed
   Its ravelled fleeces by.

He did not wring his hands, as do
   Those witless men who dare
To try to rear the changeling Hope
   In the cave of black Despair:
He only looked upon the sun,
   And drank the morning air.

He did not wring his hands nor weep,
   Nor did he peek or pine,
But he drank the air as though it held
   Some healthful anodyne:

With open mouth he drank the sun
  As though it had been wine!

And I and all the souls in pain,
  Who tramped the other ring,
Forgot if we ourselves had done
  A great or little thing,
And watched with gaze of dull amaze
  The man who had to swing.

For strange it was to see him pass
  With a step so light and gay,
And strange it was to see him look
  So wistfully at the day,
And strange it was to think that he
  Had such a debt to pay.

*

For oak and elm have pleasant leaves
  That in the spring-time shoot:
But grim to see is the gallows-tree,
  With its adder-bitten root,
And, green or dry, a man must die
  Before it bears its fruit!

The loftiest place is that seat of grace
  For which all worldlings try:
But who would stand in hempen band
  Upon a scaffold high,
And through a murderer's collar take
  His last look at the sky?

It is sweet to dance to violins
  When Love and Life are fair:
To dance to flutes, to dance to lutes
  Is delicate and rare:

But it is not sweet with nimble feet
   To dance upon the air!

So with curious eyes and sick surmise
   We watched him day by day,
And wondered if each one of us
   Would end the self-same way,
For none can tell to what red Hell
   His sightless soul may stray.

At last the dead man walked no more
   Amongst the Trial Men,
And I knew that he was standing up
   In the black dock's dreadful pen,
And that never would I see his face
   For weal or woe again.

Like two doomed ships that pass in storm
   We had crossed each other's way:
But we made no sign, we said no word,
   We had no word to say;
For we did not meet in the holy night,
   But in the shameful day.

A prison wall was round us both,
   Two outcast men we were:
The world had thrust us from its heart
   And God from out His care:
And the iron gin that waits for Sin
   Had caught us in its snare.

3

IN Debtors' Yard the stones are hard,
   And the dripping wall is high,
So it was there he took the air
   Beneath the leaden sky,

And by each side a Warder walked,
  For fear the man might die.

Or else he sat with those who watched
  His anguish night and day;
Who watched him when he rose to weep,
  And when he crouched to pray;
Who watched him lest himself should rob
  Their scaffold of its prey.

The Governor was strong upon
  The Regulations Act:
The Doctor said that Death was but
  A scientific fact:
And twice a day the Chaplain called,
  And left a little tract.

And twice a day he smoked his pipe,
  And drank his quart of beer:
His soul was resolute, and held
  No hiding-place for fear;
He often said that he was glad
  The hangman's day was near.

But why he said so strange a thing
  No warder dared to ask:
For he to whom a watcher's doom
  Is given as his task,
Must set a lock upon his lips
  And make his face a mask.

Or else he might be moved, and try
  To comfort or console:
And what should Human Pity do
  Pent up in Murderer's Hole?
What word of grace in such a place
  Could help a brother's soul?

With slouch and swing around the ring
   We trod the Fool's Parade!
We did not care: we knew we were
   The Devil's Own Brigade:
And shaven head and feet of lead
   Make a merry masquerade.

We tore the tarry rope to shreds
   With blunt and bleeding nails;
We rubbed the doors, and scrubbed the floors,
   And cleaned the shining rails:
And, rank by rank, we soaped the plank,
   And clattered with the pails.

We sewed the sacks, we broke the stones,
   We turned the dusty drill:
We banged the tins, and bawled the hymns,
   And sweated on the mill:
But in the heart of every man
   Terror was lying still.

So still it lay that every day
   Crawled like a weed-clogged wave:
And we forgot the bitter lot
   That waits for fool and knave,
Till once, as we tramped in from work,
   We passed an open grave.

With yawning mouth the yellow hole
   Gaped for a living thing;
The very mud cried out for blood
   To the thirsty asphalte ring;
And we knew that ere one dawn grew fair
   Some prisoner had to swing.

Right in we went, with soul intent
   On Death and Dread and Doom:

The hangman, with his little bag,
    Went shuffling through the gloom:
And I trembled as I groped my way
    Into my numbered tomb.

*

That night the empty corridors
    Were full of forms of Fear,
And up and down the iron town
    Stole feet we could not hear,
And through the bars that hide the stars
    White faces seemed to peer.

He lay as one who lies and dreams
    In a pleasant meadow-land
The watchers watched him as he slept,
    And could not understand
How one could sleep so sweet a sleep
    With a hangman close at hand.

But there is no sleep when men must weep
    Who never yet have wept:
So we – the fool, the fraud, the knave –
    That endless vigil kept,
And through each brain on hands of pain
    Another's terror crept.

Alas! it is a fearful thing
    To feel another's guilt!
For, right, within, the Sword of Sin
    Pierced to its poisoned hilt,
And as molten lead were the tears we shed
    For the blood we had not spilt.

The warders with their shoes of felt
    Crept by each padlocked door,

And peeped and saw, with eyes of awe,
   Grey figures on the floor,
And wondered why men knelt to pray
   Who never prayed before.

All through the night we knelt and prayed,
   Mad mourners of a corse!
The troubled plumes of midnight shook
   The plumes upon a hearse:
And bitter wine upon a sponge
   Was the savour of Remorse.

                ★

The grey cock crew, the red cock crew,
   But never came the day:
And crooked shapes of Terror crouched,
   In the corners where we lay:
And each evil sprite that walks by night
   Before us seemed to play.

They glided past, they glided fast,
   Like travellers through a mist:
They mocked the moon in a rigadoon
   Of delicate turn and twist,
And with formal pace and loathsome grace
   The phantoms kept their tryst.

With mop and mow, we saw them go,
   Slim shadows hand in hand:
About, about, in ghostly rout
   They trod a saraband:
And the damned grotesques made arabesques,
   Like the wind upon the sand!

With the pirouettes of marionettes,
   They tripped on pointed tread:

But with flutes of Fear they filled the ear,
  As their grisly masque they led,
And loud they sang, and long they sang,
  For they sang to wake the dead.

'Oho!' they cried, 'The world is wide,
  But fettered limbs go lame!
And once, or twice, to throw the dice
  Is a gentlemanly game,
But he does not win who plays with Sin
  In the secret House of Shame.'

No things of air these antics were,
  That frolicked with such glee:
To men whose lives were held in gyves,
  And whose feet might not go free,
Ah! wounds of Christ! they were living things,
  Most terrible to see.

Around, around, they waltzed and wound;
  Some wheeled in smirking pairs;
With the mincing step of a demirep
  Some sidled up the stairs;
And with subtle sneer, and fawning leer,
  Each helped us at our prayers.

The morning wind began to moan,
  But still the night went on:
Through its giant loom the web of gloom
  Crept till each thread was spun:
And, as we prayed, we grew afraid
  Of the Justice of the Sun.

The moaning wind went wandering round
  The weeping prison-wall:
Till like a wheel of turning steel
  We felt the minutes crawl:

O moaning wind! what had we done
  To have such a seneschal?

At last I saw the shadowed bars,
  Like a lattice wrought in lead,
Move right across the whitewashed wall
  That faced my three-plank bed,
And I knew that somewhere in the world
  God's dreadful dawn was red.

At six o'clock we cleaned our cells,
  At seven all was still,
But the sough and swing of a mighty wing
  The prison seemed to fill,
For the Lord of Death with icy breath
  Had entered in to kill.

He did not pass in purple pomp,
  Nor ride a moon-white steed.
Three yards of cord and a sliding board
  Are all the gallows' need:
So with rope of shame the Herald came
  To do the secret deed.

We were as men who through a fen
  Of filthy darkness grope:
We did not dare to breathe a prayer,
  Or to give our anguish scope:
Something was dead in each of us,
  And what was dead was Hope.

For Man's grim Justice goes its way,
  And will not swerve aside:
It slays the weak, it slays the strong,
  It has a deadly stride:
With iron heel it slays the strong,
  The monstrous parricide!

We waited for the stroke of eight:
   Each tongue was thick with thirst:
For the stroke of eight is the stroke of Fate
   That makes a man accursed,
And Fate will use a running noose
   For the best man and the worst.

We had no other thing to do,
   Save to wait for the sign to come:
So, like things of stone in a valley lone,
   Quiet we sat and dumb:
But each man's heart beat thick, and quick,
   Like a madman on a drum!

With sudden shock the prison-clock
   Smote on the shivering air,
And from all the gaol rose up a wail
   Of impotent despair,
Like the sound that frightened marshes hear
   From some leper in his lair.

And as one sees most fearful things
   In the crystal of a dream,
We saw the greasy hempen rope
   Hooked to the blackened beam,
And heard the prayer the hangman's snare
   Strangled into a scream.

And all the woe that moved him so
   That he gave that bitter cry,
And the wild regrets, and the bloody sweats,
   None knew so well as I:
For he who lives more lives than one
   More deaths than one must die.

4

THERE is no chapel on the day
  On which they hang a man:
The Chaplain's heart is far too sick,
  Or his face is far too wan,
Or there is that written in his eyes
  Which none should look upon.

So they kept us close till nigh on noon,
  And then they rang the bell,
And the warders with their jingling keys
  Opened each listening cell,
And down the iron stair we tramped,
  Each from his separate Hell.

Out into God's sweet air we went,
  But not in wonted way,
For this man's face was white with fear,
  And that man's face was grey,
And I never saw sad men who looked
  So wistfully at the day.

I never saw sad men who looked
  With such a wistful eye
Upon that little tent of blue
  We prisoners called the sky,
And at every happy cloud that passed
  In such strange freedom by.

But there were those amongst us all
  Who walked with downcast head,
And knew that, had each got his due,
  They should have died instead:
He had but killed a thing that lived,
  Whilst they had killed the dead.

For he who sins a second time
  Wakes a dead soul to pain,
And draws it from its spotted shroud,
  And makes it bleed again,
And makes it bleed great gouts of blood,
  And makes it bleed in vain!

*

Like ape or clown, in monstrous garb
  With crooked arrows starred,
Silently we went round and round
  The slippery asphalte yard;
Silently we went round and round,
  And no man spoke a word.

Silently we went round and round,
  And through each hollow mind
The Memory of dreadful things
  Rushed like a dreadful wind,
And Horror stalked before each man,
  And Terror crept behind.

*

The warders strutted up and down,
  And watched their herd of brutes,
Their uniforms were spick and span,
  And they wore their Sunday suits,
But we knew the work they had been at,
  By the quicklime on their boots.

For where a grave had opened wide,
  There was no grave at all:
Only a stretch of mud and sand
  By the hideous prison-wall,

And a little heap of burning lime,
    That the man should have his pall.

For he has a pall, this wretched man,
    Such as few men can claim:
Deep down below a prison-yard,
    Naked for greater shame,
He lies, with fetters on each foot,
    Wrapt in a sheet of flame!

And all the while the burning lime
    Eats flesh and bone away,
It eats the brittle bone by night,
    And the soft flesh by day,
It eats the flesh and bone by turns,
    But it eats the heart alway.

*

For three long years they will not sow
    Or root or seedling there:
For three long years the unblessed spot
    Will sterile be and bare,
And look upon the wondering sky
    With unreproachful stare.

They think a murderer's heart would taint
    Each simple seed they sow.
It is not true! God's kindly earth
    Is kindlier than men know,
And the red rose would blow more red,
    The white rose whiter blow.

Out of his mouth a red, red rose!
    Out of his heart a white!
For who can say by what strange way,
    Christ brings His will to light,

The Ballad of Reading Gaol

Since the barren staff the pilgrim bore
    Bloomed in the great Pope's sight?

But neither milk-white rose nor red
    May bloom in prison-air;
The shard, the pebble, and the flint,
    Are what they give us there:
For flowers have been known to heal
    A common man's despair.

So never will wine-red rose or white,
    Petal by petal, fall
On that stretch of mud and sand that lies
    By the hideous prison-wall,
To tell the men who tramp the yard
    That God's Son died for all.

*

Yet though the hideous prison-wall
    Still hems him round and round,
And a spirit may not walk by night
    That is with fetters bound,
And a spirit may but weep that lies
    In such unholy ground,

He is at peace – this wretched man –
    At peace, or will be soon:
There is no thing to make him mad,
    Nor does Terror walk at noon,
For the lampless Earth in which he lies
    Has neither Sun nor Moon.

They hanged him as a beast is hanged:
    They did not even toll
A requiem that might have brought
    Rest to his startled soul,

But hurriedly they took him out,
  And hid him in a hole.

The warders stripped him of his clothes,
  And gave him to the flies:
They mocked the swollen purple throat,
  And the stark and staring eyes:
And with laughter loud they heaped the shroud
  In which the convict lies.

The Chaplain would not kneel to pray
  By his dishonoured grave:
Nor mark it with that blessed Cross
  That Christ for sinners gave,
Because the man was one of those
  Whom Christ came down to save.

Yet all is well; he has but passed
  To Life's appointed bourne:
And alien tears will fill for him
  Pity's long-broken urn,
For his mourners will be outcast men,
  And outcasts always mourn.

5

I KNOW not whether Laws be right,
  Or whether Laws be wrong;
All that we know who lie in gaol
  Is that the wall is strong;
And that each day is like a year,
  A year whose days are long.

But this I know, that every Law
  That men have made for Man,
Since first Man took his brother's life,
  And the sad world began,

But straws the wheat and saves the chaff
  With a most evil fan.

This too I know – and wise it were
  If each could know the same –
That every prison that men build
  Is built with bricks of shame,
And bound with bars lest Christ should see
  How men their brothers maim.

With bars they blur the gracious moon,
  And blind the goodly sun:
And they do well to hide their Hell,
  For in it things are done
That Son of God nor son of Man
  Ever should look upon!

*

The vilest deeds like poison weeds,
  Bloom well in prison-air;
It is only what is good in Man
  That wastes and withers there:
Pale Anguish keeps the heavy gate,
  And the Warder is Despair.

For they starve the little frightened child
  Till it weeps both night and day:
And they scourge the weak, and flog the fool,
  And gibe the old and grey,
And some grow mad, and all grow bad,
  And none a word may say.

Each narrow cell in which we dwell
  Is a foul and dark latrine,
And the fetid breath of living Death
  Chokes up each grated screen,

And all, but Lust, is turned to dust
  In Humanity's machine.

The brackish water that we drink
  Creeps with a loathsome slime,
And the bitter bread they weigh in scales
  Is full of chalk and lime,
And Sleep will not lie down, but walks
  Wild-eyed, and cries to Time.

*

But though lean Hunger and green Thirst
  Like asp with adder fight,
We have little care of prison fare,
  For what chills and kills outright
Is that every stone one lifts by day
  Becomes one's heart by night.

With midnight always in one's heart,
  And twilight in one's cell,
We turn the crank, or tear the rope,
  Each in his separate Hell,
And the silence is more awful far
  Than the sound of a brazen bell.

And never a human voice comes near
  To speak a gentle word:
And the eye that watches through the door
  Is pitiless and hard:
And by all forgot, we rot and rot,
  With soul and body marred.

And thus we rust Life's iron chain
  Degraded and alone:
And some men curse, and some men weep,
  And some men make no moan:

But God's eternal Laws are kind
　　And break the heart of stone.

*

And every human heart that breaks,
　　In prison-cell or yard,
Is as that broken box that gave
　　Its treasure to the Lord,
And filled the unclean leper's house
　　With the scent of costliest nard.

Ah! happy they whose hearts can break
　　And peace of pardon win!
How else may man make straight his plan
　　And cleanse his soul from Sin?
How else but through a broken heart
　　May Lord Christ enter in?

*

And he of the swollen purple throat,
　　And the stark and staring eyes,
Waits for the holy hands that took
　　The Thief to Paradise;
And a broken and a contrite heart
　　The Lord will not despise.

The man in red who reads the Law
　　Gave him three weeks of life,
Three little weeks in which to heal
　　His soul of his soul's strife,
And cleanse from every blot of blood
　　The hand that held the knife.

And with tears of blood he cleansed the hand,
　　The hand that held the steel:

For only blood can wipe out blood,
    And only tears can heal:
And the crimson stain that was of Cain
    Became Christ's snow-white seal.

6

IN Reading gaol by Reading town
    There is a pit of shame,
And in it lies a wretched man
    Eaten by teeth of flame,
In a burning winding-sheet he lies,
    And his grave has got no name.

And there, till Christ call forth the dead,
    In silence let him lie:
No need to waste the foolish tear,
    Or heave the windy sigh:
The man had killed the thing he loved,
    And so he had to die.

And all men kill the thing they love,
    By all let this be heard,
Some do it with a bitter look,
    Some with a flattering word,
The coward does it with a kiss,
    The brave man with a sword!

MORE ABOUT PENGUINS, PELICANS,
PEREGRINES AND PUFFINS

For further information about books available from Penguins please write to Dept EP, Penguin Books Ltd, Harmondsworth, Middlesex UB7 0DA.

In the U.S.A.: For a complete list of books available from Penguins in the United States write to Dept DG, Penguin Books, 299 Murray Hill Parkway, East Rutherford, New Jersey 07073.

In Canada: For a complete list of books available from Penguins in Canada write to Penguin Books Canada Ltd, 2801 John Street, Markham, Ontario L3R 1B4.

In Australia: For a complete list of books available from Penguins in Australia write to the Marketing Department, Penguin Books Australia Ltd, P.O. Box 257, Ringwood, Victoria 3134.

In New Zealand: For a complete list of books available from Penguins in New Zealand write to the Marketing Department, Penguin Books (N.Z.) Ltd, Private Bag, Takapuna, Auckland 9.

In India: For a complete list of books available from Penguins in India write to Penguin Overseas Ltd, 706 Eros Apartments, 56 Nehru Place, New Delhi 110019.

ENGLISH AND AMERICAN LITERATURE IN PENGUINS

☐ *Emma* **Jane Austen** £1.25

'I am going to take a heroine whom no one but myself will much like,' declared Jane Austen of Emma, her most spirited and controversial heroine in a comedy of self-deceit and self-discovery.

☐ *Tender is the Night* **F. Scott Fitzgerald** £2.95

Fitzgerald worked on seventeen different versions of this novel, and its obsessions – idealism, beauty, dissipation, alcohol and insanity – were those that consumed his own marriage and his life.

☐ *The Life of Johnson* **James Boswell** £2.95

Full of gusto, imagination, conversation and wit, Boswell's immortal portrait of Johnson is as near a novel as a true biography can be, and still regarded by many as the finest 'life' ever written. This shortened version is based on the 1799 edition.

☐ *A House and its Head* **Ivy Compton-Burnett** £4.95

In a novel 'as trim and tidy as a hand-grenade' (as Pamela Hansford Johnson put it), Ivy Compton-Burnett penetrates the facade of a conventional, upper-class Victorian family to uncover a chasm of violent emotions – jealousy, pain, frustration and sexual passion.

☐ *The Trumpet Major* **Thomas Hardy** £1.50

Although a vein of unhappy unrequited love runs through this novel, Hardy also draws on his warmest sense of humour to portray Wessex village life at the time of the Napoleonic wars.

☐ *The Complete Poems of Hugh MacDiarmid*

☐ Volume One £8.95
☐ Volume Two £8.95

The definitive edition of work by the greatest Scottish poet since Robert Burns, edited by his son Michael Grieve, and W. R. Aitken.

ENGLISH AND AMERICAN LITERATURE IN PENGUINS

☐ ***Main Street* Sinclair Lewis** £4.95

The novel that added an immortal chapter to the literature of America's Mid-West, *Main Street* contains the comic essence of Main Streets everywhere.

☐ ***The Compleat Angler* Izaak Walton** £2.50

A celebration of the countryside, and the superiority of those in 1653, as now, who love *quietnesse, vertue* and, above all, *Angling*. 'No fish, however coarse, could wish for a doughtier champion than Izaak Walton' – Lord Home

☐ ***The Portrait of a Lady* Henry James** £2.50

'One of the two most brilliant novels in the language', according to F. R. Leavis, James's masterpiece tells the story of a young American heiress, prey to fortune-hunters but not without a will of her own.

☐ ***Hangover Square* Patrick Hamilton** £3.95

Part love story, part thriller, and set in the publands of London's Earls Court, this novel caught the conversational tone of a whole generation in the uneasy months before the Second World War.

☐ ***The Rainbow* D. H. Lawrence** £2.50

Written between *Sons and Lovers* and *Women in Love*, *The Rainbow* covers three generations of Brangwens, a yeoman family living on the borders of Nottinghamshire.

☐ ***Vindication of the Rights of Woman*
Mary Wollstonecraft** £2.95

Although Walpole once called her 'a hyena in petticoats', Mary Wollstonecraft's vision was such that modern feminists continue to go back and debate the arguments so powerfully set down here.

ENGLISH AND AMERICAN
LITERATURE IN PENGUINS